EVERYONE
IS LYING

BOOKS BY HOLLY DOWN

The Other Woman

EVERYONE IS LYING

HOLLY DOWN

bookouture

Published by Bookouture in 2025

An imprint of Storyfire Ltd.
Carmelite House
50 Victoria Embankment
London EC4Y oDZ

www.bookouture.com

The authorised representative in the EEA is Hachette Ireland
8 Castlecourt Centre
Dublin 15 D15 XTP3
Ireland
(email: info@hbgi.ie)

ISBN: 978-1-83525-972-6
eBook ISBN: 978-1-83525-971-9

PROLOGUE

The rain pounds the window, making it impossible to see the road ahead, and I lean forward in my seat, clutching the steering wheel in both hands and forcing myself to keep my foot on the pedal. We're not far from our destination, though I can tell it would probably be better to pull over and wait for this down-pour to pass. The windscreen wipers are working triple-time, and their swish and flick is the only sound as we sit in tense silence, teetering on the precipice of another screaming row that we both know will begin as soon as one of us says a single word. I clench my jaw to keep myself from speaking, pushing my tongue painfully against my teeth to stop it from forming words I know I will regret. I'm trying desperately not to be the one who starts us back on the path to destruction that we know so well, but another force is fighting against my will – a force I can acknowledge is malevolent, but one I'm not sure I can resist: the absolute imperative to be right.

'I did tell you...' The words spill out of my mouth before I can stop them, and a sharp intake of breath from the passenger seat tells me you are gearing up for a fight.

'We said we were going to leave it,' you snap, and a warm

flush of guilt blooms in my cheeks, but I need you to see it from my point of view. I just don't understand why you won't listen to me. Why won't you see sense?

'I'm not starting it again, but I do think it's important that we learn lessons—'

The sound that erupts from your mouth is not what I expect at all. Rather than a torrent of abuse or even a stream of denials, what spills forth is a scream so loud and so guttural, it sounds like it's come from the depths of hell; at first I wonder if it's a baby wailing and I almost laugh when I realise it has come from your lungs. But then any hint of humour is robbed from me as you reach over and grab the steering wheel.

It all happens so fast. At first, I'm peering through the sloshing rain, staring at the white line in the road, using it like a balance beam to precariously keep the car moving in the right direction. I'm grateful that most other traffic appears to have sensibly stopped and we are the only vehicle taking the out-of-town bypass. But then your hand drags us from the safety of the centre of the road and through the large puddle that has formed in the gutter. I go to slam my foot on the brake, but in my panic it slips and comes crashing down on the wrong pedal, sending the car surging forward. Now I'm the one screaming. You are strangely silent.

Using all my strength, I try to wrestle the wheel back, but all I manage to achieve is a short jerk that allows the headlights to sweep across the road and catch a glimmer of the raindrops that shimmer like needles falling from the sky in the beam of light. You pull again and we bump over the muddy bank, leaping up for a moment as if we have taken flight before slamming back down with a bone-juddering crunch and slamming through a hedge. I spot the tree only a moment before we hit it, and in that split-second, time divides into a million shattered pieces like a broken mirror, and I'm able to think so many things at once – things I wish I could say to you, only there's no time for that.

I'm sorry.
You're not wearing a seat belt.
They'll think it was my fault.
You did this.
We're dead.

ONE

I wince as searing daylight dazzles me. I'm hit by a piercing pain, like I've been shot through the head with an arrow. I'm certain that waking up shouldn't hurt this much but that's about all I'm certain of... The sharp spike is quickly replaced by a tsunami of panic that crashes over me relentlessly as I realise I know nothing. Zero. Zilch. Not only do I have no idea why my body feels like it's been through a mangle, but I also can't remember anything about myself, not a single thing. I do not know who I am.

My fear threatens to become a full-blown panic attack so I try to laugh it off, telling myself that I must be half asleep, that in a moment everything will come flooding back in the way it should, but as I lie completely still with my eyes wide open, nothing comes. My mind feels like a landscape after a snow-storm, and as I desperately try to pull an iota of information from my brain, a tightness slowly envelops my chest as if there is a band wrapped around me, and I wonder, *How is it possible not to even know your own name?*

Trying to remember feels like searching for a light switch in the dark. The more I grasp for answers, the greater my panic becomes until I fear I may vomit, so I close my eyes and dig my fingers into the surface to steady myself. Beneath me, I feel cotton sheets and a soft mattress, and I recognise that I'm in a bed. Clutching this simple fact, I try to take a deep breath, deciding the best approach is to take things one step at a time and establish any facts I can. I open my eyes once more and the pain hits again, only this time it's more of a dull throb as if my whole head is in a vice that is being slowly tightened. But at least it's more bearable, and as my mind clears I remember something important – Jen. My name is Jen.

This little piece of vital information helps and I force myself to draw in another big lungful of air, breathing out slowly, thinking, *Pull yourself together, woman*. I have no idea what type of person I am, but I tell myself I need to be one of those capable types that just gets on with things because there appears to be no one here to help me. I'm alone and something tells me I need to listen to my instincts and try to create a picture of myself, however wrong I may be, because otherwise I will be this blank person. A nothing. And that certainly won't soothe the terror I'm feeling.

It crosses my mind that this could be the aftermath of a mega drinking session. Only this does not feel like one of those 'the morning after the night before' mornings. The aches and pains are more acute as if something has actually *happened* to me – something awful. The only thing I can compare it to is giving birth – the shock of arriving at the hospital in excellent health, despite the gigantic baby bump, and leaving more like a victim of war, hobbling so as not to tear the stitches.

Panic whirls and swirls in my chest like a tornado but I tell myself to start at the beginning and gather clues like a detective. I already remembered my name – Jen. And then it comes to me, my last name, Jen Versailles. *French, but I don't feel French*, though as I ponder this, my brain resists and I'm suddenly not sure if that even is my name. I tell myself not to push it, that it will come. Instead, I try looking around the room to gather clues from my surroundings. Where am I? That feels like the place I need to start.

From my position flat out on my back, I can see an ornate ceiling rose overhead with an antique-style light fitting that looks vaguely familiar. Screwing up my eyes, I stare at the curly metal with its tulip-shaped glass lights and I feel like I can see myself trawling local car boot sales and online antique fairs until I found the exact one I had in mind. Is that a memory or am I just creating a story from the objects around me? I can't be sure, but I really want to believe that this is my own home and I'm in my own bed. Gripping the sheets tightly in my fingers, I wish desperately for a way to confirm my suspicions. I don't trust myself. It's like I'm trying to walk on fragile glass over a ravine, and at any minute I'll go crashing to the ground.

Needing to see the rest of the room, I attempt to move my neck, but my head has only turned by the smallest fraction when I hear a strange, whimpering noise that it takes me a moment to realise is coming from me. My God it hurts, but when I try again the pain has lessened as if I'm loosening up a screw that's rusted in place. I can tell that eventually it will work again, and I feel a small part of my terror ease. I'm not locked in my own body at the very least.

I see a sash window that's open a couple of inches and is the source of the gentle breeze that's caressing my face, and I send silent gratitude to whoever opened it, certain that it wasn't me, not in this state. I take in the green and gold floral curtains that match the gold patterned wallpaper, which, together, are a little jarring. *Not quite right*, I think to myself, wondering if the old me would have cared about that, though it feels immeasurably insignificant now, like worrying that your hair might get wet in a shipwreck.

As I try to work out the extent of my injuries, I slowly force myself to lift my head, vertebra by vertebra, curling up like a rusty bike chain that needs a good oiling, until I can see the length of my body. The shock hits me like a punch in the stomach. Most of me is covered by a white cotton duvet set, but my right arm is exposed and it's the tubes sticking in that have taken my breath away – I appear to be charging. Letting out a dark chuckle at this strange thought, I follow the length of tube across the bed to a stand where a bag of clear fluid is hanging and see that it appears to be dripping into my arm. Now I'm certain that something has happened to me, since unless I am one of those health freaks who orders at-home vitamins to be delivered by a drip, I am clearly receiving medical care. Who would put a needle in their arm unless they really needed to?

With even more desperation now to work out what is wrong with me, I feel pressure on my face and realise with a jolt of horror that there's a tube stuck down my nose. I may not have much medical knowledge, but everything points to something being seriously wrong with me. I run through the symptoms: horrendous aches and pains, an awful headache, memory loss so severe I can barely work out who I am. All I can think is that I must have been in a serious accident, but why wouldn't I be in hospital? And who has been looking after me, since I clearly didn't put the drip or feeding tube in myself?

Turning my head another fraction, I see the scrubbed pine door with a round porcelain door knob and a keyhole beneath it, and I wonder if it's locked. A thought crosses my mind and plants a dark seed that I fear may take over everything else: am I even free to leave if I were capable of it? Is it possible that someone is keeping me here against my will?

I wish I could dismiss this thought as totally ridiculous but everything about this situation feels wrong and I'm struggling to think of a reasonable explanation for why I have woken here, alone, feeling like this. I want to leap out of bed and test the door knob, but there is no way I can move that quickly or stretch that far in the state I'm in. I'm just wondering whether I can

even lift my hand when I hear a sound from outside the room –
a scuff or a creak – and every muscle in my body tenses and my
heart thumps in my chest as I fix my gaze on the door knob,
waiting for it to turn. I try not to let out a sound but I can't help
whimpering softly as it hits me that someone is outside the room
while I lie here, stuck in bed.

My eyes grow wide as I keep them fixed on the door, one
thought running over and over in my head: *Who is there?*

TWO

My chest tightens and I can barely breathe as the knob twitches then rotates and the door eases open. I can't be sure if it was unlocked. As I shake with fear, a vase of flowers enters the room, seeming to float in mid-air, and I force myself to exhale, telling myself I've been ridiculous and worked myself up for no reason – surely no evil captor brings flowers? I spot long, slim fingers that are wrapped around the glass, and as the person lowers the vase onto the bedside table, my gaze lands on a woman's face at the same moment she sees me looking.

'Oh my God!' she shrieks and thuds the flowers down, bending over me so quickly that I barely take in her features. 'Jen? Jen! You're awake!'

Tears swill in her big brown eyes, and I see she has a long face, framed by thick dark hair, that would be Hollywood-gorgeous were it not for the strength of her chin. It's hard to feel frightened of someone whose reaction looks so genuine, but I don't let my guard drop. I can't until I have some answers.

'So my name *is* Jen,' I manage to croak and she breaks out into a loud sob that she passes off as a laugh as the tears spill over and fall down her cheeks.

'We've been so worried,' she says, brushing the tears away with the back of her hand though more fall as quickly as she clears them.

There are so many things I want to ask, so many questions like, 'Who are you?', 'Who's "we"?' and 'Where am I?' but I start with what feels like the most urgent.

'What happened to me?'

The woman sits on the small armchair by my bedside and takes my hand, and even though it aches to lift my arm to keep the connection, I like the feeling of her warm hand squeezing my fingers. It makes me feel like I'm not alone and I tell myself that this woman is here to help me. She must be.

'Don't you remember?' she says gently, a little too gently for my liking, and I start to feel the panic fizzing just below the surface again. She knows something that I don't, something that is making her wince slightly as she waits for me to respond. Something she doesn't want to tell me. I try to shake my head, telling myself that I'm letting my imagination run away with me, but the sharp pain comes again and I let out a strangled moan.

'You need to rest,' she says and she goes to stand up, but I use every ounce of my strength to grab her hand tightly and hold her in place. There is no way I can let her leave. That's not happening. I can't go back to lying here not knowing anything again, I just can't.

'I don't remember anything,' I say through gritted teeth. The ache in my arm starts to burn like my muscles have wasted away and even basic movement requires Herculean effort.

She frowns – and I notice her eyes are now dry – before she repeats, 'Nothing?' and the tremor in her voice makes it sound like there is something I really ought to remember. She opens her mouth then hesitates and I feel like there's something she needs to tell me, and a shiver runs through me as I have a premonition that it's not going to be good. You don't wake up with no memory, feeling like you've been hit by a train, after something *good* happens.

'You really don't remember *anything*?' she asks softly, and though my neck still hurts, I manage a short, sharp shake. I wonder how I can convey the terrifying blank to her. What words do I have to express what I'm feeling right now?

'I'm Jen,' I say simply and she nods vigorously before I add in a croaky voice, 'And you are?'

Her mouth falls open in almost cartoon horror and an image of her tongue forming downward steps as it rolls out of her mouth like Scooby Doo comes to mind. She doesn't respond immediately and I can almost see the cogs turning in her head as she processes what I've just said.

'Why don't we start at the beginning?' she says.

'Please,' I rasp as anticipation churns in my stomach and I realise I'm gripping the sheet again with both hands. She could be about to tell me I'm royalty and I've been in a riding accident, or a billionaire who's crashed their private jet, only I feel instinctively that neither of these are true. I'm certain that I'm much more ordinary than that.

'I'm Rachel, your sister,' she says, putting her hand over one of mine and squeezing gently. I roll the word 'sister' around in my head, testing the word against my image of her.

I have so little to go on and tears fill my eyes as our gazes meet. I desperately try to work out if she's telling the truth. I'm not sure if this woman, Rachel, feels like someone I've known my whole life, but she looks earnest and she's here. Fighting back a sob at my utter frustration, I tell myself I have no other options right now but to trust her.

'My sister,' I say in a faltering voice, and she nods.

I'm not sure how my face reacts, but tears spring back into Rachel's eyes and she says, 'Oh Jen, I am so sorry. You really don't deserve this.'

'Are we French?' I ask.

Rachel's heavy eyebrows pull together. 'No, why do you ask?'

'My surname. Is it Versailles?'

Rachel shakes her head and that small motion is enough to make me feel like a toy train that's been knocked off the track.

'Our last name is Vincent,' she says softly, and seeming to sense my panic adds, 'Don't push yourself. It will come.'

'Where am I?' I ask.

'This is your home,' Rachel says. 'You're in your own bed. I hope that's some comfort.'

No comfort at all, I think bitterly, *not when I don't know why I'm here.* 'Why are all these wires stuck in me?'

'You've needed medical help but you're on the mend now. I'll make sure we get those removed as soon as possible.' She seems to be deflecting and I have no idea why.

'What's wrong with me?' I sound angry now, but Rachel just rises from the seat.

'There's plenty of time for talk, but you need to rest.' She says this firmly, almost as if I'm a child, and I feel a roil of anger in my stomach, wondering if I am the younger sister and Rachel has spent her whole life telling me what to do. She begins fussing with the flowers on my bedside table in a brisk way that suggests she is about to sweep from the room and leave me here alone, and I'm filled with terror again. Casting about, I try to work out what questions I should ask or what I should say to persuade her to stay, but my brain isn't working properly.

My eyes rest on the dusky pink armchair that she was sitting on only moments ago, and as my gaze drifts out of focus, I can picture the outline of someone sitting there, keeping vigil at my bedside. Was I drifting in and out of consciousness or am I completely imagining it? Did I see someone, and if I did, was it Rachel? I try to picture her there, but it doesn't seem quite right and my mind goes back to the feeling I had when I awoke, that I'd felt this battered and bruised once before when I'd given birth. Suddenly a question comes to me that I can't believe I haven't asked already, the sentiment so forceful that the words come out much louder than I intend.

'Where are *they*?'

Rachel stops stock still, her fingers jolting so much that she snaps the stem of the lily she is holding, and a strange look crosses her face that takes me a moment to place – fear.

'Who?' she asks gently and the world lurches once more as I realise in disbelief I'm going to have to say it. Surely Rachel should know exactly who I mean – the people who are obviously the very centre of my universe.

'My husband and child,' I say.

When she doesn't answer immediately, I feel a flicker of righteous anger that she's holding something back from me, so certain am I that there are two people missing who should be here. But Rachel refuses to look at me and I begin to feel a horrible doubt creep over me as I wonder what the hell is going on. As she lifts her eyes, all I see is sorrowful pity that makes me want to leap out of bed and do something, anything, to distract myself. Only I can't even move.

Tears threaten to overtake me once more as the silence stretches between us. Fighting to keep my composure, I tune into the noises outside, where I hear a car drive by and somewhere in the distance the whine of a lawnmower as people get on with their lives in whatever neighbourhood this is, while I lie here in limbo, feeling as if I'm on the very edge of a ledge without any idea of what is below or how I got here. Or if someone is standing behind me, about to give me a hard shove. Terror swells inside me as I wait for Rachel to spit out whatever she has to say but her fingers move again as she prunes a leaf from one of the long stems, buying time, and I notice a tremor that wasn't there before.

'Rachel!' I bark, panic raising my pitch into a sharp squeak.

'What are you keeping from me? Just tell me! Has something happened to them? Please.'

My voice cracks on the last word and she sighs heavily, sitting down slowly to perch on the edge of the chair. The way she takes my hand and begins rubbing small circles with her thumb in a soothing motion makes me brace myself for the worst.

'Jen,' she says, 'I'm so sorry to have to tell you...' There's an excruciating pause and I find myself holding in a silent scream.

And then she says something that makes the bottom fall out of my world.

'Jen... you never had a husband. Or a baby.'

THREE

Of all the things I was expecting Rachel to say, that certainly wasn't one of them. I stare at her with my mouth hanging open, waiting for the punchline of what must be some sort of sick joke. But it never comes.

I may not be of sound mind, but I can feel the shape of two people imprinted on my heart. I don't need to remember them to know that they exist. My husband and child – where are they? But the longer Rachel sits quietly, her expression filled with unwavering pity, the more I question myself. Clearly one of us is absolutely wrong and I fear that I am the less reliable party. I did misremember my surname after all, but surely it's not possible to forget your own baby?

The whole situation is so destabilising that when I try to form a question, to make Rachel understand that she needs to try again, to come up with a different answer, I find I can only make a strange gurgling noise at the back of my throat, and the next moment, tears are streaming down my face. The true horror of my situation settles upon me as I realise how vulnerable I am. I can't move. I know nothing. And this woman who claims to be my sister is the only link I have to the outside world.

'There, there,' Rachel says, and she leans closer to stroke my hair as the tears turn into great, gulping sobs that I couldn't stop even if I wanted to. 'Get it all out. It's OK.'

'But...' I manage to rasp, but I don't know what to say next and it starts to dawn on me that this is my new reality – alone, confused and a prisoner of my own broken mind. 'Who do I have?' I croak.

'It's just me,' Rachel says in a whisper, and then perhaps she realises how bleak that sounds because she corrects herself and says firmly, 'You've got me.'

Every fibre of my being is railing against her words but when our eyes meet, I see the depth of sorrow in her brown eyes and I tell myself that she is not faking. Clearly she is finding this difficult too. Surely my sister just wants the best for me and is trying to protect me as best she can. But her pity stings. I rub the skin of my bare fourth finger of my left hand, feeling the empty space where a wedding band would be, and try to remember if there has ever been a ring there. Despite the odd feeling that I have a husband and child somewhere, I have no real memories of either of them and my finger feels the same as all the others – there's no phantom ring or dent in the skin where one might have been. And if I were married, surely my husband would be here, nursing me back to health. And what child is kept apart from its mother?

Despite everything going on inside my head and the tumult of emotions I'm feeling, I sense my eyelids drifting down of their own accord. I'm utterly exhausted. Battling for every single thought has left me spent.

'Rest now,' Rachel says.

I want to resist because there is still so much I don't know and questions are buzzing around my head like flies, but her words have drained me. I have to fight to keep my eyes open.

'But...' I begin as I try to ask what's wrong with me; when I will get better; what town we live in; what job I do. I'm overwhelmed by the sheer number of questions I need answers to, and I can't form the words quickly enough as Rachel stands.

'Back soon,' she promises.

'Don't go,' I manage to squawk, but she just pats my cheek gently like she hasn't heard the desperation in my voice and sweeps out of the room, closing the door behind her. Straining my ears, I listen for the sound of her turning a key and locking me in but I tell myself I'm being silly. Why would my sister want to trap me? All I hear are her footsteps retreating and I scold myself for being so paranoid.

I count six thuds of her feet on the stairs before there's a louder noise. She can't have made it all the way to the bottom of the stairs unless I live in some sort of hobbit house. Could she have slipped? I can't believe she would have crashed down the rest of the stairs without crying out, but then it hits me that she must have stopped midway down. I wonder why. I picture her fleeing my room then sinking down on the stairs when she was far enough away and collapsing in a fit of... anguish, or sorrow, or could it even be mirth? Perhaps she's huddled in a ball on the stairs, laughing herself silly at the fact that I know nothing about myself, not even my marital status. But even as I think this, tears prick my eyes and I know that my situation is not funny. Rachel didn't seem like the type of person to take pleasure from another's misfortune, especially not mine. No, I have to believe that my sister is a kind woman who'll be there for me – she's all I have, after all. And as I stare again at the pink armchair, I decide that it must have been Rachel that held vigil through my darkest hours.

But even as I'm telling myself that Rachel is here for me, doubt begins to trickle in as the questions keep on coming. Why am I not in a hospital bed? And why wouldn't she tell me what happened to me? I may not remember much about my life, but

Rachel seems like a normal, straightforward woman. Could she really be involved in a massive deception? What sort of motive could anyone have to isolate an injured person and... lie to her? I think of my husband and child again – the ghosts of my past that apparently are a figment of my imagination. Even just thinking of them brings a clutch of panic to my chest and makes me want to try and get up and attempt to track them down myself. But I tell myself I'm being ridiculous. What possible reason could Rachel have to lie about something so important? And if they did exist, surely I would have more than a vague sense of them – I expect they'd be fully formed in my mind in technicolour.

I lie back, breathing deeply, telling myself to relax and allow the memories to come of their own accord. Perhaps if I empty my mind, my lost family will come rushing back to me? But as I desperately wish for a glimpse of them, all that comes to mind is a tree and I feel a bitter disappointment. What could be so special about a stupid tree? This tree is a large, old oak with a thick, gnarled trunk and wide, glossy leaves – it's a beauty – but I have no idea where or when I've seen this tree or why it holds any importance to me. Did I plant it or climb it or chop it down? Glancing again at the window, I can't be certain of the size of this house or the garden, but I have the feeling that I'm not in some grand manor house. Something about the proportions tells me that my home is smaller than that, cosy in fact, and any garden is probably not much more than a square of paving stones with a little bench to sit on under the sun with a cup of tea and a biscuit.

Turning my face towards the gentle breeze coming in through the window, I realise with a jolt that I'm not imagining my yard, I'm actually remembering it. Pride swells in my chest that I've managed to recall something as I grasp the image – it may not be particularly ground-breaking but I'm certain it's something real about my life.

The bench is an old one that I think I salvaged from the local tip. In my mind's eye I can see it set aside for firewood with a sad, crumpled note that read 'take me' and I did just that, dragging it home myself and stopping every few minutes to sit on it for a rest. Once I got it here, I painstakingly replaced the broken slats and painted the wood a nice, chirpy yellow, and although it wasn't perfect in the end, I know in my bones that it is a lovely place to sit and contemplate life in the late-afternoon sun. I'm on a roll and as I close my eyes, I remember getting home from work and sitting out there and... the image that pops into my head surprises me. It seems like a cheery place, but all I can think is that it is where I would sit and sob my heart out.

And now all I can wonder as my heavy eyes drift shut is, *What happened in my life to make me so sad?*

FOUR

I wake with a jolt to a rap on the door and all my confusion and fear comes rushing back as the knob turns and the door swings open.

'Rachel?' I say in a shaky voice, but my breath catches in my throat as a bear of a man enters in a pair of navy blue scrubs, ducking his head as he steps into the room.

I have no idea what time it is but daylight is seeping through the gap in the curtains and the man is carrying a tray with a bowl of porridge. Have I slept the whole night through?

'Your sister said you'd woken up,' he says in a soft, gentle voice that's at odds with his powerful build, and I'm not sure whether I should be scared or not. He appears to be a medical professional but why is he letting himself into my room and where is Rachel? 'That's great news. How do you feel?'

'Like roadkill,' I answer honestly, studying his face and wondering whether we've met before. I search for a glimmer of recognition, but there's nothing there, and I'm hit by a rush of disappointment that makes me feel silly – somewhere in the back of my mind, I must have been hoping that this man could be my husband. I need to accept that Rachel told me I never married.

'Who are you?' I ask as he places the tray he's carrying on the bedside table.

'I'm sorry, that should have been the first thing I said. I'm Bryce. Your sister hired me to help with your nursing care. I hope you don't mind if I carry out my observations?'

'That's fine,' I say tersely, feeling like I'm going to have to get used to being the one in the dark. 'I'm Jen.'

This makes him smile but he smothers it and I realise I have no need to introduce myself to the man who's been paid to look after me – he must know everything there is to know about me already but all he says is, 'How do you do?' and I find myself grudgingly liking Bryce. He's treating me like an adult rather than a child who is being a nuisance, which I felt Rachel was verging on, and although he's large and hairy, he has a nice face that is rather pleasing on the eye. *I can certainly imagine worse people to have around*, I think with a wry smile, wondering if this is the type of thought patients are allowed to have about their caregivers. At the very least, something about his presence sets me at ease.

'Let's see if we can make you a little more comfortable. I think we can remove this tube.' He peels off some of the tape on my face and I flinch as he begins sliding the tube from my nose. I feel an awful urge to gag and a gurgling sound comes from my throat, but in a moment it's over. I cough and splutter as he discards the tube and tape into a clear plastic sack he's brought with him.

'What's wrong with me?' I ask when I feel ready to speak again.

'The main thing is you've suffered a very bad brain injury.'

I don't need him to tell me that.

'How?' I ask.

'You really don't remember?' he asks gently.

'Really.'

'You were in a car accident,' he says. 'A bad one.'

Of course, it had to be an accident, but I find myself frowning as I think of what the usual consequences of an accident are. Surely an ambulance is called and the person is taken to their local emergency room and a doctor takes responsibility for their care. I don't want to accuse Bryce of doing something wrong, not when we've only just met, but I'm confused.

'Why aren't I in hospital?' I ask.

He runs a hand through his beard, using his fingertips to comb the hair so it all points downward, and I can tell I'm making him uncomfortable, which only makes me more muddled. Surely that's a straightforward question.

'Head injuries are complex things. I understand that Rachel has had advice that familiar surroundings might help you recover so she's decided to treat you here. It's a lot more work planning in-home care so she really has bitten off quite a bit.'

I let that comment sink in and realise that it sounds like he thinks I should be grateful to Rachel but all I feel is desperation, and it may not be fair but a small part of me blames her. Why hasn't she returned yet? She must know I'm lying here in limbo, lost inside my own empty head.

'I just need to change your pads,' he says before I can ask another question, lowering his voice to an apologetic whisper. For the first time I feel myself flushing with shame as he whips a square nappy not unlike a puppy pad from under me and we both must smell the strong, acrid scent of urine. I feel paralysed with horror, but he acts with utmost professionalism, replacing it with a fresh one in what seems like it could be record time and disposing of the dirty one in the large plastic sack. Bryce glances at me and he must notice my red cheeks and the way I can't hold his gaze because he says lightly, 'Personal care is a daily part of my job.'

Cringing, I try to act like that makes me feel better but it's impossible not to picture this attractive man wiping my bum.

'If you feel up to it, perhaps you could start using this,' and he lifts a bedpan from the floor and places it on the bed beside me. 'But no matter if not, it's baby steps for now.'

He smiles again and I see he has lovely straight white teeth, and I try not to think about what he's had to do for me while I've been unable to help myself. I flush again and vow that whatever it takes out of me, I will use the bedpan from now on.

Trying to get back onto less humiliating ground, I ask, 'Why can't I move if I hurt my head?'

'Your head bore the brunt I'm afraid to say, but you also suffered bad facial injuries, several fractures, broken ribs and lots of cuts and bruises.' I wince as he adds, 'It was a really nasty accident.'

Glancing down at my body again, I realise that while the skin I can see is rather pasty and puffy and looks like it hasn't seen sunlight in far too long, none of it bears any sign of visible injury. Surely arms and hands are the most likely places to get cut in an accident since you'd imagine your instinct would be to protect your head? I frown as I try to work out why there isn't a scratch on them.

'Now, do you think you can manage anything to eat?' He says this in a peppy voice and I wonder if he's trying to distract me – is there something he doesn't want me to know? I begin shaking my head to refuse, but the mere mention of food has made my stomach contract with hunger. Glancing over at the bowl of porridge with what looks like a swirl of honey on top, I find myself salivating.

'Yes, please,' I say.

'Let's sit you up then,' he says and puts both arms in the crooks of my armpits before saying, 'Brace yourself,' and lifting me to sitting with ease as if I'm a small child, making me gasp at the shock of it. There is no strength in my body and it feels like

Bryce is manipulating a sack of potatoes rather than a person, but strangely I feel no pain. I wonder why he didn't take slightly more care, given the broken bones and fractures he mentioned, and why I'm not suffering more.

'Sorry,' he says, perhaps seeing my frown, but despite his roughness, I'm grateful to be in a different position. I feel like blood is rushing to my fingers and toes and I wiggle my hands and feet in turn.

'That feels better,' I say. 'Thank you.'

I'm about to ask him again about my injuries, but Bryce resumes talking in that easy, laconic way of his.

'I thought we'd start you off with a little porridge and see how that goes,' he says. 'We can move on to more exciting things once you're happy that everything is working as it should.'

I nod, but I suddenly feel nervous as I look at the bowl and the spoon on the tray that Bryce has placed on the small table. How the hell am I going to navigate a spoon of porridge from the bowl to my mouth without spilling it, when I'm barely able to lift my arm for any length of time? But I don't have to worry for long because Bryce sits in the armchair by my bedside and balances the tray on his knee, serving me small spoonfuls of porridge himself. *Feeding me like the baby I never had*, I think bitterly.

I'm quickly diverted by the taste explosion as the sweet honey hits my tongue. It may be a simple meal, but as I wolf it down I wonder if porridge ever tasted this good before. Soon the small bowl is empty and I long for more, bedpan be damned. Bryce has brought a water bottle with one of those spouts for me to suck from and I guzzle water greedily before I turn my eyes on him, about to ask for more. He seems to sense what I'm about to ask and says, 'Why don't we give that a few minutes to settle and see how you feel?'

'Fine,' I mutter petulantly, aware he is probably right but annoyed that I have so little control of my life that I can't even decide how much I want to eat. Even toddlers have that level of autonomy.

'It will get easier,' he says. 'You're making really great progress.'

The only progress I seem to have made is healing broken bones in an instant, I think wryly, and then the realisation hits me like a train and it's so chilling that I actually shiver. If I wasn't so horrified, I would laugh at my own stupidity. How did I not put it together before? The signs have been right in front of my eyes – the feeding tube, my wasted muscles, my pale, puffy, scratch-free skin.

'Something bothering you?' Bryce asks, clearly seeing whatever look on my face is betraying my emotions.

'You said cuts and bruises, but I can't see any,' I say shrilly, wanting Bryce to tell me the truth without my having to ask.

He rubs his beard again and I see I've found his tic – I'm clearly making him uncomfortable again, but I'm not going to stop this time.

'And you said I'd broken bones, but you lifted me to sitting position without being very gentle.'

'Maybe you should talk to Rachel,' he says nervously.

'Why? Just answer me one thing.'

He stands and lifts the tray as if he is readying to go.

'When did the accident happen?'

'Really, Rachel would be better placed to answer all your questions.'

'Just tell me.'

He meets my gaze and I see pity and sorrow in his brown eyes, but I grit my teeth and nod once, trying to convey that I can handle whatever he has to tell me.

'Six months,' he says. 'I'm sorry, Jen, but the accident was six months ago.'

FIVE

As I gasp in shock, my mind spinning from Bryce's revelation, he quickly extricates himself from the room, saying, 'I'll be back later. You rest.' I want to beg him to stay, but he's already shut the door behind him and is stomping down the stairs.

Collapsing back into my pillows, I try to make sense of what he's just told me, opening and closing my mouth like a goldfish swimming senselessly round and round a bowl. Six months? Six whole *months*? My mind returns to its choppy, frantic state. I guess there was no particular reason why, but I'd assumed I'd been unconscious for *days*. Why didn't Rachel tell me I'd missed half a year? Surely that's an important piece of information but perhaps it got lost in the sea of unanswered questions I have.

I so wish I could get out of bed and actually do something – be proactive – but I know that's still beyond me. A wave of exhaustion washes over me and threatens to pull me under like a riptide. How can I feel so tired when all I've done is lie in bed? I fight against it, refusing to allow myself to sleep, although it would be the easiest thing in the world to slide back down under the duvet and close my eyes, to escape from the terror clutching me in its grip. I need to do something, to take control, to wrestle a small part of my life back and not feel so useless.

Scanning the room in desperation, my eyes land on a photo frame on the bookshelf, but it's angled away from the bed as if whoever was sitting on the pink armchair while I was unconscious was looking at it. I picture Rachel there while I slept, staring wistfully at a snap of us... I try to imagine the type of thing we might like but I realise I can't fill in the blank. I have no idea what I'd like to do outside this room and that terrifies me. All I can picture is these four walls, the safety of this bed.

That picture frame contains an image of a moment I felt was important enough to capture and to frame and suddenly I feel an intense hunger to hold it in my hands and devour its secrets. But all I can see from my position in bed is the cardboard back of the frame and the little hooks holding whatever photo is inside in place. I decide – that's it. I will do whatever it takes to pick up that photo and look at the picture. It may only be a small act of independence, pathetic really, but at least it's something I can do for myself, and since I now know that the accident was months ago, any broken bones or bruising should be long healed. I tell myself scornfully that all I'm suffering from now is something akin to laziness and I vow to push through whatever lethargy my muscles are suffering from. It's only picking up a photo frame after all, hardly the Olympics.

I have no idea of the time since I don't have a phone or a clock, but I estimate that it must take me an hour at least to get myself sitting fully upright and positioned so my legs are hanging over the side of the bed, battling every muscle and sinew in the process. Once I'm in that position, the frame is only across two feet of exposed floorboards, but as I look down at the stained wood floor, it feels like an impossible task. Grunting from the effort, I inch myself to the very edge of the bed and try to grab the frame, but my arm is weak and my hand falls short. I bite down and try again, gripping the duvet with my other hand to act as an anchor and levering forward. The corner of the white wooden frame is only centimetres away. Stretching further, it's just millimetres. I am almost there when the door opens behind me and I hear Rachel's voice cry out, 'Oh my gosh, Jen, what are you doing?'

I make one final grab and manage to get a finger on the frame, but I only succeed in knocking it from the shelf. It hits the floor with a loud crack as I slip from the bed, falling forward with a shriek, but Rachel makes it around the bed just in time and cushions my fall with her body. We sit there for a minute, both panting from our exertions, and Rachel keeps her arms tightly around me while I rest my head on her shoulder and enjoy the warmth of her embrace, feeling so starved of human affection that it brings tears to my eyes. It has been a long time since anyone held me – or that's how it feels anyway – and I choke back a sob before Rachel gently and firmly helps me up. With a lot of grunting and groaning, she manages to haul me back into bed.

'What were you thinking?' she asks once she's got her breath back, lightly scolding me. 'It's lucky I could work from home this morning and pop by, or else you could have been really hurt. You're not ready to get out of bed. You've had a long period of inactivity and your muscles need time to build up their strength.'

'I just wanted to look at my things,' I say.

Rachel's eyes fall on the photo frame where it landed face down on the floor and she lets out a frustrated-sounding laugh. 'You only need to ask me if you want something passing,' she says, 'it's no bother.' She bends down to pick up the frame and says, 'Oh dear, it's broken. I'll just get the dustpan and brush.'

She's gone before I can protest, taking the broken photo frame with her, and I hear her footsteps move down the stairs, then there's silence and I imagine her opening and closing cupboards, searching for the cleaning things although I have no idea how familiar she is with my house, before she returns and begins sweeping up the glass.

'Can I see the photo?' I ask and she looks confused for a moment before realisation dawns in her eyes and she lets out a laugh. 'Sorry, I'm away with the fairies. I had no idea I was still holding it.' The frame is tucked under her arm and she removes it, glancing wistfully at the photograph herself before brushing off a couple of tiny shards of glass into the dustpan and handing it to me. Inside is a faded picture of two small girls wearing matching spotty swimsuits on a very British beach with grey sky and a muddy-looking sea behind them.

'Walberswick,' Rachel says. 'One of the many summers we spent there.'

The two small girls must be roughly four and six and they're smiling broadly, but the devastating thing is they're strangers to me. I nod blankly, trying not to let Rachel see that her words mean nothing to me, but suddenly I find I can remember the feeling of sand between my toes, and as I close my eyes, an image of dangling bits of bacon from a line to catch crabs from a tiny bridge behind the caravan site comes to mind. My eyes fly open excitedly. It's like I can taste the strawberry ice cream from the shop in the village square where we'd chase each other all over the yellowing grass as the high sun baked down. Tears fill my eyes at the sheer relief of remembering something.

'Walberswick,' I say with certainty and Rachel smiles, finishing up her sweeping and sitting in the seat beside me.

'Do you actually remember?' she asks, not sounding as excited as I feel somehow.

Nodding, I whisper, 'Not much, but I actually remember.'

She clutches my hand tightly and her nails dig painfully into the skin. I try to hold on to the feeling for as long as I can, but it fades as the memories of Walberswick seem to lose their colour and drift from my mind, taking with them any hope and lightness that I felt.

'It's gone,' I say, and she releases my hand.

'Never mind. Don't force it,' she says softly. 'I spoke to Bryce. He told me that you know about the accident.'

'He said it was six months ago,' I say incredulously.

'It's been slow progress but you're getting there, Jen.' She grips my hand again and I find myself wincing. 'You're really getting there.' Tears spring into her eyes as she goes on, 'For a while we weren't sure if you...' But then she shakes her head. 'No need to even think it. We've had a couple of false starts but here you are, awake, asking questions, and soon you'll be your old self again, back trawling car boot sales every Sunday and listening to your records so loudly that the neighbours complain.'

Her description disappoints me since I didn't picture myself as the type of person who blasts music without caring what my neighbours may think; I may not have too much to go on, but I assumed I was an ordinary person, conscientious, caring, the type of person who'd make a good wife and mother, even though I'm apparently neither. I don't feel like someone who dances around to pop music or headbangs to rock or whatever they do to rap, and am I really someone who ruins the peace and quiet in the neighbourhood? I would like to think I'm more respectful than that.

'I'm just teasing,' Rachel says, noticing my creased brow. 'I think that only happened once after you found a rare Mozart recording.'

'So I like classical music?' I ask falteringly.

It's Rachel's turn to frown briefly before she catches herself and says brightly, 'Yes, you do. You play too, and teach. That's your job.'

Play and teach? I'm flabbergasted but it's also a relief to square away something about me. 'What do I play?'

'The violin. I'm sure it will come back to you when it's back in your hands. It's probably like riding a bike, although I never got to grips with it. Funny that when we both tried it, you couldn't get enough, whereas for me it was like I'd been introduced to an instrument of torture.'

As she says the words, I find I *can* picture the size and weight of a violin tucked under my chin, and the idea of playing is not wholly alien to me. With a jolt of clarity, I realise now why I thought there was something strange about the house last night – it was the silence I found odd. Music must have been a huge part of my life for many years and suddenly I feel a strong yearning to hear some. Perhaps it will help bring me back to myself.

'Could you bring my record player up here?' I ask and Rachel's proper smile suddenly breaks out. It's like the sun coming through the clouds – my sister really is a beautiful woman. I wonder if I look like her or if I've always been in her shadow.

'Of course I can,' she says.

'Rachel, before you go, how old am I?'

She lets out a strangled laugh, 'I'm sorry but I keep forgetting we need to start at the very beginning. You're forty-one. We had a lovely barbecue for your fortieth birthday in the garden last year. Now, I'll just go and get your record player.'

She leaves the room and as I run through what she's just told me something snags in my mind. Most people have barbecues in the summer, so it seems likely that my forty-first birthday has taken place while I've been in this room, unconscious. Goose-bumps appear on my arms and I try to rub away the chill while I wait for Rachel to return.

It doesn't take long before she has the portable record player set up on the small table beside the bed and we're putting on a Mozart symphony that she says is one of my favourites. Trying not to focus on the string of words on the well-worn sleeve that

mean nothing to me, I close my eyes and let the music's undula-
tions wash over me. It doesn't create the explosion of memories
that I'd hoped for, but quickly I feel calm and it takes me away
from my own worries for a moment. At the end of the
symphony, I open my eyes and see Rachel is watching me with
a happy expression on her face, and when I touch my cheeks, I
realise they're wet with tears.

'It's a lovely piece,' I say and Rachel nods in agreement.

'It is. Although I always was more of a Radiohead kind of
gal.' She laughs and I join in a beat later, not having the heart to
tell her that I have no idea who or what Radiohead is. The next
track begins and Rachel gets up. 'I'll just pop down and get your
lunch ready for today before I head to work, then Bryce will be
here later to look after you.'

I nod because I realise she needs to get on, but I wish I
could demand that she stay so we can talk everything through
until I am all out of questions.

As if reading my mind she says, 'I'm sorry I have to dash
again, I need to get to a meeting. They've been really understanding, but I've missed so much lately.'

A pang of guilt hits me that I've caused so much trouble and
I say quickly, 'Of course, you must go. What is it that you do?'

Rachel looks at me and blinks then says, 'I'm going to have
to get used to telling you everything from the beginning, aren't
I? Nothing glamorous, I'm afraid – I'm in insurance.'

I have no further questions about Rachel's job in insurance
so I simply smile and nod and say, 'Can we talk properly soon?
When you have more time.'

'How about this evening? I can come straight after work and
bring a Chinese takeout.' Perhaps seeing my brow knit as I
consider whether my stomach can handle gloopy, sugary sauces,
Rachel adds, 'It's your favourite,' so I smile and nod because I
don't want to disappoint her.

'That sounds wonderful.'

She bends over and kisses my cheek.

'Great. You just relax until Bryce returns later,' and then she goes, leaving me listening to my music, feeling slightly more like myself.

I lift the photo and examine the two small girls we were who have turned into two very different women by the sounds of it, and I wonder what type of sisters we are – the type that tell each other everything or those that keep their secrets firmly clutched to their chests? I may not remember much, but sharing memories with her today has filled me with warmth. I feel grateful that she's stuck by me through these past six months – at least someone has.

But as I study the frame, I notice that the photograph is a little smaller than the aperture. It's very difficult to tell without the glass, but I wiggle it around and hold it up and I'm sure that this picture would leave a sliver of the backboard visible, a brown line of chipboard that would stand out a mile off. This photo does not fit the frame. Wrinkling my nose, I wonder if I am the type of woman who could live with such an imperfection in front of her every day, staring at her from her own bedroom. But I don't need to give it too much thought. Instinctively, I know that no, I'm not, and the budding sisterly love I was feeling shatters in an instant.

SIX

I hear Rachel moving around downstairs until the front door slams and I feel a rush of relief. Any comfort I felt from having her here has evaporated. Now, all I can think is, *Why are you lying to me?* Panic tightens my chest. I feel like I can't breathe.

I try to tell myself that I'm being silly but I can't get over the fact that she took the picture frame with her when she went downstairs and took longer than you'd expect to pick up a dustpan and brush. She had time to substitute the photo, and more than that, her deception provides some evidence that I'm not going crazy – the doubt that's been creeping up on me since I woke up is justified, and it intensifies as it dawns on me that it's possible that she's keeping me here, isolating me from the world, and not telling me the truth about what happened to me. But what could she possibly be so desperate to keep from me that would make her go to such lengths?

I wrestle with the possibilities in my mind but I can't quite believe that the woman who seems so nice and kind and has been looking after me so patiently could do anything so sinister. My sister is apparently all I've got, so it would make sense that I have a framed photograph of the two of us in my bedroom, unless... I try not to get carried away, but the sense that I was married is hanging around like a scent in the air. The possibility that my husband and child could be real is thrilling but also terrifying, because if they are somewhere, out there, then what's happened to them? And what am I doing here, alone, with Rachel? And why is she lying to me?

A shudder passes through me as I look around the bedroom and realise that it shares similarities with what I picture a prison cell to be like. There's only one small window, and from the angle of the sky I can tell we're above the ground so it would be difficult to escape that way; there's a bed, a bedpan and a lock on the door that gives me the chills just looking at it since it makes it possible that Rachel and Bryce are locking me in.

There's a vase of flowers and a shelf of books, but they could just be window-dressing – there's nothing useful and certainly no connection to the outside world. I'm trying not to have a full-blown panic attack but it feels like the walls are closing in as I consider that perhaps I'm a prisoner in my own home. Pushing myself up, I tug open the drawer of my bedside table, half hoping there will be a mobile phone waiting for me to check back in with the world and I can laugh off all these terrifying thoughts, but all I find is a brand-new puzzle book and a biro. I must admit it feels like a stage set rather than a bedroom.

I decide it's time to have a proper look around, however tired I may feel, and I swing my legs around the side of the bed, moving them slowly, one at a time, like a person dragging dead weights. Once I'm in sitting position, I consider testing my weight on my feet, but I feel nerves joining the worry that's swirling inside me. Something tells me that if I try to stand, I'm going to end up in another heap on the floor, and a squeeze in my bladder makes me pause. It takes me a moment to realise that not only is my bladder full, but it must be close to bursting point because I am suddenly desperate for the toilet. I process that the dull ache has been building for a while and I let out a groan of frustration. It's so difficult trying to get my mind in order when my body is in constant need of attention too.

As I reach across for the bedpan that Bryce left on the small table within grabbing distance of the bed, I can almost hear my own voice saying, *Tell me when you need a wee-wee*, and I smile despite the fact that I'm about to pee all over myself and my pyjamas like an excited puppy. It's like I can hear myself potty-training a small child. I can almost remember the frustration of the multiple failures and the joy of seeing them finally grasp it. But I live alone, and I have no children... Shoving the bedpan beneath me at the same moment as I can hold on no longer, I manage to get most of it in the container, and I'm just wondering how to extract the full can when I hear the door open downstairs and what sounds like Bryce arriving.

My face flushes as I try to pull the full bedpan from under me while tugging at my pyjama bottoms. I hear Bryce's heavy tread on the stairs as urine sloshes onto my hand and the smell of it hits my nose. I feel more wary of him than I did earlier – if Rachel is the brains of this strange situation, then Bryce must be the brawn, but I realise I'm in no position to reject his help. Not when I'm holding an overflowing bedpan.

'Hello...' Bryce's voice trails off as he pushes open the door and sees the position I'm in. '... again,' he finishes as he rushes forward and grabs the bedpan. 'Let me help you with that.'

He whisks it out of the room and into the bathroom and a moment later I hear the flush of the loo as I rearrange myself and the bedclothes and I desperately look around for anything I could use to protect myself. Bryce may be acting nice but I have no idea what he's truly capable of. There's nothing heavy enough to do any damage and I wonder if that's intentional. Perhaps Rachel and Bryce don't want me to be able to defend myself. Bryce doesn't return right away and I hear the whoosh of the tap before he comes back carrying a plastic bowl filled with foamy water.

'I thought you might appreciate a freshen up,' he says with a knowing glance at my hand, which I'm holding out at an odd angle, currently covered with drying pee. I think about challenging him but it's hard when he's being so helpful. And when I imagine telling him about the issue with the photo size, I realise it sounds petty so I decide to continue trying to gather information myself. I just know I need to be on my guard.

'You read my mind,' I say, and he grins beneath his large beard and brings the bowl over to the small table, moving it as close as possible to the bed so I can reach the sponge.

I stare at it for a moment, wondering what's the best approach for a sponge-bath while lying in bed fully dressed, before Bryce takes the lead.

'Usually I would remove a patient's clothing and sponge from top to tail.'

The description makes me cringe and I feel my whole body growing hot, aware my face must be painfully red. I have a very strong feeling that I do not want Bryce to remove my pyjamas, not while I look and smell like this, but I feel silly saying it – he is my nurse after all. And I'm sure he's seen it all before if I've been here for six months already although I don't like thinking about that.

'We could just do top half today?' he suggests, and I nod quickly. 'I'm sure you'll be ready for a shower soon. Your bones have all healed nicely so we just need to build up your strength.'

I let him help me remove the pyjama top and find I'm wearing a greying sports bra underneath. I'm glad I'm not nude as he squeezes out the sponge and gently swabs my skin. We avoid making eye contact and Bryce starts idly chatting about a film about a famous conductor that he thinks I might enjoy, but my mind drifts as the sponge glides in long strokes down my neck and along my arms. Despite how worried I've been, there's something strangely sensual about the whole experience and I close my eyes, trying desperately to halt my thoughts and stop myself from blushing further. This man is being paid to be here, I remind myself, and he is certainly not enjoying himself. I tell myself it's only because I've been starved of affection that I'm feeling anything towards him at all but it doesn't stop me feeling desperate.

I think we're both glad once it's done, and he wraps a towel around me and disappears to empty the bowl, leaving me alone with my thoughts. Why does this man feel closer to me than my own sister? I fear it may be a product of a dirty mind and I feel heat rising to my face again when he returns to the room.

'Everything OK?' he asks.

'Yes!' I squeak. Clearing my throat, I say in a more even voice, 'Yes, fine. Please can you push the window open as wide as it will go? I need some air in here.'

He shoves the sash window upwards and I enjoy the waft of fresh air it brings. Returning to the side of the bed, he says, 'Since you're eating and drinking and your system is clearly working, we can remove the drip if you feel up to it?'

'Yes, please,' I say quickly, imagining the lightness of my arm once the needle is removed, the freedom of not being attached to something even though I can't imagine I will be leaping straight out of bed. My muscles still feel seriously wobbly. Suddenly I can barely wait another second, but I breathe slowly in and out and force myself to remain calm as Bryce carefully unwraps the bandage that's wound around the crook of my elbow and then gently peels off the tape until he can slide out the needle.

I'm expecting it to all be over in a moment, but he seems to take longer than is necessary, fiddling with the tube as I wince and a trickle of blood runs down my arm. I'm expecting him to tug out the needle and press a bandage against the wound, but he glances at me and I swear I see fear and confusion in his round brown eyes, before he yanks out the needle and blood spurts out of my arm. It's almost comical as red droplets land in an arc on the white sheets and he leaps back so far that he crashes into the bedside table, where the vase of flowers stands. We both cry out as the glass orb rocks then teeters and falls to the floor with a loud crash.

In another moment, the farce has ended and Bryce is chalk-faced but pressing a piece of gauze to the wound and saying, 'Keep the pressure on, I'll just clean that up.'

He hurries out of the room, leaving me to wonder what the hell has just happened. It was almost as if he was frightened, but what nurse is afraid of needles? Now a little voice is whispering, *Maybe he's not a nurse?* But that feels like a big leap to make given, apart from this incident, so far he's behaved with the utmost professionalism, whereas I have objectified him from start to finish. Perhaps I've made him so uncomfortable that he felt unable to do his job? Worried that I might have landed on the answer, I mentally scold myself, but when I glance down at the smashed vase, my thoughts come to a juddering stop.

There, in among the shards of glass and bedraggled flowers, tucked in between the stalks and no bigger than a book of stamps, is a small card that must have been delivered with them. I'd assumed Rachel brought the flowers but why would she write a card and not mention it? I feel a thrill of excitement that perhaps it's from someone else and my thoughts begin to race as I try to work out who it could be from, and I find myself thinking of my husband again. This strange presence on the edge of my mind. Of course, I want the flowers to be from him but is that just wishful thinking? Imagining a wonderful man by my side certainly doesn't make him real.

Hearing Bryce on the stairs, I realise I have two options: ask him to pick up the card for me or get it for myself. After what happened with Rachel and the photo frame, I don't trust anyone else, so I move as quickly as I can, sliding out of the side of the bed and feeling the balls of my feet land on a sodden patch of carpet, but I only manage to push up for a moment before my legs give way and I slither into a heap on the floor. I land in the crush of flowers and glass and feel the inevitable slice of pain as the tip of a shard connects with the soft part of my thigh – but my fingers close around the soggy piece of card just as Bryce enters the room. His face twists as he takes in the scene before him, and he rushes forward and heaves me back onto the bed.

'What are you doing?' he asks. 'Surely you can see there's broken glass.'

We both stare at my leg where a short neat slit oozes blood.

'Sorry,' I say contritely as he presses another piece of gauze against my thigh. 'I thought I would try and help clear up.'

Bryce sighs heavily. 'That's what I'm here for. I don't think that cut is too bad, so I'll just go and grab a plaster for it and then I'll get everything put to right.'

'Thank you,' I breathe.

'Don't you go being the hero again,' he says and he tramps back downstairs.

The moment he's gone, I gently open my fist and peer at the small card clenched inside. The edges are soft and curled but I can clearly see that it's a standard florist's card with a bland bunch of flowers on the front and the shop's logo on the back. For a moment I'm hit with disappointment, but then I realise that it's a card you can open. My heart thuds as I carefully attempt to peel apart the pieces of wet card without tearing them. My first try results in a small, soft piece of pulp falling onto the bedsheet, but just as I hear Bryce start back this way, I manage to peel open the remaining front half.

Inside, written in cursive script, the blue ink bleeding into the white paper, are two words that make my insides turn over.

I'm sorry.

SEVEN

Bryce leaves again after he's made sure I'm comfortable and my body feels heavy and my eyelids struggle to stay open. I spend my afternoon drifting in and out of consciousness, battling fitful sleep as my thoughts rage, going over and over what might have happened to me or my disappeared family, who could be sorry, and what for.

But it's impossible to colour in a picture when you don't even have an outline. I'm still no closer to understanding myself or what happened and I feel furious as I think about what Rachel has done for me – or rather, what she hasn't. Since I woke up, all she has done is given me a faded photo of two little girls and painted an overexposed picture of us playing on the beach but I can't even trust that. She's deliberately evaded all of my questions. And how do I even know she's telling the truth about being my sister or about Bryce being a nurse? I shudder involuntarily at the sheer horror of it. I'm doubting everything and everyone but it's hard to picture them as cold-blooded kidnappers when they've been so attentive.

When I hear Rachel return, I make sure that I'm sitting as upright as I can, facing the door, ready to demand that she tell me everything that she knows the moment she arrives. I can't bear another second of being alone with my own thoughts when the voice in my head is a stranger's. Her footsteps come up the stairs and I set my jaw, readying myself for whatever comes. If I have to battle this woman for the truth, then I'm prepared. I will do whatever it takes within my power.

The door opens and Rachel enters carrying a white plastic bag filled with cartons of Chinese food, and she has a big smile on her face.

'Jen, darling, you've got so much more colour in your cheeks.' She comes over and kisses me and my anger catches in my throat as I'm unsure how to respond. It would be easier to hate her if she was horrible.

'Thanks,' I mumble gloomily as she begins spreading the plastic cartons on the small table, peeling off the lids and filling the room with a sweet and aromatic smell that makes my mouth water and stomach growl in hunger. She has definitely over-ordered but it seems like a long time since I last ate.

'Shall I just give you a little bit of everything?' she asks, starting to load a plate without waiting for a response, and I'm struck by the absurdity of the situation. Here Rachel is, faffing with a takeaway while I lie next to her, doubting everything she has told me so far and stewing in questions.

'Just sit down!' I burst out and Rachel's head snaps up and her hand stills.

There's a pause before she says in an overly calm voice, 'There's no need to shout. What's wrong?'

'Don't you get how weird this is? How terrifying?' I feel desperate now, my eyes meeting hers as I search frantically for a glimmer of understanding. 'I don't know anything. *Anything*! It seems like you are all I have in the world, the only person who can help me figure things out. And all you seem to be worried about is Chinese food.'

Rachel plops in the chair next to me, sighing. 'I'm trying not to overwhelm you.'

I snort at this. 'You didn't even tell me I'd been in a coma for six months!'

'I'm sorry,' she says. 'I honestly thought it was better not to bombard you with details the moment you opened your eyes. But I'm here now and you can ask me anything you want.'

'Fine. Why are you keeping me here alone?' The words rush out of my mouth in an accusation before I can stop them and Rachel's mouth falls open.

'Is that what you think?' Tears fill her dark eyes and I feel a hit of guilt that I've upset her when there is still the possibility that she has only ever been trying to help me.

'Why aren't I seeing a doctor?' I ask in a strangled voice.

'You are!' she guffaws. 'Dr Marsden is a wonderful physician who specialises in brain injuries; she's one of the best neurologists in London. She was the one who advised that we could look after you just as well at home and that your chances of recovery would be improved by being away from the hospital environment. She said patients often recover quicker when they are in familiar surroundings, and look at you! Plus there's much less risk of you catching one of those awful superbugs here when it's just me and Bryce coming in and out. And Dr Marsden of course.'

'But I've never met Dr Marsden,' I say in a whiny voice and Rachel lets out a strange laugh that rankles me but I keep my annoyance from showing on my face. I suppose it must be funny to see a fully grown woman who knows about as much as a puppy. She loads a forkful of sweet and sour chicken and I allow her to feed it to me.

'You've been unconscious, Jen. She's been here once or twice a week for months. I called her as soon as you woke up and she came to check on you yesterday afternoon, but you were sleeping. She didn't want to wake you but she said she'll come back as soon as she can.'

Rachel continues feeding me forkful after forkful and smiling at me with her big square teeth, gleaming like a Cheshire cat, but I'm not satisfied. By my count, I woke up yesterday afternoon so it hasn't been long, but I feel so alone. The only family member or friend I've seen or even heard about is Rachel and that doesn't seem right. Where are all the cards, texts and real-life people calling or rushing to my bedside? All I've received is a mystery apology that I had to find myself in among shattered glass and broken stems.

'Don't I have any other family or friends?' I ask in a small voice.

'Of course you do!' Rachel says, sounding shocked.

She leans forward and I catch a whiff of cigarette smoke covered by her perfume, and I wonder whether I knew that she smoked or if that's another thing she's kept from me. She takes my hand and looks at me beseechingly. 'You're going to have to trust me that there are lots of people out there who are thinking of you and will jump at the chance to visit when I give them the say-so, but right now, you're just not well enough to have people traipsing in and out of here. You were in a very serious accident, Jen. I'm not going to sugar-coat it – you almost died, so we need to listen to the doctor and only open the door when we're sure your immune system can handle it. Does that sound OK?'

I nod but I can't help but ask, 'Don't we have parents?'

Rachel looks startled and pauses on the force-feeding for a moment, staring at me, and I know what she's about to say isn't good news. 'There's no nice way to say this so I'll just tell you. Dad died five, no six, years ago now. Pancreatic cancer. You and he were very close. You both loved music and painting. You spent a lot of time with him at the end.'

Tears fill my eyes, but I have no memory of my father, only

a sense that yes, I did share my love of music with someone close and perhaps that's why I find playing my records so comforting. My sadness springs from the knowledge that there's an empty space in my memory where someone I love should be rather than the loss of my dad, since it's impossible to miss what you don't know.

'And our mum? Is she dead, too?'

Rachel looks into the distance for a moment, then cocks her head and says, 'No, she's not dead, but she's not well. It was a pretty hellish time when Dad died because Mum was acting so strangely and it took us a while to realise it was early-onset dementia. She's in a specialist care home. I'll take you to visit her when you're strong enough.'

Nodding, I take this in and Rachel resumes feeding me sticky rice that I chew in silence. I almost don't want to hear any more but after a couple of mouthfuls, I force myself to go on. 'What about other family? Aunts, uncles, cousins?' I don't dare mention my phantom husband and child again.

Rachel smiles, 'Yes, they're all fit and well, thankfully. There's Auntie Georgina, Dad's sister, and her kids, Emma and Danny, up in Sheffield – well, Emma moved to Pontefract but she's still nearby. They've been messaging almost every day and I know they will come down and visit just as soon as I give them the green light. Then there are the Australian cousins...' She looks at me quizzically, I assume checking to see whether I know who the Australian cousins are, so I just give my head a single shake and she continues, 'Mum's sister, Auntie Veronica, married an Australian, Brian, and they moved to Melbourne years ago. They have three kids, Rich, Paul and Sarah, our cousins, who now all have families of their own. We took Mum for a visit just before Dad got sick, but you've been talking about going back out there to meet all of our new second cousins – I think they've had six or seven babies between them in the last few years. Maybe we can go together when you're recovered? That would be something to look forward to.'

I give a noncommittal grunt, feeling less certain than Rachel sounds that seeing my cousins with all their new children is exactly what I need right now. The pang of sadness I feel when I think of their families and the fact that I haven't got any children of my own makes me wonder whether visiting might just make me feel worse not better. There's a lump in my throat, but Rachel loads up another fork with shredded beef this time and I gulp it down, grateful the plate is almost clean and Rachel seems satisfied by the amount I've eaten.

'What about you?' I ask, dropping my gaze since I'm not sure if this question will upset her. 'Are you married with kids?'

Rachel surprises me by smiling and shaking her head. 'Nope, that wasn't on the cards for me. I've got a partner, a lovely woman called Laura, but I've known since I was a kid that I would be happier child-free.'

Her eyes rest on my face and she lifts her chin almost as if she is daring me to be shocked by her revelation that she's gay with no desire for children, but I find I'm not surprised at all. I'm sure I've known for years. I'm glad my sister is living the life she wants to, but I can't help feeling disappointed to hear about my own lonely existence. I can't believe that's what I dreamed of as a kid.

Rachel sighs. 'You still seem sad, Jen. Is there anything else I can tell you that might help?'

'Have I always been alone? Was this the life I wanted?'

Rachel sighs once more and I wonder if she feels sorry for me or is frustrated by my question. And a little voice whispers that maybe she is stalling for time as she works out how best to answer.

'You've had several relationships over the years but I'm afraid you never met the right man. But there's still time!'

'What about children?' I probe. 'Did I want them?'

'We didn't really talk about it,' Rachel says. She must see me frown as I wonder why sisters close enough for one of them to take full responsibility for the other's health wouldn't discuss such a fundamental part of life.

'Maybe you felt I wasn't the best person to talk to about it since I never wanted any,' she offers, but this still feels hollow. I realise I can't be angry with her for not knowing but I still feel simmering resentment that I need to address.

'Did you swap out the photo from my frame?' I ask and Rachel gasps. A look of hurt flashes across her face and my anger curdles slightly. When she speaks, she sounds genuinely emotional. 'Why would you think that?'

'The Walberswick photo doesn't fit the frame properly.'

Rachel picks it up and holds it in front of her eyes, wiggling the picture and frowning. 'I don't know what you mean. It's a good fit.'

'No, it's slightly small.' I sound churlish but I need to ask her. I want to hear her deny it.

Rachel purses her lips. 'I can't see anything wrong with it, but you have always been a perfectionist.'

There's a contradiction in her words – if I'm such a perfectionist, why would I frame a too-small photo? – but I can see I'm not going to get anywhere by challenging her further. Rachel is starting to look angry so I decide to move on. I wonder what else I should ask but the weight of how much I don't know is overwhelming, like trying to work out which pebble to pick up on a beach, and I bite my lip, frustrated at myself that I can't form the right question. Resting my hands by my side, I feel the card that I found in the bunch of flowers and I caress the edge before pulling it out and offering it to Rachel.

She examines the card quizzically, taking it from me and reading the message before saying, 'Where did you get this?' in a stern voice that sounds almost accusatory.

'The flowers,' I say, and when she doesn't react, I add, 'It was stuck between the stems.'

She reads the message out loud, 'I'm sorry,' then tuts and adds, 'Well, I'm sorry too but I have no idea who sent this or why. I imagine it must have been an error by the florist not to include the name of the sender, but you have received lots of cards and flowers so perhaps they got complacent.'

I can't let that one go by without asking so I cut in, 'Where are they all then?'

'All what?'

'The cards and flowers from all of my many friends?' I glance pointedly at the surfaces in the room that are mostly bare apart from the single photo frame containing the photo of me and Rachel.

'Well, that's a funny thing to say.' Rachel says her words carefully and I feel like she's trying to hide her annoyance. 'You know that flowers don't last forever and I've put all of the cards on display downstairs. I didn't want to overwhelm you by putting them all in here, but I thought they'd be nice for you to read when you were feeling up to it. Would you like me to go and get them?'

'Not now,' I say, 'But later, please. And where's my phone?'

Rachel holds up her finger and disappears from the room. She crosses the hallway but doesn't go downstairs and a moment later she returns with a smashed-up smartphone and a charger.

'It got broken in the crash, I'm afraid. I'll leave it here for you, but if you can't get it working, let me know and I can take it to the repair shop.'

I clutch my phone to my chest since, despite the obliterated screen, it still feels like a lifeline, a tangible connection to my old life, but I don't feel quite satisfied. 'There's something still bugging me,' I say, and as she lifts her eyes to mine it's almost as if she's wincing, waiting for something specific.

'Why would the person who sent the flowers be sorry? If it was an accident, surely it wouldn't be anybody's fault?'

Rachel folds her arms and I can see how angry she is now. I don't know how much further I can push her until she snaps, but maybe that wouldn't be a bad thing. People spill their secrets when they're upset.

'It's probably just a generic "I'm sorry", like people say when someone's hurt or ill. You know how English people overuse the word.'

It seems like whatever question I ask, Rachel always has the answer, but I never get any closer to the truth.

'I can see that's not what you wanted to hear and I'm sorry.' She laughs and the sound grates on me. 'There I go, doing it myself.'

I grit my teeth. 'I know there's something you're not telling me.'

We glare at each other, suspicion and fury radiating between us. How can she even pretend that everything is all right when there's so much unsaid? Rachel looks away first and starts fiddling with her fork. She purses her lips as if she's wondering how much to say and my heart skips a beat. Could this be the moment? I'm sure she is holding back. I've felt it from the very second I woke up and she walked into the room. I can tell there's something she wants to say.

'Tell me,' I say, forcing myself to breathe evenly.

'Jen,' she says with a sigh and puts her face in her hands before looking up at me. I can't put my finger on exactly what it is but I feel like finally, thankfully, she's going to level with me. 'OK,' she says, 'Dr Marsden advised that I take my time in telling you things to give your brain a chance to heal, but I can see you're not going to rest until I tell you everything I know.'

I'm so relieved that I'm finally going to get the truth that I feel like bursting into tears, but a sliver of steel passes through me as I realise that there must be a reason that Rachel has been holding back. She must have thought that I was too fragile to handle whatever she's about to tell me. It must be bad. I feel a shiver of premonition as I wait for the news that might break me apart...

EIGHT

I force myself to keep my face passive and act as if I'm not so desperate to hear what Rachel has to say that I feel like shoving my hand into her mouth and ripping the words from her throat myself. But something tells me that it's time to practise patience; best to lie back and wait and act like I'm not on tenter-hooks. Play it cool since I have a sense that my sister doesn't like to be rushed. I can tell that Rachel likes to be in control and that seems like one thing we have in common. Perhaps it has been the source of trouble between us – both of us desperate to be the one who shuffled and dealt the cards, sat in the front seat, went first in the bath. Maybe that competitiveness extended beyond childhood.

I count back from ten, trying to maintain an air of noncha-lance, but thankfully I don't have to wait for long before she clears her throat and begins in a quiet, wavering voice, 'It was back in March, a Saturday. You'd been in town shopping and you were driving home, and the weather was God-awful – wind, rain, freezing cold, you name it. You took the bypass route even though the main road must have been quiet because no one would've been out in that weather if they could help it and…' Rachel falters and narrows her eyes at me. 'Are you sure you want me to go on? You've gone a bit pale.'

Her hand goes to my forehead and she purses her lips in a way that annoys me rather than makes me feel comforted, so I grit my teeth and say with as much determination as I can muster, 'Keep going.'

'OK… so we don't know the exact time but it was around six in the evening. It would have already been dark at that time of year, and maybe it was the rain, or another car's headlights, or perhaps an animal, but something caused you to leave the road.'

Leave the road? That's a strange way to describe a car crash. I furrow my brow, trying to remember anything from that evening, but it's like trying to remember the plot of a film you haven't seen. I run over her words, but I simply can't bring any pictures to mind, as if I'm hearing someone else's story.

'Did I crash?' As soon as the words leave my lips I feel silly because, of course, I must have, since you don't spend six months in bed if you career into a field and roll to a gentle stop. To Rachel's credit, she doesn't laugh.

'You hit a tree,' she says and we both wince.

'What type of tree?' I ask and now Rachel does laugh, a soft and gentle laugh that diffuses the tension in the room.

'You always want to know the gory details, don't you?' And then she realises what she's said and her hands go to her mouth. 'Sorry, "gory" was the wrong word.'

'Don't worry,' I say, just waiting for her to tell me the type of tree, and without really thinking it, I suddenly know exactly what she is going to say before the word leaves her mouth.

'Oak,' she says, and I nod as something falls into place in a satisfying way that makes me happy that my brain is working as it's meant to for once. The oak tree I dreamed of wasn't one that I planted, nor did I frolic high in its branches – it was the tree that almost killed me.

'What do you think happened?' I ask.

'Only you can tell us that, Jen,' she says. 'But don't worry yourself about it now. You've got other more important things to focus on. Like getting better...'

'Is that it?' I ask, feeling confused and disappointed, because I thought Rachel was going to reveal something that might jolt my memory, but all she's told me are details that I might have guessed. My car went off the road in bad weather – what's the big deal about that?

Rachel bites her lip. 'I'm trying to tell you that it's not clear why you left the road.'

'You must have a theory,' I probe, not willing to give up on it yet. 'Didn't anyone see what happened or hear anything?'

Rachel shakes her head. 'No one went by until around quarter past six when the engine was already drenched with rain and almost cold. That road is usually busy on a Saturday evening, but the rain really was torrential. The driver who found you said they'd stopped at the garden centre for half an hour and it was still raining when they gave up and got back in their car.'

I wonder why I didn't stop like everyone else – why did I think I was special? – and a little voice tells me that this is all my fault. By carrying on recklessly, I put myself in bed for six months and gave Rachel a dependent to look after, but even just thinking the word 'reckless' grates. It's hard to imagine myself as a reckless person. I don't know very much about myself but I feel like I'm cautious, boring even, the type of person who catalogues their spice collection and stores all their sweaters in plastic bags, I imagine. Now why would I have been merrily zooming along the road in what sounds like almost a typhoon?

I can't think of a good reason but then another idea pops into my head and I blurt out, 'There must have been skid marks on the road. The rain doesn't wash those off. That would at least show if there was something I swerved to avoid?'

Rachel begins to look more uncomfortable, shifting in the

soft pink armchair and wincing as if she's sitting on a slab of stone. 'Why don't we talk about this in a few days. It's getting late. You could do with some rest and there's absolutely no rush on this. Neither of us is going anywhere.'

'Rachel, whatever it is, just tell me.'

She sighs and a resigned smile crosses her face. 'I can never keep anything from you, can I?'

I don't know how to respond to this since it feels like she's doing her best to keep an awful lot from me, but I swallow the bitter annoyance that rises inside me. It's not the time for another argument.

'Look, we don't know what this means and there's no one who can say what happened other than you, but there were no skid marks.'

'No skid marks?' I echo, quickly running through why this could be. My head aches from desperately trying to make sense of what she's saying.

'Could the brakes have failed?' I ask, suddenly hopeful that all this can be explained away by a simple piece of bad fortune, something that could have happened to anyone. Maybe I was driving an old banger that conked out at precisely the wrong moment, but I see Rachel is looking doubtful.

'It's possible,' she says, 'but you'd only had the car a couple of months, and although it wasn't brand-new, you made sure the MOT was up to date and you'd had the logbook checked over by a mechanic.'

'Why else, then?' I ask. 'Do you have a theory?'

Rachel sighs again and shrugs. 'Really, I'm hardly an expert, but I suppose I've had some time to think about it and I guess I've come up with two possible explanations.'

'Yes?' I say eagerly.

This time Rachel meets my gaze and says directly, 'The first is that you fell asleep at the wheel.'

I quickly dismiss this. It was early evening, after all, and I don't have young children who might be keeping me up at night, plus Rachel would surely have mentioned if I have any illness or condition that would make me susceptible to daytime sleeping.

'And the second?'

Rachel looks away and fixes her eyes straight ahead, rubbing the side of her nose. 'I'm not saying this is what happened, just one possibility, and we won't know unless you remember yourself.'

Rachel is stalling – what she's about to say must be what she believes is the truth, from the way she's dragging out the words. I just nod and wait for her to go on, open to any possibility that brings me closer to the truth.

'But I guess that another reason that people don't brake is that they don't *want* to stop in time.'

I open my mouth to ask why someone wouldn't want to stop in time but, of course, the answer hits me first between the eyes as if someone has thwacked me with a hammer, and then again in the gut, like they've followed up with a drop-kick right to my stomach. Of course the reason people don't brake is that they want there to be an accident – they want to get hurt. It shocks me that my own sister thinks it's possible that I was trying to kill myself. But I realise I have no idea whether she is right or wrong. I don't know anything about the woman I was that day...

'Do you think I did it on purpose?' I ask and the pause Rachel leaves before she answers says it all. I feel like all my stuffing has come out.

'All that matters to me is that you're here now and you're getting better,' Rachel says, pasting on a bright smile that both of us know is fake, and I can see concern shining in her eyes as she's clearly trying to work out how I'm reacting to this news. No wonder she kept it back – she probably didn't want to trigger whatever hopelessness or depression I must have been in to drive my car into a tree. I know people have their ups and downs, and I've felt many things since I awoke – sad, confused, frustrated, angry even – but I haven't felt suicidal.

'Was I really miserable before?' I ask in a small voice, trying to picture how desperate I must have been, how utterly alone I must have felt. The news that it's likely I did this to myself has sent my mind into freefall, spinning out of control. Perhaps I was so desperate to have this imaginary husband and baby I've been convinced were mine that I decided to give up trying.

'No!' Rachel exclaims. 'You've always had so many passions in your life.'

Passions but no passion, I think sourly.

'I guess I must have been lonely,' I say, and Rachel slams her hand on the bed. 'You have a ton of friends. Look, I'm going to fetch all your cards and you can read them. That will show you just how loved you are.'

And she sweeps from the room, leaving me to stare up at the ceiling rose overhead, feeling utterly deflated as I try to accept that the reason I have become this shell of a person was probably down to my own choices all along.

NINE

I wake, still completely drained, to a swirly-whirly feeling in my guts that tells me that my stomach definitely *wasn't* ready for the Chinese food. In the bright morning sunlight, I feel a little ashamed of the level of suspicion I reached about Rachel. I'd been so convinced that she was keeping my happy family a secret from me that her news of my crumbling mental health was a blow. I'd been expecting her to reveal something, but not that; hearing that all this is down to me is hard to take.

Rachel did seem to have an answer for everything, but for some reason I still don't trust her. I try to pinpoint any proof I have that she's lied but the only evidence I have is the Walberswick photo which was slightly too small for the frame, and I don't feel like that's enough. Sighing loudly, my stomach gurgles and my guts clench and I realise with dawning revulsion that I'm going to need to use the bedpan immediately. I hastily manoeuvre it into position, managing to empty my bowels without spilling this time, but filling the room with a putrid smell that I'm sure will linger. The whole process is horribly undignified and my skin prickles with shame as I place the full bedpan onto the bedside table, trying not to look at the brownish liquid inside, and wondering whether I can carry it safely to the bathroom.

Before I attempt it, the front door downstairs opens and my heart drops as I hear Bryce entering, whistling softly. His timing is always impeccable... It's bad enough being confronted so directly by my own bodily functions, but it's so much worse that I have to share them with a man I find attractive, however inappropriate that may be. I quickly run over my options, trying to find any possible course of action other than having to call out to Bryce for help, but the realisation settles like lead in my stomach – I need him.

'Bryce? Can you come up here when you have a moment, please?'

I try to sound casual, but he immediately rushes upstairs and flings open the door.

'What do you n—' He stops short as he takes in the situation, sniffing first, his eyes resting on the bedpan as I wish that a huge sinkhole would open and take down the whole house. To his credit, he only misses a beat. 'I'll just sort that out for you.'

He whisks the bedpan out of the room while I lie in bed feeling hot and cold all over, with a strong urge to pick up my phone and scroll to distract myself, even though I know it's broken. There's a horrible sloshing sound from the bathroom that must be Bryce emptying the bedpan, and I glance around the room for something to do, desperate to be busy with something when he comes back in so I won't need to make eye contact.

My gaze lands on the stack of cards that Rachel returned to my room last night and left on the bedside table for me to read when I felt up to it. I was too tired then, and too hopeless after hearing that the crash was my fault, but now I feel ready. Picking up the top one, I see it has a cartoon elephant on the front and its trunk is holding a sign that says, 'Get well soon.'

Inside reads, 'Dear Ms V, get well soon, from Tom.'

I remember that Rachel said our last name is Vincent and my job is teaching the violin, so I deduce that the card must be from one of my pupils. It's nice to be remembered, but it's hardly a revelation, so I pick up the next one, a card with a photo of the New York skyline on the front. I open it and read, 'To Ms V, sorry to hear about your accident and wishing you a speedy recovery, love Violet.'

Another pupil. Frowning, I quickly flick through the pile and find that there are ten addressed to 'Ms V' – it's nice that I'm a popular teacher, but all I can feel is a sinking disappointment that there isn't anything more personal. The loo flushes in the bathroom as I reach the bottom of the pile and discover a handful of cards addressed to 'Jen', which must be from friends. But when I open them, they all contain only generic wishes for me to 'get well' or 'feel better'. Not a single person has written a personal note or added a titbit of information that suggests they gave me more than a second thought.

The final card on the pile has a bouquet of flowers on the front and is addressed to 'My darling Jen'. When I read the words, I feel a brief lift of hope – this must be someone close, someone who really cares – and my mind goes again to the mystery man I can't quite accept isn't real. But quickly I see that written at the bottom of the card is a single word, 'Mum', which makes me realise how pathetic I'm being. Not even my own mother thought to enhance the greeting card's printed 'with love', but Rachel did say that she's suffering from dementia so perhaps that explains why she didn't write more. I can't think of an excuse for any of the others.

Bryce returns to the room with the now clean bedpan and puts it back on the table within reach of the bed just as I cast aside the cards and slump back against the pillows.

'Everything OK?' he says and I wonder how obvious it is that I feel like bursting into tears. Maybe this is how I felt before the accident? Low and lethargic, conscious that the only people who care about me are students who I teach violin to.

'Fine,' I say flatly.

'Are you in any pain?' he asks.

'Not really.'

'I hope you don't mind me saying, but you don't seem quite yourself this morning,' he says, then flushes a little and adds, 'Sorry if that's overstepping.'

'I'm just feeling a bit...' I search for the word and land on, '... blue.'

'Fair enough after what you've been through.'

'Rachel told me a bit more about the crash. She thinks that I was trying to kill myself,' I say, watching for his reaction but he barely flinches. Rachel must have told him already, and I think bitterly that this virtual stranger knows more about me than I do myself. I wonder what else he knows.

'I'm sorry to hear that. Are you having suicidal thoughts now?'

My instinct is to answer 'God, no' right away but it feels like Bryce is asking in his medical capacity, so I let the thought sit with me for a moment and really examine it, turning it over in my mind. I am feeling low after everything I've discovered, but I definitely do not wish I wasn't alive.

'No,' I say, 'I want to get better.'

'Good, then let's you and I focus on that, what do you say?'

I meet his eyes and find myself nodding vigorously.

'Physically, what exactly is wrong with me?' I ask.

'You've been through a long period of inactivity. We kept moving you so you wouldn't develop sores, but we couldn't prevent muscle wastage. It's going to take you a bit of time to get your strength back, but you'll soon be up and about.'

I feel a slow smile spread across my face as I realise that is exactly what I want – some freedom.

'That's good,' I say forcefully.

'With your head injury, I'm afraid it's not quite as straightforward but I really ought to let Dr Marsden discuss that with you directly.'

I sigh, feeling like there's always a reason for everyone to keep something from me. I want to argue, but I don't have the energy for it, so instead I say, 'OK, fine. I'll wait to speak to Dr Marsden, but in the meantime, can you help me with something?'

Bryce smiles hesitantly. 'What did you have in mind?'

I answer so forcefully that Bryce bursts out laughing. 'I need to get out of this goddamn room.'

TEN

Bryce insists I eat something and try to take a nap first but it doesn't take much persuading for him to agree to try to help me get up. I think he must see how desperate I'm feeling and when he returns to my room later that day, he says brightly, 'Ready?'

'Ready,' I say, not telling him that I've been ready since the moment he left, sitting here, waiting with my heart thrumming in my chest. I am beyond excited for a change of scene.

'As soon as you feel a hint of tiredness, we are returning you to bed, promise?' he says and I find myself nodding along and saying, 'Scout's honour,' even though I have absolutely no intention of getting back into that bed any time soon. I know that without his help I won't get far, and I long to feel the sun on my face and breathe fresh air into my lungs. I picture my sunny yellow bench that I'm positively convinced is out in the small paved garden at the back of my house and feel a sudden longing that makes me start trying to scramble to my feet.

'Hold your horses,' Bryce says and he rushes over to help me. 'Let's do this together.'

With Bryce's help, I make it to a sitting position, facing the door with my legs over the side of the bed. He passes me a lovely, silky dressing gown to put over my tatty nightdress, which I'm grateful for. There are no mirrors in the room and although I've been excruciatingly aware of how my unwashed body smells, for the first time it crosses my mind just how awful I must look, but I tell myself that it's not time for vanity. Bryce must have seen all sorts in his role as a nurse, and I have been in a life-changing accident so I'm sure he will cut me some slack. But even as I try to convince myself that there's no reason to feel embarrassed, I still feel a mortifying rush of shame when I catch a whiff of the tangy, sweaty smell coming off me.

'Maybe I can try a shower later?' I say, trying to laugh off my embarrassment.

'One thing at a time,' Bryce says gently. 'Baby steps.'

His calm response makes me grateful Bryce chose this career path, and it seems incredible that I doubted him earlier. He's dealt with every hygiene issue with pure professionalism and he seems to have the perfect temperament for caring. It's not his fault that I'm finding his presence a little distracting. He must have quite the fan club among the little old ladies of the town if they are his usual clientele, and I find myself blushing at the idea that I'm only one of many who admires the way his arms look in his scrubs. Maybe fate has put this man in my path? Although I realise I have no idea of his marital status. He doesn't wear a ring, but then not all married men do. It would be awful if he has a wife and kids at home and I'm here lusting after their husband and father.

Bryce slides his arm around my waist and I tell myself I need to get a grip on my thoughts. He holds me so tightly it feels like I almost won't have to put any weight on my feet at all and turns to give me a steely look, his face only inches from mine.

'Ready to stand?' he asks.

'Ready,' I say, my wandering thoughts silenced by the burst of excitement I feel about the prospect of seeing the rest of my house, which is plainly ridiculous since I'm the one who decorated it and I must have seen everything hundreds of times before. But my mind is still a terrifying blank, and seeing someone's decor can tell you a lot about a person, of that I am certain. A person's home is like a window to their soul.

'On three,' Bryce says. 'One, two, three.' We both inhale and push up to standing, although if I'm honest it's more that he stands and lifts me with him, but either way, the important thing is that we make it to our feet and remain there. I feel myself swaying as the blood rushes around my body and I'm suddenly light-headed. Fingers of black creep into the edges of my vision but I squeeze my eyes shut and take several deep breaths, willing myself not to faint because if I do, Bryce will surely force me to return to bed and I simply cannot take it any more.

'All OK?' he asks.

'Yes,' I say through gritted teeth, 'let's walk to the door.'

'I like your attitude,' he says, and we stagger the few steps. As we get closer, I notice there is a key in the lock that I haven't seen before, only it is on the inside. I wonder what reason I could have had to want to lock myself inside my room when I live alone, but before I can wonder too much, Bryce twists the knob and the door swings open. I feel a lurch of excitement as I get my first glimpse outside the bedroom.

My hallway is painted a dove-grey, but there are no windows opening onto it so it does feel rather gloomy despite the lights being on, and I wonder if a brighter, lighter colour would have been wiser. *Perhaps I chose the colour to reflect my mood*, I think dourly, but I refuse to dwell on those thoughts when I'm so close to tasting freedom. As I peer down at the stripy stair-runner on the steep set of stairs, I feel like I'm standing on the edge of a mountain, staring down a black run, and I realise that there is no way I can walk down. But I can't give up, not now.

'I'm going to bump down,' I say, and Bryce gives me a

quizzical look before I add, 'Yes, like a toddler, on my bottom – I don't think my legs are quite ready for stairs.'

Bryce is smiling like he thinks I'm joking until it seems to dawn on him that I'm serious and suddenly he nods and says, 'OK then,' sounding like he's impressed, but I'm not doing it to show off. My mental health may have been bad before, but it's certainly not going to get any better unless I do something other than lie in bed feeling sorry for myself.

We make it to the top step and I slump onto my bottom; then, gripping the banister, I slowly yet surely descend the stairs, one at a time, using the seat of my silky dressing gown to slip down more easily. Bryce joins me on his arse and we end up half giggling, half groaning, and by the time we've both landed on the wooden floor at the bottom, we're falling about in hysterics. It feels good to laugh, and for a moment Bryce seems like a friend rather than someone being paid to be here. And any thought that he might be an enemy feels frankly ridiculous.

My laughter quickly fades as I peer around at my surroundings, intrigued to learn as much as I can about myself. The front door is straight ahead with a wooden shoe and coat rack to one side, the kind with ornate hooks and neat cubby holes for shoes; on the other side is a small table with a wooden bowl full of what looks like trinkets and keys. I take everything in while Bryce brings me a glass of water which I drain in one go after my minor exertion that felt like a marathon. There's nothing particularly unusual or personal in view, save for a few pairs of shoes and a couple of jackets hanging up, which I notice are all women's apparel so I presume are all mine. Beyond wondering how the leopard-print trench coat would look on, I don't see much of note and I'm impatient to get outside into the yard.

'I'm ready for the next bit,' I say, and this time Bryce doesn't even ask if I'm sure, he just clamps his arm around my waist and supports me as we reel through the door that leads off the hallway into a lovely, sunny room that runs the full length of the house; it has a sofa and telly at the front and a kitchen and dining table at the back. It's a fantastic space, truly the heart of the home, and although it's a small house I do wonder whether it's all a bit much for one person. A small family could be well and truly happy here and I think of my imagined husband and child, picture us sitting around the table or curled up on the sofa watching a movie together, and I feel a pang of sadness. The things that feel almost within touching distance are always the things that torture us the most.

I've continued the traditional look downstairs: the kitchen has lovely navy blue kitchen cabinets and there's a big wooden table, but as I look around, my smile falters as I realise that there are hardly any personal touches at all. Where is my personality here? It looks more like a kitchen showroom than a home; there aren't any pictures or letters lying around and there are certainly no toys. *A child wouldn't have much fun here*, I think bitterly as Bryce gives me a questioning look and says, 'Ready for the last push?'

I nod, focusing on crossing the wooden floor to the back door. Bryce half carries me the last few yards because my legs are turning to spaghetti. When we make it out into the sun, I feel a huge rush of elation that reminds me of cresting a hill on a bike. The feeling is more solid and I realise with a jolt of pleasure that it's probably a memory. I'm suddenly sure that in my normal life I'm a cyclist – ironic that my accident was in a car when I bet people have spent my whole life warning me about the perils of being on the road on a bicycle. I wonder if I'll ever make it back onto two wheels, but I tell myself that I can do whatever I put my mind to. I'm sure I'm one of those determined people that some may call stubborn.

I'm pleased to find that my backyard is almost exactly as I pictured it – a small paved area with a chest-height fence on both sides, separating my yard from the neighbouring houses in the terrace, and a wall at the end that is covered with climbing plants. But the yellow bench is nowhere to be seen and I feel a churning disappointment that makes me want to sink to the ground and curl into a ball. Is this the type of melancholy I suffer from? As I cast about looking for it, my gaze falls on a strange, scorched patch of paving about six feet wide by two feet across that has the distinct blackened look to mark where something has burned down. Could my bench have once been there? I turn to ask Bryce, but he's busy putting cushions on a plastic garden chair and brushing off cobwebs.

'Take a seat,' he says, pushing the chair behind me, and I sit down gratefully.

'I'll just go and freshen up your room while you're out here,' he says and disappears off while I tip my head back so the sun bathes my face. I breathe deeply through my nose, smelling my marigolds and petunias in their planters and listening to the soft buzzing of the bees as they drift from flower to flower. Rachel's revelation about my mood from before the accident feels like she's talking about a different person because as I sit here, even despite my endless questions and uncertainty, I can't help but take pleasure in my surroundings. It's a lovely day and despite the grime covering my body and my aching legs, I feel fantastic for a change in scene and some fresh air. They do say that a change is as good as a rest, and now I've had both and I feel ready to face my recovery head on.

Closing my eyes, I allow myself to rest a little since I'm exhausted from the sheer effort of getting from my bed to this seat, but I do feel rather pleased with myself that I've made it this whole way, deciding that it won't be long before I'm back on my feet again whatever this Dr Marsden or Rachel or even Bryce has to say about it.

I'm just drifting off when a piercing whisper snaps me back to reality.

'Oh my Lord, Jen, is that you?'

ELEVEN

It takes me a moment or two to locate the speaker's head poking above the fence because she's tucked away behind an apple tree, peering at me through the glossy green leaves, and I can even see a number of small green apples that aren't that far off being ready to be picked. It tells me that the whole summer is almost past and soon the dark nights will be drawing in and the temperatures will be dropping and I'll have missed it all, and I shiver at the thought.

Trying to smooth my greasy hair and arrange my dressing gown in a way that looks more presentable, I focus in on the person staring right at me with a smile on her lips but a quizzical look on her shrewd face. She must be mid-fifties or thereabouts with a pair of funky red glasses and her grey hair worn in a stylish cropped hairdo; as she watches me, she takes a long drag on a cigarette.

'Don't go telling my Ian about this, will you now?' she asks, blowing a stream of smoke into the air and grimacing. 'He'd have my guts, I tell you. Promised him I'd stop but I just have the odd one every now and then as a little pick-me-up. And lucky I did today, because I've spotted you out here. First time I've set eyes on you in ages.'

I give her a smile to try to convey that I'm pleased to see her too and I certainly won't tell Ian, but I don't want to admit that I have absolutely no idea who Ian is, or her for that matter.

'Listen to me, wittering on, when it's you I want to hear about. How *are* you?' The emphasis she puts on this question suggests she knows I've been unwell, but I have no idea whether she knows the full extent of it or what's happened to my memory. She's clearly realised that I've not been around much, but does she know I've been upstairs in my bedroom the whole time, unconscious? Somehow I don't get the feeling that Rachel has told her everything since she's looking at me as if I've just got back from a nice, long holiday rather than with wide-eyed horror that the notion of a six-month coma should bring.

'I've been better,' I say breezily. 'Have you spoken to my sister at all?'

A frown creases her brow and I think I see a shadow of dislike pass across her face before she says, 'I've seen her coming and going but we haven't said much beyond "hello" and "good morning".'

It's my turn to frown as I wonder why Rachel hasn't taken the time to tell my neighbours about my accident. I know not everyone is close to their neighbours but this woman seems to know me quite well and it's not like I have a family of my own to rally around me. She looks over my head and appears to scan the house behind me before dropping her voice and continuing in a stream of whispers.

'Not that it's any of my business, but I have been wondering what's been going on at yours. Obviously there was all that business a while back, and then, well, I won't dredge all that up, but I was worried about you and then you went and totally disappeared. It was like you dropped off the face of the planet and then Rachel appeared. My Ian said I should just stay out of it…'

With each word my heart rate increases a notch as I wonder exactly what 'all that business' was and what it is she doesn't want to 'dredge up'.

'Ian said you're not one of those people that likes to gossip and he said if you wanted help, then you would ask for it, so I should keep my beak out.'

Her words make me wonder whether I had a friend, just next door, across the fence, who might have been there for me, someone to visit me who wasn't on Rachel's payroll, who might have helped with my recovery if this apparently well-meaning Ian hadn't got in the way. Trying to keep the bitterness out of my voice, I say, 'Can I just ask, exactly how well do I know your husband?'

The woman coughs mid-drag and gives me a long, searching look before stubbing her cigarette out on the fence post and saying, 'I should think you don't know Chris at all since we divorced almost fifteen years ago after he ran off to Málaga with a man called Nigel from the golf club.' We both stare at each other and her eyes grow rounder and bigger and she says slowly, 'You do know who Ian is, don't you?'

I can see that this is important to her and I don't want to let her down but I have absolutely no idea who she's talking about.

'Ian,' I say slowly, stalling for time, 'well, let me see. Ian, Ian, Ian...'

The woman lets out a small snort and darts out of view, and I'm hit with a deep, crushing disappointment that I've let her slip away without relearning a single thing. I go to call after her, but I don't even know her name, and a choking sob of frustration rises up my throat – I've gone and failed again. But before I break down completely, she reappears, coming further down the garden towards me, and leans over the fence, thrusting a framed photo at me.

'My Ian,' she says and I take in the handsome young man in a blazer and tie. 'He's at university now but this was his last year of school. Prefect, he was,' she says, clearly puffed up with pride. 'Ringing any bells? He ought to be familiar, you did see him every Tuesday evening.'

I try to keep the confusion from my face but this boy in the photo is a stranger.

'You did say he was your best student,' the woman prompts, before adding with a knowing grin, 'Although you probably say that to all the mums.'

Of course, violin lessons. The fact that I'm a teacher is going to take some getting used to. 'I'm sure he was brilliant!' I swallow hard before launching into an explanation, deciding that honesty is the best policy if I'm ever going to get anywhere. 'I'm afraid, though, that I don't really remember very much about him at all. I don't remember much of anything, if I'm honest. I was in a car accident a while back, a bad one, and I hit my head and my memory has been affected.'

The woman looks aghast: her mouth falls open and she clutches the framed photo to her chest as if she's shocked that anyone who's met him would ever forget her Ian. 'I'm so sorry, Jen, how awful. How bad is it?'

'It's bad,' I say. 'I'm not really sure of anything any more. I didn't even know my own name when I woke up.' I try to laugh it off, but I give up and let my face fall; there's nothing funny in my situation.

'You poor thing,' she says, shaking her head. 'And has any of it come back?'

I try to think about the little bits and pieces that I've put together but there's nothing substantial. I've got the 'get well soon' cards and I've got Rachel, but that's about the sum of it.

'Not much,' I say honestly.

'Do you know who I am?' she asks and I find my face growing warm. A horrible feeling of shame slides over me as I'm forced to shake my head, and she quickly says, 'Don't worry, I'm Cathy.'

She smiles brightly but I can tell she's unnerved and she glances around as if wanting to slip back inside. A stab of panic hits me – I can't let her go, not yet.

'Cathy, if you know anything about me, anything at all, I'd be so grateful if you could tell me. It's scary not even knowing if you like wine or don't drink, or whether you prefer cats to dogs, or who your friends are. Anything you know might jog a memory or two and help me get back to me.'

'Well, I can tell you for sure that you like a glass of wine,' she says with a glint in her eye. 'You and I would have the occasional glass outside and set the world to rights. I'd come over and join you on your bench... Well, that was before the fire.'

'Fire?'

I see her eyes lift above my head and go to the house again before she looks back at me, and when she speaks again there's an edge of disbelief in her words. 'You don't remember the fire?'

I glance at the scorch marks on the paving stones, certain it was my bench that went up in flames but finding I can't even imagine a single reason why. A bench is hardly a good target for arson.

I shake my head but instead of launching into the story, Cathy says uncomfortably, 'Really, it's probably best if you talk to Rachel about it. I know she's been taking care of you.'

'Yes, she has.' As I say this I feel the urge to tell her about the medical staff who've been assisting, since my recovery hasn't just been down to Rachel. 'Along with my neurologist.'

'Neuro-whatsit?' she asks.

'My doctor. She specialises in brain injuries.'

'She? I've seen that man coming and going, but not a woman.'

I frown in confusion. I'm sure Rachel said Dr Marsden has visited me twice a week for six months, but perhaps Cathy has just missed her. It's not like she keeps a log of everyone coming and going at my house, I'm sure.

'I'm surprised Rachel didn't tell you more about what's been going on.'

Cathy doesn't respond right away, but her lips pucker as if she's sucking a very sour lemon.

'It's not that I didn't want to know,' Cathy says haughtily, almost as if she's offended. 'I'd talk the hind legs off a crocodile if I could get close enough, but Rachel's not exactly the chatting type now, is she?'

I shrug at this, realising I still have no idea what 'type' I am, let alone my sister.

'No, I think I could get more out of the crocodile than Rachel.' We both laugh at that and I try to work out how I feel about sitting here, making jokes about my sister with Cathy. Somehow, the way she's leaning on the fence and cackling suggests to me that it's a position she's used to being in, and perhaps this isn't the first time Rachel has been the subject of our wrath. I feel a bit of guilt, but then maybe Rachel deserves it. She's wrapped me in so many layers of cotton wool that I feel like I might spontaneously combust if she's not careful, and then there'll be even more scorch marks on my patio.

As our laughter fades, I catch Cathy's eye and say, 'You know what Rachel's like. She's a hard nut to crack. I'd love to ask her about the fire, but I fear she might decide not to tell me for my own sake or something ridiculous like that.'

Cathy's eyes fill with indecision, but she doesn't break my gaze. 'If I tell you, do you promise not to say where you heard it from? I don't think I could face a knock on the door and a dressing down from Rachel.'

I wince at the sound of that, but I want her to keep talking so I nod my head vigorously and say, 'I'll just say I remembered. That when I came out into my garden, it all came flooding back.'

Cathy grins at this. 'Fantastic. She can hardly object to that and it's not like I'm telling you anything you don't already know.'

Biting my lip, I keep nodding, waiting for her to spit out whatever it is that she knows about the fire, but she doesn't say anything and a burst of anger makes me snap. 'Cathy! Please!'

Her tongue darts from her mouth and dabs her lips and I can tell she's nervous as the words rush from her mouth. 'You know that bench was your pride and joy? You found it God-knows-where, dragged it home and spent weeks sanding off all the rude words that had been carved into the wood, then painted it that specific shade of yellow that you searched out. You insisted it was going to be your happy place, and it was, for a whole summer, until one night – Bonfire Night it was – I heard the most almighty row coming from your place.'

She glances at me apologetically as if embarrassed to be mentioning my antisocial behaviour, but I couldn't care less. In fact, a feeling of exhilaration is rushing through me as I realise this may be the truest thing anyone has told me since I woke up. I can almost hear the fizz of the argument as words were fired back and forth. I glance over my shoulder at the back door and try to imagine myself in the kitchen with another person, gesticulating, raising our voices. But the harder I try to picture it, the hazier it becomes.

'Was it me and Rachel?' I ask, and a frown clouds Cathy's face before she says in an uncertain voice, 'No, not Rachel. Don't you know who?'

Cathy is staring at me intensely and I will her to tell me exactly who I was fighting with, but as she opens her mouth to say the name, a low voice from behind me stops her and squeezes all the air out of my chest.

'What is going on out here?'

Our heads snap around and there, standing in the doorway, illuminated by a shaft of sunlight, is Rachel – looking positively murderous.

TWELVE

Rachel stands with her hands on her hips, glancing from me to Cathy with fury on her face, and we both fall silent. I feel oddly giddy as I catch Cathy's eye, and she wiggles her eyebrows before saying, 'Lord, is that the time? I need to get back to my washing. Lovely to see you, as ever, Rachel.' She gives me another pointed look before her head disappears from the top of the fence and she slips back into her house.

'What was that all about?' I ask, feeling my hackles rise as Rachel continues to stare me down. I'm not a teenager who's been caught smoking a fag out of the bathroom window, and as the thought crosses my mind, I find I can picture the two of us, Rachel and I, huddled together in a small bathroom that overlooked a lovely large back garden, taking cheeky puffs on a cigarette that we passed between us and blowing plumes of smoke out of the window until Dad suddenly appeared with the lawnmower and yelled up at us.

Despite my anger, the memory surprises me and I can't help but blurt out, 'Do you remember that time when Dad caught us smoking?'

Rachel's eyes grow wide as she says, 'Do you?'

I tilt my head on the side and close my eyes, remembering that he came pounding up the stairs while we stared at each other, ashen-faced, trying to push the cigarette into the other's hand before Rachel flushed it down the loo and doused us both in her expensive perfume. By the time Dad banged on the bathroom door, it was like a perfume bomb had gone off in there and Rachel pulled out a handful of tampons that she waved at him. 'Jen was just asking me to show her how these work,' she said, and Dad's face turned puce before he muttered, 'That better be all you two were doing in there,' and he stomped back downstairs.

'I remember he was too embarrassed to tell us off,' I say now, my voice wistful.

'Silly sod,' Rachel murmurs and a smile crosses her face. It's almost like the awkwardness with Cathy is forgotten until she shakes her head and the serious expression returns. 'Listen, Jen, I don't think letting too many people back into your life all at once is a good thing for you.'

'Cathy is one person,' I say indignantly, 'and I can't stay locked in my room for the rest of my life. How am I ever going to get better if I don't get out there and meet people again?'

'Dr Marsden says it's better if you take things slow. Baby steps.'

A snort escapes my nose and I think how much she sounds like Bryce. Everyone keeps saying 'baby steps' only I'm not a baby. I'm a fully grown woman and I need to start taking responsibility for myself.

'Well, since I've never met Dr Marsden, I don't really care what she says. Cathy is my friend and I'm going to keep talking to her whenever I feel like it.'

'You don't even know her,' Rachel says quietly.

'I do. I know her and Ian.' I'm proud of myself for remembering her son's name but it has the opposite effect on Rachel and she winces before drawing herself up to her full height and saying, 'You don't know the full background but you need to trust me, nothing good will come from talking to Cathy or Ian.'

I can't believe what I'm hearing and I feel rising frustration that Rachel is continuing to talk in riddles. 'Why don't you fill me in?' I say. 'We've got time.'

Rachel sighs. 'Jen, I promise, I will, soon, but right now you just need to trust me.'

I almost laugh out loud at this since it's impossible to trust someone who won't tell you anything, but I realise that challenging her is only going to result in an argument and I don't want to offend her – Rachel has been looking after me, after all, plus it seems like I'm not going to get anywhere with her. I vow to pick up my conversation with Cathy as soon as I possibly can and I nod meekly. 'OK, Rachel, I trust you.'

A smile flickers on her face and she comes closer, offering me an arm. 'Come on, then, let's get you back inside. Bryce says you've been up and about for a while now. You must be tired.'

I *am* feeling tired – a yawn takes over my whole body and I stretch loudly, making Rachel laugh and say, 'I think that confirms it. Come on.'

I accept Rachel's arm and she hauls me to my feet, and together we shuffle back inside to where Bryce is in the kitchen, loading a tray with a cup of tea and a stack of sandwiches for my evening meal. There's even a piece of cake in a cardboard box that Rachel must have brought with her as a special treat and she follows my gaze and says, 'Coffee and walnut.'

She's smiling expectantly and I find myself asking, 'My favourite?'

'Your favourite,' she confirms, and we both laugh and I find my anger at Rachel melting away like a piece of ice in a glass of water on a hot summer's day. We may not see eye to eye on Cathy, but sisters don't have to agree on everything – in fact, they rarely do, but that doesn't mean we don't love and support one another, and it is nice that she's giving up all her free time to visit me and bring me little treats. I tell myself to focus on the positives of my situation; concentrating on the negatives might lead me back to the headspace I was in that resulted in the accident.

'Bryce, will you help Jen back upstairs and I'll bring her tray up?' Rachel asks, and Bryce moves over to my side.

'Of course,' he says, taking Rachel's place.

'You must be knackered by now,' he says and I find myself nodding. I think I'd usually be too proud to admit it but something about Bryce makes me want to tell him the truth. He strokes his beard and looks sideways at me and I can tell he's wondering how to ask something before he clears his throat and says, 'You can tell me to buzz off but if it would be easier, since you've had a long day already, I could lift you back to bed if that would help?'

I'm touched by the thoughtful way he's phrased the question and a warm feeling spreads through my chest as I think how lucky I am to have both of them here. If I'm honest, it would be nice to be back up in bed without having to heave myself up there. 'You know, if you think you can manage, I would really appreciate it.'

No sooner have the words left my mouth than Bryce hooks one arm under my knees and the other behind my back and he sweeps me off my feet. I may never have been carried over the threshold by my groom, but Bryce does a good job of making it seem like he's carrying a feather pillow as he manoeuvres me from the room, and I can't help but imagine that we truly are newlyweds. I glance back to give Rachel a grin over his shoulder, but I see she's not paying me any attention. She's moved over to the back door and, as I watch, she purposefully locks the door, checks the handles a couple of times to make sure, and then puts the key into her pocket.

'Stop!' I yell, and Bryce jolts to a halt in the doorway.

'Did I hurt you?' he asks, sounding panicked, but it's Rachel who looks up with guilt clouding her face.

'What's wrong?' she asks, putting on an innocent voice.

Righteous anger is rising inside me and I have to fight to stop myself from yelling. 'I saw you.'

'Well, I've been standing right here so that's hardly surprising,' she answers in a sing-song voice that sets my teeth on edge.

'You locked the door.' I grit my teeth and keep my voice low, hoping she will laugh and say it was a mistake.

'It's my job to keep you safe,' she replies coolly.

A burst of fury overtakes me and I find myself yelling, 'Rachel, this is my home. You can't lock me in here like a prisoner. You have no right...'

I try to scramble out of Bryce's arms, but he holds on tight and the strength in his broad chest and shoulders takes my breath away. Any comfort I felt evaporates. Now, all I feel is fear.

'Put me down!'

But Bryce glances at Rachel rather than setting me back on my feet, and he holds firm as if I'm encased in concrete. It's obvious now how easily he could overpower me if he chose to, and as much as I struggle, only my arms and legs flail but he does not loosen his hold. After thirty seconds of wriggling, I give up with a groan but I'm livid.

'Sorry to do this, but I'm not letting go for your own safety,' Bryce says. I would hit him if I had the strength.

'You're being ridiculous,' Rachel says.

'You put my key in your pocket,' I reply, my voice sounding high and tight and I can feel I'm close to tears.

'I'm just looking after it for you until you're feeling a bit better,' Rachel says.

I try to get either one of them to look at me, but neither will meet my gaze.

'You do realise how crazy this is?' I say.

Rachel barks out an odd laugh and says, 'Jen, you barely know your own name. Don't you realise how vulnerable that makes you? Someone could tell you anything, literally anything, and you'd believe them.'

That 'someone' could be you too, I think. I try once more to wriggle from Bryce's grip, but his arms clamp down and I realise that even in full health I would be unlikely to get away from him. The thought terrifies me. This man is in total control. I bite my next retort back and force myself to stay silent, my anger boiling slowly inside me like a can of Coke that's been shaken, but I realise I'm not going to win this one right now.

'You're not my mother,' I hiss, allowing myself one barb before saying to Bryce, 'Take me upstairs please.'

He starts moving again, gently lifting me step by step up the stairs as I close my eyes and will him to hurry up and let me go.

Behind us, I hear Rachel say one last thing. 'You're right, but I'm the closest thing you've got right now.'

THIRTEEN

Bryce deposits me in my bed, but the moment he leaves the room, I slide silently onto the floor, positioning my back up against the bedroom door, feeling like I need to regain some control of the situation. How dare they treat me like a child? I'm exhausted, but I can't let myself fall asleep. I want to know if either of them returns; I no longer feel safe in my own home and suddenly a chilling realisation hits me: I've felt this way before.

Fear makes my breath unsteady as I strain my ears, trying to hear what they are doing downstairs. Something is very wrong about this situation, but I'm not exactly sure what it is or who I can trust. Surely my sister wouldn't be keeping me here against my will, but the way Bryce held me so tightly in his arms and the fact that Rachel locked the back door and put the key in her pocket certainly makes me feel that way. And Rachel was not happy about me talking to Cathy. What could be making her so worried?

I try running through all the possible justifications in my head, but I quickly hit a brick wall, and if I'm honest, I'm sick of searching my broken mind for answers when I don't seem to have any. I give up, letting my thoughts spool freely into a sea of nothingness, but I don't stop listening. Downstairs, I hear their footsteps moving around, and after five or ten minutes, one set – the lighter tread, which I presume to be Rachel's – moves through the house, and then the front door clicks as it opens and clunks as it shuts. Now there's only Bryce left, but I can't relax. I certainly don't want to confront him. My arms still ache from where his fingers were digging in and I pull up my sleeve, checking for a bruise, but the whole area is just a bit pink.

After another couple of minutes, I hear Bryce's footsteps in the hallway, but instead of leaving the house, they come towards me and my stomach drops as I realise he's coming up the stairs. Hauling myself back into bed, I just get sat up in position and throw the cover over my legs when he knocks once and enters without waiting for a response. I feel a flicker of irritation through my fear – there is no point in knocking if you don't wait for an answer. I feel like giving him a piece of my mind, but I bite my tongue as he places the tray of sandwiches on the table with the slice of cake that I'd like to hurl against the wall.

'I'll leave these here for you,' he says.

I wordlessly stare straight ahead, waiting for him to go.

'I'm heading home now,' he says, moving towards the door but importantly not walking through it, and I think, *Well, go on then*, but again I don't speak and Bryce continues to hover in the doorway.

'Look, I can tell you're pissed off about what happened downstairs,' he says and my gaze flicks to him as I think, *No shit, Sherlock*, but I just give my eyes a small roll and look away. Bryce takes this as an invitation to move closer to the bed.

'I don't know Rachel well,' he begins, and I feel him looming over me. He must be six foot three or four and he's heavy-set. When he grabbed me earlier, I felt the strength in his grip and it hit me that if Bryce wanted to hurt me, he could. Easily.

I begin to edge away from him and look around for something I could use as a weapon – the bedpan is the only thing near enough for me to grab hold of – but he seems totally oblivious and continues earnestly, 'But I do know that your sister really cares about you. While you were unconscious, she was here twice a day, coming before and after work, and she stayed all day whenever she had a day off. She's advocated for your care like a tiger, refusing to accept anything but the best. Do you think most families would be able to care for a family member at home, giving them the level of care they would need to make such an impressive recovery?'

The question is rhetorical, but I feel a flash of doubt that anyone would describe my recovery as 'impressive', and part of my problem is that Rachel has kept me at home in this cell-like bedroom, like a prisoner, shutting me off from the world. Raising my eyes to his, I feel like I might contest some of his sentiment, but before I say anything I notice there is genuine emotion reflected on his face and I'm floored. Either he's a big teddy bear of a man, a real softie, or Rachel has somehow managed to bewitch him.

'What happened out there must have felt strange to you, but your sister is just being extremely cautious with your mental health – and after what happened, can you blame her?'

The 'what happened' hangs over me and I feel another rush of shame that I caused all this, but I try to put Rachel's actions into perspective and find that they still don't feel reasonable. Is she going to stop me talking to anyone other than her and Bryce for the rest of my life? Why would a short conversation with my neighbour be a risk to me? And what happened with the fire? Whatever she's worried about, she could sit and talk to me like an adult rather than lock me up and throw away the key. My anger returns and I will Bryce to shut up and leave.

Finally he says, 'I'll be off, then, but please think about all that Rachel has done for you and try to understand that she's got your best interests at heart.'

He lumbers to the door and just as he walks through I feel the urge to ask something that I can't ignore, and I call out, 'Bryce?'

He pops his head back in and I see a hopeful look in his eyes until I say, 'Why do you care?' and his face falls. It takes him a moment to compose himself before he looks me in the eyes and says, 'Jen, you may feel like we have only just met but I have been coming to your home and caring for you for six months. I care about you and your sister – that's why I'm good at my job. It's part of the profession. Whatever you do or say, that won't change, and I'll keep showing up until you don't need looking after any more.'

Or until Rachel stops paying you, I think but I feel guilty at my uncharitable thoughts. As far as I know, Bryce has been nothing but good to me. Perhaps I am overreacting to this whole situation. But then again, feeling the tenderness of my arm, perhaps not.

'Just try to give Rachel the benefit of the doubt and focus on your recovery,' he says.

'OK, I'll try.'

Bryce breaks out into a grin and says, 'You superstar. I will see you bright and early tomorrow.'

I return his smile and he finally leaves the room. I listen to his footsteps stomp downstairs and there's a moment of quiet – probably while he gathers his things – before I hear the front door open and shut with a bang. I'm bone-tired and aching all over, but I throw off the duvet and drag myself back out of bed. I can't lie around while Rachel and Bryce decide what to tell me, or not as the case may be. It's time for me to take control of my life, starting with my home. There must be some clues here about the real me, and if I need to rip this place apart to find them, well, that's exactly what I'll do.

FOURTEEN

I don't bother starting with my bedroom since I've spent hours staring at these four walls; instead, I go along the hallway on my hands and knees to conserve my strength and enter the second bedroom. It's a few degrees cooler in here because it's at the back of the house and doesn't appear to get much sun. The window is cracked open, letting some fresh air in. The walls are painted a boring white and the bed has a white-and-grey striped bedspread that appears to be brand new. Sniffing, I wonder if I can detect a whiff of that heady new paint smell, but I tell myself I must be imagining it since I've hardly been in a fit state to do a spot of decorating these past six months.

I wonder if I thought when I bought this house that one day I would use this room as a nursery, and without warning, the image of a tiny baby with a shock of red hair comes to mind and an ache of longing slices through me that feels so sharp and so deep it must surely go to the bone. I can't tell if this is a memory or a figment of my imagination, but the pain is real. Who could this child be if not my own? I feel like bursting into tears and I can't shake the feeling that it must be my baby, and I suddenly wonder if I have red hair too. It wouldn't prove anything, but it feels like something, and I tug at the bun on the top of my head, pulling a greasy strand in front of my eyes, trying not to grimace at how dirty my hair is. My heart sinks – my hair is almost black, exactly like Rachel's. And nothing like the phantom baby I keep imagining.

Letting out a ragged breath, I give myself a mental shake and try to dispel the image. I need to get on with things if I want to get any answers. This room is clearly a guest room, though judging by how pristine it is, it doesn't look like I have many visitors. Starting with the built-in wardrobes at the end of the bed, I find a stack of Lycra cycling clothing piled on one shelf and bike parts and cycling paraphernalia such as a pump and helmet stacked in the bottom of the wardrobe. So I was right – I am a cyclist.

Disappointed to have discovered nothing new about myself with my first find, I move on to the small bedside tables either side of the double bed, but they are totally empty apart from a coaster on the top that says 'keep calm and drink gin'. It's the same story with the chest of drawers that's pushed against the wall – empty, other than the top drawer which contains a couple of beach-read romance novels with hot-pink covers. It is a spare room, but I'm surprised that it's so utterly anonymous, and as someone who appears to be so interested in interior design, I'm shocked I haven't made seemingly the slightest effort with the decor.

I'm about to ram the top drawer of the chest closed when something at the very back catches my eye and I ease the drawer out as far as it will go. Wedged into the joint between the bottom and the back of the drawers is a half-burnt stick of incense. Lifting it out, I give it a sniff and wrinkle my nose at the smoky, perfumed scent, instantly certain that I detest incense. Why would I have something I hate in my home? I can't imagine a situation where I would choose to burn it since it reminds me of those shops in town that always smell funny and seem to be mostly selling wind chimes and magic mushrooms to teenagers, but it's hardly an offensive item. Perhaps one of my rare guests brought it with them but I can't picture the type of person who travels with incense sticks in their wash bag.

Setting it aside in confusion, I finish the room by scouring the floor and remaking the bed to see if anything has got tucked inside the sheets, but there's absolutely nothing and I leave feeling deflated. It's the same story in the bathroom – the only other room upstairs – and all I find is a handful of products a woman my age would use, like tampons and lipsticks, in the small mirrored cabinet. Deciding to test one of the lipsticks, I look at my face in the mirror and I freeze as I take in the person staring back.

My hair is slicked back with dirt and oil and I look much worse than I imagined. Somehow I'd convinced myself that my appearance matched how I've been feeling – tired and a bit battered but not catastrophic – but I realise I was way off the mark. I do share some similarities with Rachel, the square jaw and dark hair, though mine is shot through with wiry greys, but where she is bright-eyed and her skin seems almost glossy, I look pale and drawn and my eyes are dull with heavy bags underneath. Of course, it's understandable, since I've been inside for most of the past six months, but still, looking at myself it's like my spark has gone out.

Trying not to burst into tears at the sight, I fiddle with my hair, smoothing out some of the greasy clumps and trying to pinch some colour into my cheeks. With a shaky hand, I apply one of the lipsticks, a deep purple that's almost black, and notice instantly that it looks horrible with my skin tone. Frowning, I wonder why I bought it, but perhaps I'm just not a good judge of what suits me, or maybe my face has changed so dramatically since the accident that I need new make-up. I certainly need a makeover.

Tossing the lipstick in the bin in disgust, I make my way

downstairs, sliding on my bottom again and ignoring the worry I feel about how I will get back up – I'll just have to find a way. It feels ridiculous without someone here to laugh with and I miss Bryce for a moment but then I remind myself that he hauled me up to bed earlier against my will so I need to be wary. There's something off about him, there must be. Nurses don't manhandle their patients.

The house is a classic two-up two-down, and there's not much of it to search but I keep going – there must be something that will shed some light on my life. Outside it is pitch-black by now and glancing at the kitchen clock I see it's just gone 10 p.m. The tiredness I feel is overshadowed by grim determination. This is my chance to take control.

I work methodically, starting at the front window and working my way backwards, checking every nook and cranny in between. The living area has a sofa, an armchair and a small coffee table, plus a TV in the corner on a wooden stand. In the opposite corner is a small desk and desk chair, plus a folded music stand. Hung on the wall are several violins of different sizes and I lift one down, feeling its fragility as I hold it to my chin, but I have no desire to play. I feel a stronger urge to smash it against the desk due to the fact that I've learned nothing new, but I return it carefully to the wall, assuming it must be my pride and joy since it's hung in such a prominent place.

On the TV stand I find a couple of old copies of interior design magazines, and down the back of the sofa are a penny and a button, but otherwise there is barely any indication that the house is lived in. Any hope I felt that I might discover something about me has slowly trickled away, and continuing the search is a struggle since all I want to do is return to bed and pull the duvet over my head. But I force myself to finish what I started.

In the desk drawers, I find reams of sheet music, and beneath the desk I discover my shredder, which is one of the only things that makes sense – for a person to live in such a way as to leave so little evidence of their life, I must do an awful lot of shredding. Where are all the bills, the receipts, the little scraps of paper you pick up here and there and scrawl notes to yourself or write shopping lists on? I already had an inkling that I'm house-proud but going through my home it feels like that impulse might have become a monster that took over my entire life. Perhaps I even suffer from OCD given the level of sani- tising that I've clearly committed to – it appears like I've tried to erase my entire life.

Completing my search of the kitchen, all I find is a pile of takeaway menus and I notice that the one for the local Chinese does look more crumpled than the others as if it's got more use – so Rachel was probably telling the truth about one thing, I do like Chinese food. On the windowsill is a framed photo of me in cycling gear holding a bike, which makes me wince – it feels pretty sad that the only person I have to put in a frame is myself. Leaning my forehead against the back door and looking out at the yard, I feel utterly defeated. I can still make out the burn marks on the paving stones in the dark and I stare at them for a few minutes, wondering if I'll ever remember what happened or if that's one of many things that is probably consigned to the depths of history. If I can't remember them, do they even matter?

I search the gloom for any sign of my bicycle, realising that I have found my Lycra but not the bike itself, but there's nowhere it could be. Perhaps Rachel has removed my only means of escape as well. Tears prick my eyes as I realise I have made no progress. I'm still as clueless as I ever was. *Clueless and useless*, a small, vicious voice whispers inside my head and I feel myself falling into the depths of despair. It's as if my feet have got stuck in thick mud. I wonder if this is how I felt when I was driving the car; perhaps something crossed my mind and my legs became so heavy I couldn't lift up my foot to press the brake?

Taking a deep breath, I force myself to go back upstairs, using the banister to haul myself up, one step at a time, until I make it back to my bedroom.

The air inside feels thick and heavy and I crawl across to the window to open it and let in a breeze. I've held it together so far, but I know that as soon as I'm in bed, the tears will come, and I plan to curl up into a ball and cry myself bitterly to sleep. Why has this happened to me? I don't feel like I deserve to be here, alone, lost in my own head. I haven't done anything wrong. I steel myself for one last effort to push myself up to standing so I can get back into bed. I put my hands out and grab the bookshelf to use as a lever, but as I test my strength, the bookshelf moves forward by an inch and there's a thud as something falls. My heart leaps into my mouth, but I tell myself to stay calm, it's probably nothing interesting. But it does look like there is something jammed between the back and the wall that has slipped, and as I peer closer, I realise that it's a photo album.

The album is an old family collection, starting with photos of first one chubby baby, then a toddler and another, with their parents. Although I don't feel much more than a gentle hint of recognition, I know immediately that these are my parents and the babies are me and my sister. We progress from toddlers to little girls and then to teenagers and I study each photo in turn, trying to make sure that I am one hundred per cent certain that the child is Rachel, but I can't quite get there. The girl looks like her – she is dark-haired and pale-skinned just like Rachel – but the photos are old and yellowing and most of them are a little fuzzy.

In the final picture, it's her birthday and she's blowing out candles on a cake – with 'Happy 6th Birthday' in frosting – surrounded by lots of other little children. I study each face in turn – a dark-haired girl with wild curls, a little blond boy, a girl with thick glasses – but the only one who is familiar is me, kneeling on a chair next to my sister, trying to blow out her candles before she can. I try to work out if this could be photos of someone else's childhood, another of Rachel's lies, but I realise that I'm clutching at straws.

I can barely keep my eyes open, and outside the dense blackness of the sky and quietness of the street tell me it's very late and I decide it's time for bed. I'm about to return the album to its hiding place, but as I lift it up, something drops out of the bottom and lands on my lap. Lifting the slip of paper, I see it's a glossy brochure for somewhere called 'The Hollies': the picture on the front is of a red-brick building set back from a rolling lawn where a handful of grey-haired people are doing tai chi in a circle.

It doesn't take a genius to work out it's a care home and, scanning the text, I see it has a wing that specialises in care for dementia patients. My best guess is that this is where my mother lives now. Quickly I look for the address and it says it's in Surbiton, which may be near or far from here, but I decide it doesn't matter. My mother may be unwell, but surely she can help me fill in some details, and most importantly, if I can get myself to wherever Surbiton is, I can speak to someone who isn't Rachel.

FIFTEEN

I wake after a difficult sleep in which I dreamed of a ginger baby crying the whole night long. I don't know why the baby is haunting me, but I tell myself it's a manifestation of my stress and worry. After what happened yesterday, I'm on edge as I listen out for Bryce's arrival; he no longer seems like my white knight. If anything, he's the dragon at the door, keeping me locked in my tower, only today I am determined to break out.

I flinch as I hear the front door open and I brace myself as he thumps around downstairs, and it's not long before his footsteps come this way. It's his usual routine but I can't help wishing I'd slipped out first thing and didn't have to face him, only I don't want to raise his suspicions. Better to act normal and leave after Bryce departs. I have no idea how long it might take me to get to Surbiton or how exactly I'm going to get there – it could be the other side of the country for all I know – but I'm going to figure out a way. Visiting Mum is the only idea I have.

'Morning,' Bryce says easily as he enters the room carrying a tray with a bowl of Weetabix and a jug of milk. There's no hint that he feels bad about yesterday or even remembers restraining me to the point that I couldn't move my arms or legs. Doesn't he realise that's akin to kidnap or is he a really good actor, pretending like he has no idea that anything is wrong? I find myself studying his every move as he sits next to me and offers to help me with my breakfast.

'I can manage,' I say and I am feeling stronger. He places the tray on my knee and I slowly feed myself, feeling a burst of pride but also relief that I can do this small thing without needing Bryce. Soon I won't need him at all.

He must be able to tell I'm in a bad mood because soon he excuses himself but instead of saying goodbye he says, 'I thought I might do some batch cooking today and put some meals in the freezer for after I stop coming daily so if you smell food, you know why.'

Crushing disappointment hits me and I try to work out how to ask him to leave but his kindness has me flummoxed. Instead, I sit in my bed, seething as I listen to him moving around my kitchen and sure enough, it's not long before a delicious aroma wafts up the stairs. I close my eyes and somehow through my fury I manage to fall into a fitful sleep and I'm woken by Bryce entering the room.

'Sorry to wake you, I'm heading off now. I just wanted to leave your lunch here. It's a bit later than usual I'm afraid.'

'What time is it?' I ask, feeling panicked that I might have slept the whole day and have lost my chance.

'Three o'clock,' Bryce says. 'I'm heading off for the day now, but Rachel mentioned she will pop by after work.'

I feel relieved that there may still be a small window and I'm determined to try and I manage a weak smile. 'Bye.'

'See you tomorrow,' Bryce says.

Finally, I hear the front door shut and I'm alone. I leave the plate of what looks like shepherd's pie untouched and I heave myself out of bed and over to my wardrobe and flick through the clothes that all feel a bit bland and impersonal. There are jeans and sensible sweaters but nothing pretty or individual. It's almost as if I wanted to disappear. I select the nicest blouse I see – a pale blue cotton with tiny white flowers – and a pair of jeans and make my way slowly to the bathroom. My legs feel heavy but I already feel a tiny bit stronger than I did when I woke up a few days ago. I block out any doubt I have about how I might make it to The Hollies – if I have to get there by determination alone, then so be it. I'll crawl if I have to. But first, I need a wash; I can't go outside unwashed and in my pyjamas and have people think I'm some crazy woman escaped from an asylum.

Kneeling on the floor in the shower tray, I let the water wash over me and instantly feel miles better with the grime and grease gone from my body. I wash my hair and although the soap stings my eyes, it's the best I've felt in a very long time. I feel like I could stay in here all day, but after a good amount of time I make myself get out – I need to save my energy for the rest of the day.

It must take me around an hour to get ready but when I look in the mirror, I feel something stir inside me. It's like I'm glimpsing the old me. I don't feel like an invalid and that makes me smile wider than I have since I returned to the land of the living. I'm moving slowly, but I'm getting my strength back and it crosses my mind that very soon I surely won't need a nurse at all. My physical injuries are mostly healed, Bryce told me that himself. Why would Rachel keep paying for someone I don't need? Unless... I let out a shudder. Perhaps he's providing another service like spying on me and keeping me shut up in here.

Before I make my way downstairs, I have one last look around my bedroom – the small box I've been stuck in for the past six months – and find myself hoping I never return. Taking out the photo album, I select one of the photos of my family where we look happy, the four of us huddled around a snowman that's taller than I am in the picture. It's one of the better-quality photos and I clutch it in my hand to show Mum. If she's as unwell as Rachel said, then at least I'll have something with me that could trigger some old memories although I try not to get my hopes up about her revealing anything since I have no idea how far her dementia has progressed. I'm sure even just being in her presence will be a comfort to me.

I wonder whether to take my broken phone, but since I can't turn it on, it would be pointless. I'm apprehensive to leave the house without a mobile or any cash but I haven't found any in the house and there's no way I can ask Rachel or Bryce. I'll just have to survive on my wits and the kindness of strangers if I need anything. Somehow that feels more reassuring than relying on my so-called carers.

Taking the stairs gingerly, I make it down to the front hallway and take a moment to catch my breath before trying the front door with gusto. The handle won't turn and although I'm not surprised, my stomach churns and I feel rising nausea – the door is locked. Bryce and Rachel are trapping me here and I have no idea why.

It's for your own safety, I hear Rachel saying and I feel a rush of anger that makes me bite down and grind my back teeth as I wonder if she's trying to protect me from the outside world or vice versa. The key isn't in the lock and I know from my search last night that there are no spares in any of the drawers or cupboards around the house. Slumping down on the bottom step, I put my head in my hands, fighting back tears, and try to think – do I have a secret place where I keep a spare key? Maybe Rachel doesn't know everything about me. I rack my brains but all I succeed in doing is giving myself a headache. I quickly abandon that idea but I refuse to give up. Instead, I consider the alternative: where is the best place to break out of?

The back door seems like the obvious answer since the fence to access the neighbours' gardens is relatively low and I could probably climb over, at a push. Cathy would surely let me go through her house and out the front door. But would she also feel the need to call Rachel to let her know what I'm doing? I'd like to think that she'd keep it between us, but I can't be sure... And there's no way to exit my garden at the back since the wall at the end is far too high to climb and I have no idea what's on the other side of it; it could back onto a railway line or a ravine for all I know.

Instead, I turn my attention to the front window, but I quickly question whether I have the strength to break through double-glazing in my current state. Just as I'm working out whether it would be better to hit the window with a high stool or the music stand, my gaze lands on the leopard-print coat hanging in the hallway and I feel a tug of familiarity. Perhaps it's my favourite coat or one I wore regularly but something draws me to it. Hauling myself back to standing, I unpeg the coat from the stand and slide my arms into it, tightening the belt around my waist and checking out my reflection in the hall mirror. Out of habit I put my right hand in the pocket and my fingers touch something metal that makes me pause. I feel a rush of anticipation as I pull it out and immediately recognise my keys. I let out a triumphant laugh – Rachel may think she's outsmarted me, but she didn't check everywhere.

There's a Yale and a deadbolt that I know right away open the door to this house, a smaller key that I am pretty sure must be the key to my bike lock, and another large, gold key, but I have no idea what it's for. All of them are held together by a key ring that is a miniature Eiffel Tower, which is strange because I feel no special affinity to Paris but that might explain why I felt I might have a connection to France when I first came around. Rachel hasn't revealed anything that would link me to the place, but then again, Rachel hasn't told me very much at all.

There are too many loose threads making my head hurt, so instead of trying to work anything out now, I put the photo into the pocket of my coat and decide to put one foot in front of the other, taking an umbrella from the rack to use as a walking stick and letting myself out of the house. I may be hobbling and have no idea where I am or in what direction I should be going or even whether I can walk to The Hollies at all, but I still feel free and my heart soars as I leave what feels like my prison behind me.

SIXTEEN

It's a lovely day and I step out onto my street, squinting into the sun and trying to establish what looks familiar. I'm nervous but I feel my confidence building with every step I take – out here, I am master of my own destiny and there's no Rachel or Bryce to try and stop me. I can hear a main road not too far away so I set off in the direction of the engine sounds, using the umbrella as a walking stick. I have no idea how my body will hold up since I've barely tested my strength, but I'm pleased that I'm moving freely enough, and the adrenaline and excitement of being somewhere new seem to carry me along at a decent pace.

Reaching the main road, I look both ways and realise I have no idea which way to turn, but in the distance I spot an elderly lady with a shopping trolley and I decide she is probably as good a person as any to ask.

'Excuse me,' I say as I approach and she turns slowly. 'Where am I?'

She narrows her eyes in distrust and glances about as if looking for someone to protect her from me. I decide to just brazen it out and act like a lost tourist.

I rephrase my question. 'What's the name of the town?'

'Surbiton,' she says and I find myself smiling, which earns another frown. It's not too much of a leap that my mother would be in a care home in the town where I live but it's a huge relief that Surbiton isn't in another county, or country even. 'Main street is that way,' and she nods in the direction we're going, turning away from me and continuing on her way.

'Sorry, one more thing. You don't know the way to The Hollies, do you?'

She immediately thaws and gives me a stream of directions that sends me back the way I came, past my own road to the outskirts of the town in the opposite direction. My heart sinks at the thought of such a long walk, but I try not to be too despondent since at least I know where I'm going. I can't give up now so I set off at a slow, determined pace, trudging along until eventually I reach the residential road she mentioned. I manage to speed up at the sight of a long driveway cutting through a well-kept lawn with a white sign at the end announcing 'The Hollies' in bold, black lettering.

I take in the impressive, red-brick building with benches outside where a couple of elderly women are enjoying the afternoon sun. I feel a stab of excitement that one of them could be my mother but as I shuffle closer and they squint at me, I begin to doubt myself. Would I even recognise her? I don't even know her full name. I decide the best thing to do is find someone who works here – they should be able to direct me.

Pushing open the heavy wooden door, I enter the reception area, and as the door closes behind me, I'm struck by the airlessness of the place as if I'm inside a tightly sealed Tupperware box. I feel like it's harder to breathe in here although I know that's silly. There's a table with a visitors' book by the front door and a second set of sealed doors that require a code to enter, so I set about signing in and hover by the glass partition, peering inside at the carpeted hallways and the large wooden staircase that runs through the centre of the building.

After a few minutes of waiting, I spot a doorbell and, kicking myself, I push it. It's not long before a carer with bright pink hair cut in a severe bob appears and opens the door, a smile breaking out on her face.

'Jen! Wow, it's been a while.'

I smile back, although I feel heat rising to my face as I wonder how much she knows about what happened to me. It must be common knowledge that I was in an accident, but does everyone think that I tried to kill myself? I try to detect whether there's sympathy in the woman's kindly eyes but it's hard to tell since she turns quickly and walks along the hallway, all the while talking to me over her shoulder.

'Your mum will be thrilled to see you, utterly delighted. Visitors always lift her, though I must warn you that she's taken a bit of a turn since I last saw you here. You must have heard, but I wouldn't like you to go in there expecting to see the same Rose as the last time.'

I nod along as she leads me up the stairs and along the corridor, saying hello to residents as we pass and scooching around the tea trolley that's being pushed by another carer. The whole place is familiar, but I can't work out if it's just that this is exactly what I'd have imagined of an old persons' home, with its odd smells and constant background noise of telly droning from somewhere. I'm peering into every room that we pass, studying every resident and trying to catch a glimpse of a face that I recognise, but everyone stares back with a slightly vacant expression apart from one old lady who yells, 'Sandra! Sandra! Is that you?'

Ignoring her, I hurry to catch up with the woman walking ahead. She doesn't slow or pause for breath but she keeps glancing at me expectantly, and after a moment I realise that she must have asked me a question.

'Sorry,' I say, 'I missed that.'

'I just asked if things have got better? I remember last time I saw you there were things going on at home…' She tails off as if I should know immediately what she means but obviously I come up short. My mind is still mostly blank.

'What exactly did I tell you?' I say but instantly I regret being so direct. The woman's face flushes and she picks up her pace.

'None of my business, of course,' she says as she reaches a locked door with a sign that says 'Tulip wing' and types the code to open it for me.

I reach out and rest my hand on her arm. 'Please, anything you can tell me would be a real help.'

She hesitates and I wonder what she's weighing up but then another carer appears and gives her a brisk nod and the woman says, 'We all go through ups and downs, that's just life.'

I want to continue the conversation but she ushers me inside.

'You head on in,' she says, and I step inside expecting her to follow me but she closes the door, leaving me inside the Tulip wing alone.

I stand for a moment, wondering what conversation I might have had with that woman before I give up trying to remember and walk along the corridor, studying each door for any sign of my mum, but the doors are closed and the numbers mean nothing to me. I'm about to find somewhere to sit since my feet and back are killing me, but something about the final door makes me pause. I study the number 28 and something makes me lift my hand and knock quietly. There's no answer so I take a deep breath, open the door, and inside I see her.

Sitting up in bed is a woman who by all rights should be outside gardening or getting a coffee with friends. She can only be in her seventies and she is immediately recognisable as the woman with long, dark hair in the photograph with the snowman, although her hair is short and mostly a dark grey but with some brown still that makes her look younger than her years.

'Mum?' I say softly but she doesn't look up. As I get closer, I see her fingers are worrying a small square of fabric and I reach out and touch the back of her hand. Finally her eyes lift to mine and she smiles.

'Jen?' Her voice comes out croaky and she clears her throat. 'Jen? Is that you?'

She breaks out into a wider smile and I clasp her paper-dry hand in both of mine, pulling it to my lips and trying not to fall apart.

'I'm sorry it's been a while,' I say.

'Oh, my darling girl.' She seems happy to see me although confusion seems to be her main emotion as her expressive eyebrows draw together and she says in a small, desperate voice, 'But I don't understand. Where have you been?'

An arrow of pain pierces my heart as I wonder, probably uncharitably, whether Rachel hasn't told her, but I tell myself it's much more likely that she's forgotten because of her dementia.

'I haven't been well, but I'm here now,' I settle on and this seems to pacify her.

Taking a seat in the wipe-clean armchair by her bedside, I nod along as she tells me about her routines here and a carer she doesn't get on with. I look around the small room as I let her ramble and feel a pang of sadness that she's confined here, and then I'm hit by the realisation that this room is not that dissimilar to my bedroom at home. There's a bed, a window and a chair, plus a wardrobe and a bookshelf filled with books. Sure, I have my record player and my room is slightly larger, but we're both stuck within the confines of our four walls with not much to see or do. Only where Mum is trapped by her dementia, I've been locked in by Rachel.

Mum gives me another odd look and says, 'Are you even listening to a word I'm saying?'

I lean forward, bowing my head. 'Sorry, Mum.'

'Now tell me, what did they give you for lunch today?'

It's a strange question but I know mums are interested in their offsprings' eating habits and old people always like talking about food so I answer truthfully, 'I skipped lunch today so I've just had Weetabix so far.'

Mum's eyebrows draw together even further and her face flushes with anger. 'No lunch yet!' she squawks. 'I've never heard such an outrage.'

'Really, it's fine,' I say, not really wanting to get into the full explanation.

'How will you focus on your afternoon lessons if you haven't had any lunch?'

Mum stares at me indignantly as I process her words and horror trickles through me. It's as if I thought I was standing on the beach, but I've looked down to find quicksand beneath my feet.

'I'm not at school, Mum,' I say gently and anger flashes across her face again.

She snaps, 'Yes, yes, yes, I know that.'

I feel tentative relief as I nod and say, 'School was quite a long time ago now.'

'Do you think I don't know what my daughter is doing?' she asks.

I shake my head and say reassuringly, 'No, of course you do.'

'It's college now, isn't it,' she says firmly. 'That's why you're wearing those God-awful jeans,' and her eyes rake from the top of my head and down my body and she wrinkles her nose. 'You know I detest denim.'

I nod, since I'm not sure what else to do, and I realise that this is probably what the carer and Rachel were trying to warn me about. Mum may be here, but her mind is somewhere a long way away, and as she launches into a dissection of my terrible haircut and dirty nails, I begin to wonder whether she's always been so critical or if this is a symptom of her dementia.

'You must know the conclusions men draw when they see a low-cut top,' she says and I feel a familiar sinking feeling that suggests this is a pattern of conversation that I'm used to, and perhaps my mother has never been one of those warm, fuzzy types but has always been on the more difficult side. Although I'm still angry with Rachel, I can picture us both on the same side, banding together to see the lighter side of our mum's distaste for our lives, finding ways to laugh rather than let her sniping drag us down.

'Heaven knows that you don't get a good example from your sister,' Mum huffs and I feel a surprising pang of sympathy towards Rachel. Mum clearly isn't an easy person to get along with. She gives me a long look, tilting her head to one side and saying, 'Has your dad been filling your head with nonsense again? Telling you fairy stories about making a living from playing the violin?'

I shake my head half-heartedly but as she continues listing out my dad's failings, I stop listening and start mentally listing the reasons why Rachel cannot be a bad person: she's hired Bryce, she's visited me twice a day for a whole six months, she's sorted out my bills and my shopping and everything else that running a household requires, and she hasn't complained even once when she's got all of that on her plate plus whatever her usual responsibilities are. Could I have totally misunderstood her motivations yesterday for locking the door? Maybe the reason she wants me to stay in my bed is very simply what she has told me it is – because she wants me to get better.

Mum moves on to a rant about the woman in the room next door and as I listen to her complain about everything and everyone in her life, I vow that as far as it is within my control, I won't let myself become like her. I need to shake off whatever funk I've been in, focus on getting well and getting my life back. However sad I may be about my choices or lack thereof that have meant I've landed living alone in my early forties with no family to speak of, I need to focus on the positives that I have a roof over my head and a sister who loves me. I need to get myself back out there.

As the words continue to pour out of Mum's mouth, her voice begins to rasp and eventually she breaks out coughing. I hoist myself up to pour her a glass of water from the jug on her bedside table and take the opportunity to remain standing, although my body is aching from head to foot. The walk here has taken a lot out of me and I start to make my excuses. 'I think I better go now and let you get some rest.'

'Don't you worry about me,' Mum cuts in, 'I'm as strong as an ox. It's you that looks like a wet weekend although I'm sure you haven't done your homework yet so you better buck up.'

'Yes, Mum,' I say meekly, and as I shove my hands deep into my pockets, my fingers brush the smooth, slippery surface of the photo I slid in there.

'I don't suppose you remember this?' I ask, placing the photo in her lap.

She picks it up with her bony fingers and studies it for all of two seconds before saying briskly, 'Of course I remember this. Heaviest snowfall in twenty years. Not the type of thing that slips one's mind.'

'No, of course not,' I murmur, hoping she'll say more.

'You were five and your sister was seven and you spent all day running about in the garden, throwing snowballs at each other. One of you would come in every five minutes in floods of tears but then your dad would go out and get you organised. That snowman was one of his more impressive creations.'

I wonder how my dad put up with her for so long but then I chide myself that perhaps this is the illness talking and none of us can judge a marriage from the outside, especially not someone with as little experience in marriage as me.

'Did Rachel and I get on?' I ask, hoping for more information, anything really.

'Rachel?' Mum barks.

'Yes,' I say.

'Who's Rachel?'

Trying not to sigh, I say gently, 'Rachel, my sister,' and I point at the small girl in the dark blue snowsuit who is grinning from ear to ear.

Mum's heavy eyebrows sink down and she stares at me as if I've taken off all my clothes and covered myself in the pot of jelly that's been left festering on her bedside table.

'That's not Rachel,' she says. 'Your sister's name is Amy.'

SEVENTEEN

Rushing out of Mum's room, I clutch the photo in my hand and stare at the little girl with Mum's words echoing around and around in my head and worry churning in my stomach. Of course, it's entirely possible that she got muddled – she thinks I'm still at college – but something is niggling at the back of my mind, telling me that she seemed to be very clear on my childhood, almost as if she was still living in those days. And when I pressed her, she said it herself: 'Don't you think I of all people would know my own daughter's name?'

After all my doubts about Rachel, I can't put this down to an absent mind. I know I need to establish exactly who Rachel is and what it is she wants from me. I slip past the carer's station, where a young woman is scrolling on her phone, until I reach the central staircase again. I feel a rush of relief as I plod down and hit the exit button to open the door and step outside, where I take big breaths and stare up at the darkening sky, trying to make sense of what I've just heard.

Has Rachel – whoever the hell she is – gone to my house and discovered I'm gone? A ripple of fear passes through me as it crosses my mind that not only do I have no idea who that woman is, I don't know what she's capable of. Perhaps she will have called the police and they'll be out here looking for me, or maybe she prefers to deal with me herself. Bryce's muscle feels intimidating not reassuring and I decide I'm not ready to face either of them, but I have nowhere else to go.

Retracing my steps back towards my street, I weigh up all the options open to me. I could return to The Hollies and sleep in the armchair by Mum's bed, but I immediately rule that out: I don't think I can face another dressing down. Then there's Cathy next door – I'm sure she would let me in, but could I get there without Rachel seeing me? It feels like too much of a risk to get so close without a proper plan, so I rack my brain for alternatives, but all that comes to mind are vague ideas about calling the police myself or going to a shelter, but nothing feels quite right. My leg muscles are beginning to cramp; I need to sit down quite soon or else I'm going to fall. It's obviously the furthest I've walked in months, and tears spring to my eyes that my body isn't up to it. I'm a broken person, inside and out. But I fight back sobs and tell myself to stop feeling sorry for myself and concentrate: now isn't the time to fall apart.

Halfway along the main road, I pass a pub lit up by a golden glow that spills out onto the pavement, looking warm and welcoming. I can practically smell the beer-scented air and hear the roar of chatter in my ear. I feel a sudden longing that surprises me and realise how much I want to be around other people, to feel like I'm part of something bigger than my own little life. Feeling drawn to it like a moth to a flame, I decide that what I need is some time to think and a place to sit down, and what better place is there to do that than a pub?

I step gratefully into the warm, boozy air that whooshes towards me and welcomes me inside and I take a deep, satisfied breath. I walk towards the bar before the flaw in my plan hits me and I remember that I'm carrying no cash or card. Disappointment floods through me but I swerve the cash register and make for a table, deciding that I will act as if I'm waiting for someone to give me some time to work out what to do next. Taking a seat, I fold my coat over the second chair before looking around in wonder.

The pub is busy for what I presume is a mid-week night, although even as I think this I realise it could be Friday or Saturday since days have no importance when you're in a coma. There are the regular old men sitting up at the bar, making their way through a pint and talking to no one. On the front table is a rowdy group of what could be work mates, yammering at each other and gently swaying as if they've been there for a while. Peering behind me to the back of the room, I spot a table filled with teenagers and I'm struck by the thought that most of them don't look old enough to be in here. In fact, some of them look like they'd struggle to get into a 15-rated film at the cinema, but I'm not the landlord.

My gaze is drawn to one of the girls. Her hair is jet-black, so dark it must be dyed, and she's bent at the waist, her head in her hands and her shoulders juddering as if she's sobbing. Two of her friends are leaned over, whispering in her ears, no doubt trying to reassure her about something her latest boyfriend has or hasn't done this time. She lifts her head briefly and I see her thick mascara streaking down her face; she looks so young beneath the layers of face paint. I can't help but wonder what could possibly have happened in her short life to make her so sad and I feel an urge to rush over and wrap her in a hug.

It strikes me that I'd like to lay my head down on the table and sob too but I don't have friends around; there's no one here to pick me up, so I tell myself I'm just going to have to get on with it. I make a decision – there's only one thing for it really: I have to confront Rachel, or Amy, or whoever she is. I wrap my arms across my chest, wishing I had a tenner in my pocket so I could buy one drink, a bit of Dutch courage to send me on my way and an anaesthetic for my aching muscles.

It's hard to know what to think but I can't deny that something about Rachel has felt off since the moment I woke up and saw her at my bedside. If I'm honest, it's felt like she's been lying to me the whole time. But if she's not my sister, then who is she? And why would she lie? I put my head in my hands and press my fingertips into my skull, wishing I could reach inside my brain and pull out the memories that must be stored somewhere inside there, locked in grey matter like something in the deep freeze just waiting to be thawed.

'What are you drinking?' a male voice says from above me and my head snaps up to see a young, handsome man looking down at me. 'Looks like you could do with one.'

I take in the sweep of dark hair and his smooth, fair skin that suggests he probably couldn't grow more than a wispy moustache even if he wanted to, and I guess his age at eighteen or nineteen. My mouth waters at the thought of a nice glass of red – I guess Cathy was right about my liking wine – but I feel uncomfortable about accepting one from this youth. God knows what his motivation is for offering a woman old enough to be his mother a drink, and as I glance at the table of young people at the back of the pub and catch a couple of them looking over at us, it hits me that this could be a dare, or maybe I'm being filmed for an online prank.

'I'm waiting for someone,' I say sniffily, but instead of walking away, he pulls back the chair that's housing my coat and slides into the seat.

'Come on, Ms V, let me get you a glass of wine and you can tell me why you've done a runner.'

I narrow my eyes as I stare at the boy, but I try not to let my shock show on my face as I wonder how it is he knows all that about me.

'I have no idea what you mean.'

'Rachel called round at my mum's an hour ago saying you are meant to be at home, but you left without telling anyone.' He grins and waggles a finger in the air. 'Naughty, naughty.'

'Ian?' I say, and his grin widens. It's easy to imagine that the girls from the table of teenagers weren't looking over here because of anything to do with me; they are probably all infatuated with this boy – I can't deny he's very good-looking.

'That's my name,' he says, 'don't wear it out.'

'I'll take a glass of red,' I say decisively.

It doesn't take long for him to slip to the bar and return with a glass of wine for me and a half an orange juice for him. 'I'm driving,' he says, lifting it to his lips and taking a sip at the same moment as I take a long, luscious gulp from my glass. The wine goes down rather too easily but I force myself to slow down and put the glass on the table. I haven't touched alcohol in more than half a year and I don't want it going straight to my head. Something tells me that perhaps Ian might be able to shed light on some part of my life – he was my student at least.

'So,' I venture, not sure where to start. 'How well do we know each other?'

Ian looks at me, his handsome face creased with a frown before he breaks out into bemused laughter, and I feel indignant heat rising up my body, threatening to engulf my head in flames.

'This is bizarre! Are you seriously telling me you don't know anything about me?'

His obvious disbelief that someone might not be a grade-A student in Ian Studies makes me shake my head at the arrogance of youth, but it is refreshing to see someone respond to my current situation with the shock and horror I feel it deserves rather than trying to placate me with reassuring words about brain injuries taking time.

'I was in a car accident. I don't remember much about before.'

Ian sweeps a hand back through his hair, opens his eyes wide and says, 'Jesus Christ,' in a performative gesture that feels as if it might be more for the teenagers at the back table than me, and I catch a couple of them elbowing each other in the ribs and sniggering. 'Mum did tell me, but I didn't think it would be quite so... thorough.'

'What else did your mum say about me?'

'Just that you've been in an accident and your brain has been fried.' He glances at me and ducks his head. 'Sorry, I mean, you've suffered a bad head injury and it's going to take some time until your memories come back. Apparently, Rachel asked us to be careful what we tell you.'

My head snaps up and my hands start to feel clammy and a cold sweat breaks out on my back as I take in that Rachel has been out there controlling what people say to me. It hits me that it's entirely possible that she is coordinating a campaign of lies and there is no way of me getting to the truth. My heart thumps hard in my chest but I try to ignore it, telling myself that this sounds like a conspiracy theory rather than a way that normal people behave. And I really want to believe that I'm a normal person who lives in a normal house on a normal street, although that is getting harder and harder to swallow the more I discover about myself.

'What do you mean "be careful"?' I ask, choosing my words delicately.

Ian's face goes blank and he seems lost for a moment before he says, 'Just, you know, not talking about the accident or your injuries. That kind of thing.' I have another gulp of wine while Ian sips his orange and adds, 'I think she's just trying to protect you.'

'It's fine, you don't need to keep things from me. To be honest, I think Rachel has got it wrong. There's nothing you could tell me that would be worse than living with this black hole inside my head where my life should be. And the weirdest thing is...' I break off. I was about to tell him about my imaginary husband and child that I feel sure should be sitting at home now, waiting for me to get back, instead of that empty house with its too-tidy cupboards and too-clean surfaces, but I realise that I'm not ready to say that aloud, especially not to this boy who is currently looking at me like a science experiment.

'Go on,' he says with obvious glee, 'what's the weirdest thing?'

I settle on something else to say. 'The weirdest thing is that Rachel is the only person I have, but I don't feel like I can trust her.'

'Rachel's cool,' Ian says suddenly and I frown. What the hell does he know about Rachel? 'She's been looking out for you.'

'Is she my sister?'

Ian stares at me like I've just asked if Rachel is a unicorn and says, 'I'm pretty sure she's your sister. Mum says she's been the one looking after you.'

'And she was before?'

'I don't know if you've always been best friends, but she's been around.'

I wonder what he means by that. Perhaps Rachel and I weren't close before and she's used my accident as a way to get back into my life. I can't help but think of my yellow bench – the place where I sat and sobbed. Was Rachel the cause?

'Your mum said that I'd been arguing with someone. Bad enough that they started a fire in my garden.'

Ian snorts and shakes his head, which is not the reaction I expected. Before I can carry on, he says, 'You know my mum is batshit, don't you?'

I feel the urge to tell him not to speak about his mother like that but I still need this boy, so I just shake my head.

'Of course she let you think you were arguing with someone else. She didn't want you to know the truth.'

I frown, wondering what he means.

'She did it.'

My mouth falls open and I stare at the twisted smile that's appeared on his face. 'Cathy?'

'She likes to pretend to be normal but sometimes, you know,' he clicks his fingers, 'it's one flew over the cuckoo's nest time.' He glances at my almost empty glass and says pointedly, 'The wine didn't help but you two got into, let's just call it, a heated debate and you stormed off. Next thing you know, Mum is out there with a jerrycan and a box of matches. She's lucky the whole house didn't go up.'

I struggle to form words – I'm not sure exactly what to say. Cathy certainly didn't mention she was the one who I was arguing with, but maybe she was too embarrassed to admit that she was involved.

'Why were we arguing?'

Ian smirks. 'I think you said something offensive about Mum's pride and joy...' He can tell I'm trying to work out what he means, as he grins and adds, 'Me.'

'I'm sure that's not true,' I offer quickly, but even as I say it, I realise I can imagine getting frustrated with this young man probably bringing friends over at all times of the day and night and playing music too loudly.

'I'm actually a very considerate neighbour,' Ian says as if reading my mind.

He laughs, but I feel more confused than when I walked in. As well as questioning my relationship with Rachel, I'm now also questioning my relationship with Cathy. Has anyone told me the truth? Suddenly I feel a burst of anger that surprises me, and as it rages through my body, I drain the dregs of my wine, slam the glass down and push myself to my feet, determined to get home and start getting answers from someone.

'I'm going,' I say.

'Woah,' Ian leaps up, 'I've got my car outside. Let me at least drive you, Ms V. I don't think you should be walking in your condition.'

I want to refuse, but something tells me I may need to conserve my strength if I'm going to confront Rachel – or Amy, or whoever she is – and finally get some answers.

EIGHTEEN

Ian pulls up outside my house much more slowly and carefully than I'm expecting, and he leaves the engine idling as we peer out at the dark windows.

'Are you going to be OK getting in?' he asks and I realise he's expecting me to move but my whole body feels as if it's seized up after the day's exertions. I'm surprised that there are no lights on and I feel an unexpected disappointment that Rachel isn't waiting by the front door, ready to rush out and help me inside like a wounded solider returning from the front line. I wonder if this is what Stockholm syndrome feels like.

'I'm fine,' I say to Ian. 'Thank you for the lift. Aren't you going home?'

'Nah, the night's still young,' he says with a grin and I glance at the clock on the dashboard and see it's only nine thirty. I wonder if I would have been going to parties and clubs when I was Ian's age, but something tells me I was much more sensible than that.

Using the door to hold on to, I haul myself to my feet and stand in the driveway, swaying in the cool breeze that is swirling in the air, making it feel like autumn is very much on its way. I put my hand in my pocket and squeeze the Eiffel Tower key ring in my fist as I stagger the few steps to the door. I've barely lifted the key to the lock when the car pulls away, and Ian gives a light beep of the horn before I hear the tyres squeal as he puts his foot down. He doesn't seem like a bad kid, but I do feel a rush of sympathy towards Cathy as I picture her waiting for him to come home and worrying about him – he certainly seems like a handful – but I quickly tell myself to stop feeling sorry for my neighbour. She's the one who torched my bench after all.

I turn the key in the lock and open the door, stepping into the silent, dark hallway and expecting Rachel to come rushing out of the kitchen demanding to know where I've been, but nothing happens.

'Rachel?' I call out. 'Bryce?' There's no response and I feel half relieved that I don't need to confront them right away and half disappointed that I have no outlet for the churning rage I feel.

The stairs look like a sheer cliff face after my day of exertion but as I stare up at the striped, navy blue runner, I know I need to make it to the top, so I grit my teeth and start the slow climb. By the time I reach the landing, I'm breathing hard and sweating. The swirl of anger has returned, and when I step inside my bedroom, I'm struck by the thought that if I don't grasp control and actually do something, I'm going to be stuck at the mercy of others forever. The only thing I know is that I need to find a way to make Rachel be honest with me since even Ian admitted she's holding things back and I've had enough of being protected.

Glancing around the room, my eyes land on the key in the lock and an idea begins to form; it sends a thrill of fear through me that makes my hands shake but somehow the more scared I feel, the more sure I am that this is what I need to do. It's time for drastic measures, something I'm sure the old, sensible me would never even dream of. Something to shock Rachel into telling me the truth.

Returning to the hallway, I stomp through into the spare room, grab a couple of pillows from the bed and take them into my bedroom, arranging them in a lump in the middle of the bed as if there's someone sleeping. Perhaps with the lights off it might work, but with the lightbulb blazing overhead there's no doubt that it could be anything other than a pile of cushions, so I set about dressing one of the pillows in my T-shirt and ruching the duvet to give a glimpse of my clothes. Shaking my head, I sigh in aggravation. It's still impossible to look at the pile on the bed and think that a real human is lying there so I glance around the room, searching for something to add to the realism, but nothing comes to mind. Until a strand of my long, dark hair slips in front of my face and I tug it back in frustration – an idea hits me.

My hands go to my head. I feel my long hair held back by a scrunchie and ease it free, letting the strands fall loosely around my face. It feels lifeless and limp but as I hold a clump between my fingers, I feel an attachment that suggests I once cared very much about these dead cells and I try to imagine the trips to the hairdressers and hours I probably spent styling and brushing it. Making my way to the small bathroom, I feel more certain with every step that what I'm about to do is a good idea, and perhaps it's the only thing that is going to make my plan work – and what I need right now more than long hair is a plan.

Inside the bathroom, I turn on the light and take one long last look in the mirror. My hair is below my shoulders and heavy, like a thick curtain that's fallen at the end of a play. Although my skin is dull and pale from being inside for so long, my eyes are bright and a lovely deep brown, with nice long eyelashes and a good brow line. Laughing slightly manically, I think to myself that perhaps it is time for a change – new me, new hair – and I open the bathroom cabinet. My hand immediately lands on what I need: a pair of nail scissors.

Holding up small sections at a time, I snip away at the strands, leaving about two inches of hair at the root and letting the long strands fall into the sink. With each scratchy cut, I feel as if I'm getting lighter and lighter, almost like I'm swallowing bubbles of helium. By the time I'm done, it's like I could float right out of the window and up into the sky. In the mirror, a woman I don't recognise looks back at me. I stare at her. She meets my gaze with an edge of defiance in her dark eyes and a small smile playing on her lips. I like this person – I've shed my skin and a new me has crawled out.

'Hello,' I say and I laugh at the sound of my own voice echoing in the empty bathroom, then I chide myself for being silly when there is work to be done.

I grab the shorn hair in my fists and hurry back through into the bedroom, where I carefully arrange it at the head of the bed, letting it fall across the pillow as if I'm lying in bed on my side, turned towards the window – the same position I've spent countless hours in. Stepping back to admire my handiwork, I decide that it looks almost too realistic and I wonder what Rachel will think of me when she discovers what I've done. But it's too late to go back because in that moment, I hear a noise downstairs that makes me freeze. Someone has opened the front door.

NINETEEN

I try to stay calm as I strain my ears and hear footsteps as someone rushes through into the kitchen. Next, I hear my name being called.

'Jen? Jen?' It's Rachel's voice. It's edged with worry, but I can't think about that now. Instead, I set my plan into motion and hit the lights, positioning myself behind the door so that when it swings open, the first thing she'll see is the bed.

Rachel's footsteps start on the stairs and there isn't much time to think before she is at the door to my room, still calling my name. Then the door opens and I hear the breath leave her body in a huge exhale of relief.

'Oh my gosh, Jen, there you are.' She rushes inside and almost dives onto the bed, bending over the cushions, but I don't wait to see her reaction when the hair comes off in her fingers and slides to the floor. Instead, I slip out of the room behind her, close the door and turn the key in the lock with a loud clunk.

There's a moment of silence before Rachel says my name again although now her voice is filled with shock, not worry, and her footsteps cross the room before the doorknob begins to rattle.

'Jen, what the hell is going on?' she demands.

I sink to the floor, stretching my legs out in front of me and resting my back against the door as she pounds on it with her fist.

'Please, Rachel, let's not disturb the neighbours,' I say, surprised at how calm I sound when my whole body is churning on the inside like the sea in a storm.

'Have you lost your mind?' she says.

I start to laugh, fighting against the impulse to burst into frustrated tears, and I say, 'Yes, that's exactly what's happened. I lost my mind six months ago and I need you to help me find it again.'

'That's what I'm trying to do,' she says. 'I've been trying to help you and how do you repay me? You lock me in your fucking bedroom!'

Rachel sounds mad now and she starts slapping the door before the noise stops. She moves across the room before I hear her yelling, 'Help! Help! I'm locked in! Call the police!'

'Rachel,' I call out, 'it would be better if we could just talk without the police coming, but if that's what you want, then fine by me. Perhaps then we'll get to the bottom of why you've been keeping me here and not at a hospital when I clearly need medical treatment.'

'You've got Dr Marsden,' Rachel practically shrieks but that only makes me laugh harder.

'Come on, do you think I'm a simpleton? Clearly Dr Marsden isn't real, or I would have met her by now. I've been back in the world of the living for four days now and the only time you ever mention her is when it's convenient for you.'

'Convenient? You think any of this is convenient? Let me tell you that this has been a nightmare from start to finish and I have been the one trying to pick up the pieces, like I always am. Forever the big sister.'

I let out a snort. 'You know I went to see Mum today?'

Rachel falls silent and I wonder if she's been struck down by the fear that I might have found her out, but then I hear a scraping sound, like she's dragging the armchair across the floor. All I can think is that she is trying to climb out of the window.

'It's a long way down, Rachel,' I call, hoping that she won't attempt it, but deciding that it's her choice if she does. I am not to blame for her actions just like she's not to blame for mine. We're grown women after all.

'If you fall, I'll nurse you back to health, don't you worry. You're welcome to stay in that room for as long as you like.'

She doesn't laugh at this. I hear the scraping sound again, moving closer to the door, and then there's a creak that could be her flopping down in the chair.

'OK,' she says, 'I'm listening.'

The silence thrums in the air as I realise I have her where I wanted her, but now I have no idea what to say.

'Look, this clearly means a lot to you,' she continues. 'What the hell have you done to your hair?'

I let this one slide and settle on my first question. 'What's your real name?'

An anguished cry comes through the door and Rachel groans, 'This is ridiculous. I'm sorry you don't trust me, but I am being honest with you. My name is Rachel Vincent and I am your sister.'

'Mum said my sister's name is Amy.'

Her voice drops and there's a slight quiver in it when she speaks again. 'Mum thinks I'm eighteen and have missed my grades for uni. Every time I see her, I have to relive that day, and the crazy thing is, I got into my second choice through clearing and had an absolute blast, and I've gone on to have a sensible, lucrative career, exactly as she wanted. But all she can fixate on is the day I disappointed her.'

This picture of Mum rings true and it does seem wrong to think of the woman inside my bedroom as anyone other than my sister but I can't just swallow her words without question. I *know* she's lying to me; somewhere, deep down, I can tell.

'You must have seen that she wasn't all there,' Rachel says gently. Of course, that much was evident and I drop my gaze, feeling a little embarrassed that I've rushed in with my accusations. Perhaps I should have been a bit more measured given Mum's dementia.

'She thought I was still at college,' I admit, 'and that my top was too low.'

Rachel laughs softly. 'That sounds like Mum... It does hurt that you would believe her over me,' she says, leaving the 'after everything I've done for you' unsaid although I'm sure we both hear it.

'Maybe it's because...' I start to say and then stop, holding back what I think for fear of hurting Rachel or perhaps for fear of what she might say.

'Go on,' her voice comes back.

Clearing my throat and hugging my knees tightly to my chest, I say, 'Maybe it's because I know you so well that I can tell you're keeping something from me.'

She doesn't respond to this and we sit there as time stretches out, and I wonder if it's seconds or minutes or even an hour that have passed.

'I bumped into Ian. He said you told Cathy not to tell me things,' I say finally, breaking the silence.

'That little shit! I only ever wanted the best for you and to help your recovery. But you know what, I'm done trying to protect you. I'm tired and I want to go home so you need to promise, once I've told you exactly what happened to you, you will open this door and let me leave.'

I feel a jolt of terror and excitement as I realise that what I've been wanting is finally about to come to pass, and all I can manage is a small squeak as I brace myself.

'You need to say, "I promise",' Rachel demands.

And I force my mouth to move as I say, 'I promise.'

TWENTY

'I want you to know that this has been an absolutely awful time,' Rachel begins and I nod even though she can't see me, absolutely agreeing with her on that. 'I never wanted any of this, and every decision I've made has been with you in mind, although it may take you a while to understand.'

I grip my knees, clutching the denim in my hands as I hear Rachel draw in a long breath.

'It's hard to know where to start...' she says and I sense her trailing off as if she's looking for a way out.

'The accident,' I hiss, 'start with the accident.'

She sighs, 'OK, so on the night of the accident, I was in my flat in Kingston, which is only around a ten-minute drive away, and it was truly awful weather outside. The type of weather that makes you look out of the window and thank your lucky stars that you're inside a warm building with a roof over your head. I'd just been watching the rain bounce off the road outside when I got a call to say that you'd been in an accident, that you'd come off the road and crashed into a tree, and that it was bad.'

I nod since I already know this bit.

'I asked if you were OK and they said it was too early to tell but they also told me... Look, Jen, are you sitting down? This might come as a shock.'

'Yes, I'm sitting down.' I want to scream, *Just tell me, tell me*, but I hold the words in, fighting with all my strength to stay calm and give her words the space they need to keep flowing from her lips.

'They told me you weren't alone in the car.' My mouth falls open, but I don't need to ask because she goes on. 'Do you remember when you asked me where your husband was?'

My whole body begins to tremble. I know deep down what is coming, almost as if I've known since the moment I woke up but I just didn't want to think it. 'Yes,' I say shakily.

Jen pauses for what feels like a long time but is probably only seconds. My heart is pounding. Is she about to confirm everything I've been thinking? Is she about to explain everything that's seemed so wrong? All the gaps I've been confused about?

'I know I said that you never married, and Jen, I'm truly sorry for so many things I've said, but I'd had medical advice that it was better not to bombard you with all the horrible details the moment you regained consciousness. You would find out soon enough anyway, and actually apparently for most patients it's a gradual thing, where memories come back to you slowly when your mind and body are ready for the facts.'

I can hear she's weeping now, and although I'm shaking, I feel a grim determination grip me. I know that I need to hear it. In order to start my recovery, I need the truth. 'I'm ready,' I say softly, aware she's about to tell me something life-changing.

'I'm not sure you are... Oh, Jen...' She breaks off in quiet sobs that sound like a mewling kitten and tug at my heartstrings before she seems to pull herself together. When she starts talking again, it's in a steady, steely voice. 'You *were* married, to Marc, a Frenchman who you met yonks ago on a trip to Paris for a concert. Marc was training to be a teacher and you fell in love. It was a whirlwind romance and you were engaged before any of the family even met him.'

Although I can't picture Marc, truth rings through her words as I remember the male presence I've felt has been missing since I woke up. My connection to France that I suspected but couldn't explain. My initial thought that I have a French name despite not feeling French. My key ring.

'So, Ms V *does* stand for Versailles?'

'You never actually changed your name because you were already teaching under your maiden name, but you liked to be called Ms V since it could be either Vincent or Versailles. Marc was desperate for you to change it, actually.'

'Were we happy?' I ask, the question bursting out of me before I really had a chance to think it. I want the answer to be yes, that we were happy and in love, that we had this perfect marriage I crave.

'At times,' Rachel says and I sense there's more behind her words than perhaps I want to hear. 'You were together a long time and there were ups and downs as there are in all marriages. You'd been having a bit of a down phase and he'd gone back to France to stay with his mother for a little while, to give you some space.'

I try to ignore the words 'separation' and 'divorce' that spring to my mind since I want the strong supportive feeling I've been imagining to return; that's exactly what I need right now.

'That's why I was so surprised to hear that he was with you, in the car.'

And the slow dawning of where this conversation is going finally erupts like a firework has exploded inside my head and is burning me from the inside out.

'Is he dead?' I cry. 'Tell me! Is he fucking dead?'

'I'm so sorry,' she says and now we're both sobbing. Tears

and snot are running down my face and dripping onto my top, but suddenly I sniff hard and wipe my face with the back of my hand.

'And my baby?' I say, suddenly certain that not only was I right about having a husband, but that the red-haired baby that has been haunting my dreams is real, is my flesh and blood, half me and half Marc.

In an instant, her name hits me. It's as if lightning has come through the roof of my house. I can't believe I could ever forget.

'Noelle,' I shriek, 'tell me what happened to Noelle.'

TWENTY-ONE

The silence in the house is deafening. I picture Rachel on the other side of the door, on her knees on the floor, her head in her hands. I can't see her, but I can almost feel her there, willing herself not to say the words she's about to but knowing she has to. It's time. We both know it's time.

'I'm so, so sorry,' Rachel says through sobs. 'I don't know how to say it... Noelle was with you, too. I'm sorry, Jen, she didn't make it.'

I try not to think of the cherubic baby that's been confounding me, but a crystal-clear image of her pops into my brain. A gummy smile, face smeared with ice cream, wispy red hair framing her face. I see how beautiful she was and how happy. Silent tears roll down my cheeks and I'm gripping my knees so tightly that my hands are aching. What is the point of anything any more? Why bother getting to know myself again when I will never know Noelle? I slump forward and wish for a moment that I'd stayed in my blissful ignorance, bouncing around the world in my pain-free bubble where all I had to worry about was what I didn't know. Why couldn't I have just accepted that Rachel knew best?

But a little voice inside is telling me that I needed to know, that I couldn't go on without truly understanding what I'd lost. It would be like tearing myself in two and discarding half, and it's almost impossible to understand why Rachel kept it from me. How can you tell a lie like that? Drawing myself up, I take a deep breath – Noelle and Marc deserve more than to be forgotten. They need bringing out into the light and remembering properly. Closing my eyes, I want to ask about whether they had a funeral, but another thought overtakes me, a thought so urgent it fills my brain and tears its way out of my mouth in that same moment. 'Why didn't I brake?'

'Oh, Jen.' I hear Rachel's voice is close to the door now, as if she is pressed up against it, trying to reach me. 'I don't know, honey, no one knows. It's one of the reasons why I've kept this from you for so long. I was hoping it would all come back to you on your own and you would be able to answer that question for yourself. It was an accident. I'm sure you did all you could, but sometimes things just happen and we can't explain them.'

'What did the police think?'

There's a long pause and I lift my head, suddenly wondering if I'm at risk of being arrested. Do the police think I murdered my own husband and baby?

'The investigation is ongoing,' Rachel says finally. 'They'll want to speak to you when they hear that you've woken up, I'm sure, although they told me off the record that with the weather that night, it's very likely to be concluded to be an accident.'

I let out my breath. My brain is struggling to keep up with what Rachel is saying. First, Marc and Noelle are dead, and second, I'm the subject of a police investigation.

'It *was* an accident, wasn't it?' The uncertainty in Rachel's voice breaks my heart and I wish I could obliterate it with words, but I know that doesn't work. 'Jen?'

'It was an accident,' I say. 'What else could it be?'

Rachel doesn't answer and we sit in silence again, listening as a car pulls up with a screech of brakes; its door slams and I wonder if it's Ian getting home. I can't help but feel a little tug of envy that Cathy is next door, having her baby return home to her, while here's me, left alone in an empty house.

'Will you let me out now, please?' Rachel says.

I manage to clumsily push myself to standing and turn the key. The door opens and Rachel rushes from the room; she immediately wraps me in a warm hug that makes me feel even worse that I locked my own sister in a room when she's been nothing but kind to me, desperately trying to protect me from the monster I am. A woman who killed her own family. How am I ever going to recover from that?

I step out of Rachel's arms and stagger the few steps to my bed, brushing the hair onto the floor and removing the pillows so I can sink onto the mattress, my hair now the last thing in the world that matters to me. Rachel remains in the doorway as I get under the covers fully clothed and pull the duvet up to my chin.

'Where are all their things?' I say as it hits me that this house is the relic of a single woman, not a mother and wife. Rachel must have cleared it from top to bottom and I find myself unable to compute how she could bear to do that.

'On the doctor's advice, I put their things into storage, just to give you the time to adjust to what happened,' she says and I'm aware I'm frowning, thinking back to when I searched the house and the whiff of fresh paint I smelled in the spare bedroom.

'Did you redecorate?' I say, my voice hollow with shock.

There's a long pause and I hear Rachel sniffling until she says, 'I really thought I was doing what was best for you. How could I tell you the truth when you've been so poorly? I wasn't sure you'd survive it.'

I try to let her words sink in but it's hard to get beyond the depth of Rachel's deception, and my head is swimming. Was it really in my best interests to keep Noelle from me? Something inside me hardens as I look at her and wonder what type of person she must be to hide such secrets.

'I kept a box of each of their things in my car so as soon as you wanted them I could give you the items that I think mattered the most.'

How on earth could you judge that? I find myself thinking, balking at the audacity of going through someone's home and sifting through their treasured possessions based on some strange idea that you are helping them, but I swallow my anger for now. I can't take any more pain. Right now, I want to sit with the knowledge that Marc and Noelle were here, that this was our house. I wasn't alone and I wasn't crazy – I did have a husband and baby, only they're gone now.

'Would you like me to bring you those boxes?' Rachel asks.

'Yes, please,' I say and I close my eyes while she disappears from the room. My body is aching from mental and physical exhaustion and I long for the comforting blackness of sleep to overtake me, but my mind is too active. The only thing going round and round in my head is, *They're dead, they're dead, they're dead.*

It takes two trips and five minutes until there are two small cardboard boxes stacked against the wall of my room – they're all I have left of my child and husband but having them there is a small comfort. After the day's excursions, I long to sleep, to enter a world where I can escape the knowledge, even if only temporarily, that Marc and Noelle have died.

'Bryce will be here in the morning and I'll come and check on you in the afternoon.'

I grunt, but of course I no longer care who visits me. My life has shrunk to the space inside those boxes – the only thing that matters to me now.

'You'll be OK,' Rachel says and she bends over the bed, pressing her lips to my forehead, before backing out of the room.

All I can think before I slip into sleep is, *Maybe I don't want to be OK.*

TWENTY-TWO

When I wake the next morning, I find Bryce sitting in the chair by my bed, reading aloud from a book in his deep bass voice and it takes me a moment to work out where I am and *then* I remember. The two cardboard boxes sit one on top of the other, exactly where Rachel left them, and I stare at them for the longest time, barely listening to Bryce as I wonder, *does he know what I did?* I finally got my truth – *Yay me*, I think sarcastically – but it's irrelevant because the two people who were missing from my life are actually gone forever, and the hardest part to accept is that I may have caused their deaths.

Bryce reaches the end of the chapter and pauses before asking, 'Would you like some toast and tea?'

My stomach rumbles at the mention of food and I realise how long it's been since I ate. 'That would be nice, actually,' I say and he smiles. 'And even better if I have any Marmite.'

'I'm sorry,' he says, 'it breaches my professional duty to serve anyone Marmite. You must have heard the medic's motto "first do no harm"?'

I let out a weak laugh and he shrugs. 'Sorry, not my best joke, but it's good to see you smile. I like your hair.'

My hand goes to my head and I feel the mop of short hair of all different lengths that must be sticking up in every direction. I grimace as last night's chain of events comes back to me one after the other, ending up at the point where I'm back in bed feeling utterly miserable.

'Suits you,' he says.

'I doubt that, but thanks.'

'Don't be too hard on yourself,' Bryce says and I wonder if he's talking about the hair or the accident, but he's gone before I can ask.

I hear him moving about downstairs, and it doesn't take long for him to return with a tray of tea and toast and a small vase with a single sunflower bursting into life.

'I thought you could do with something to brighten up the room,' he says, and I smile because it's thoughtful, but Bryce doesn't realise that the darkness I'm feeling is beyond lifting with a cheerful flower.

'You missed Rachel,' Bryce says. 'She popped by early doors and asked me to let you know that she couldn't stay for long, but she said she'll be back later this afternoon and she's arranged for Dr Marsden to come.'

He says this as if he's announcing a lottery win or like some other elusive prize is being bestowed upon me, but I can barely raise a smile as I say, 'OK.' The mention of Rachel fills me with mixed emotions because I do believe that she is my sister and she was doing her best, but it's very difficult to understand how anyone could tell such a monumental lie to their own flesh and blood. She let me think that I was crazy.

'I know you've been looking forward to meeting her?' he says, more doubtful now.

'Yes, OK,' I repeat, wishing I could summon the enthusiasm for Dr Marsden, but now I know about Marc and Noelle, getting better really doesn't seem that appealing. Maybe not remembering anything is the kinder option and I can start a new life as this person with no history. A blank slate. But it's hard to picture a future without a past to learn from and even worse to imagine Marc and Noelle going unremembered.

'It will get better,' Bryce says and I try not to sigh at the sheer improbability of this unless Dr Marsden possesses a time machine, but before I can feel too despondent, Bryce is helping me to sit up to eat my toast, which is pleasingly covered in a thick layer of Marmite.

'Would you like me to pass you anything?' Bryce says, his eyes darting towards the boxes, but I hurriedly shake my head.

'No, thanks.' I'm not ready to face the contents.

He stands by my bedside awkwardly while I munch my toast until he says, 'I'll pop downstairs then.'

Something compels me to blurt out, 'Stay, if you don't mind? I could do with the company. If you have time on your shift, that is?' And it's a relief when he sits back in the chair and folds his arms across his broad chest, tugging at the short sleeves of his scrubs.

'I'm sorry about your loss,' he says and I incline my head to thank him, aware that if I try to speak, I may not be able to get the words out.

'Shall I carry on?' he asks, lifting the book, and I nod as tears fall down my cheeks. 'I'm not sure how much you've heard, but we're halfway through *Persuasion* by Jane Austen.'

I nod, indicating him to go on; I had no idea he'd read so much to me. His deep voice soon begins to soothe me back into sleep, but just as I'm drifting off my eyes fly open.

'What is it?' Bryce says, leaning over me concerned, but I just shake my head.

'Nothing,' I murmur, letting my eyelids flutter shut again.

After a moment, he continues, and I peek over at him in the chair, realising that the person I'd seen in my mind's eye sitting vigil by my bedside wasn't Rachel, nor was it my husband, Marc, because that would be impossible. No, it was Bryce, and despite everything I've learned, I feel a little lift because it's nice to know that at least there's someone in my life who cares.

I don't know how much time has passed but I finished my toast a while ago and we've made good progress through the book, when we hear the noise of the front door opening and Bryce breaks off mid-sentence. There are two female voices and I guess Dr Marsden has arrived with Rachel; I feel a mild twitch of interest that I'm finally getting to meet the woman who orchestrated all of this – an interview with the puppet master – and questions begin popping into my head.

Bryce excuses himself politely while I sit up in bed since although I know I'm not going to change anything by grilling Dr Marsden, I feel like this is my opportunity to take my pain out on someone else. Is it really better for someone with such a serious injury to be at home with no medical support beyond a nurse who pops in and out? Do you really think anyone deserves to live believing that their nearest and dearest never even existed? There's a word for what they did to me: gaslighting. My own sister and my doctor gaslighted me to the point where I don't even know if I can trust myself.

I almost laugh out loud at the absurdity of it, and it's at that moment I hear what sounds like a scuffle on the stairs. My heart thumps. *What is going on?* As I'm trying to decipher the shushing sound, two words suddenly burst from the mire and explode up the stairs. 'Just go!' It's Rachel's voice and it strikes me as a strange way to speak to a doctor, but I suppose they have gotten to know each other quite well in the six months since the accident. They've probably had many conversations about me, especially given the unorthodox approach they've taken. I wonder if Dr Marsden is going to answer back, but I hear footsteps stomping up the stairs and then there's a little knock on my door.

'Mrs Vincent?' a voice says softly and I fight the urge to call back, *Ms V*, which seems to come as a natural reaction.

I just say, 'Yes?'

The door opens and a blonde woman steps inside the room and comes over to my bedside. She's much younger than I expected, perhaps mid-thirties, with her hair tied up in a perky ponytail and a scattering of freckles across her nose that make her look even younger. I was sure she'd sweep in with gravitas and brush off any doubts I raised, but now I'm less certain. This woman has the air of someone who wouldn't say 'boo' to the proverbial goose.

'You're awake,' she breathes, and somehow I think she sounds disappointed but I tell myself I must have imagined it as she carries on, 'Do you mind if I take a seat?'

I shake my head and she pulls the armchair up to my bedside and sits down, taking out a notebook from her bag and turning to a clean page in the middle. Rachel slips into the room behind her, but she hovers by the door, seemingly unwilling to get too close to me, but after last night I don't blame her. I can't bring myself to meet her eye and I feel a flush of shame that I actually imprisoned my own sister. Another crime to chalk up to my name after murder?

'So, how are you feeling?' Dr Marsden asks in a soft voice.

'Dreadful,' I say and I watch her pen race over the page as if I've said something captivating. I wait until she finishes whatever insightful note it is she has made and then she looks up and asks, 'Anything in particular bothering you?'

'Oh, nothing particular comes to mind,' I say icily and I see Rachel wince as I continue, 'Only the deaths of my husband and daughter, which I happened to find out about yesterday when they've been gone for half a year.'

There's an uncomfortable silence in the room and I swear I hear Dr Marsden swallow as she writes something in her notepad again. We wait, listening to the scratch of the pen.

What the hell can she be writing – is she working on her novel?

After what feels like an age, she rests the pen in her lap and says, 'Are there any physical symptoms you can tell me about?'

I want to shriek, *Is my mental pain not enough for you?* but I bite my tongue, telling myself that it's best to be polite, and I say, 'Do you not want to do any tests?'

'Bryce handles those,' she answers quickly and dismissively as if the idea of her taking out a stethoscope is utterly ridiculous. 'He shares all of your results with me so I know exactly how you are tracking.'

'And how am I tracking?' I ask innocently, wondering what type of trend my doctor can plot through this shitstorm of misery.

'You're getting better,' she says brightly. 'One day at a time.'

Her platitude feels like a slap in the face and a wave of disbelief rises up and crashes down on my head. 'Better? You think this is me doing better? I'm a husk of a person with no memories, no history and no knowledge. Apart from the fact that I know that I killed my own husband and child, so I'd pretty much say this is rock-bottom, wouldn't you?'

There's a long silence while I glare at Dr Marsden and I swear her eyes seem to fill with tears. I have a sudden lurch of fear that she might be about to burst into messy sobs, which is the last thing I need. *This is my tragedy*, I think selfishly as she seems to take a deep breath, but Rachel cuts in before Dr Marsden can speak.

'At least you're alive, my darling Jen.'

I snort softly at this, feeling it is scant comfort right now.

Dr Marsden composes herself and adds, 'Head injuries can take a very long time and improvement isn't always linear. Your physical recovery has been really great and I think soon you could manage without a nurse.'

I feel a rush of panic at the thought of Bryce not coming any more. He may be Rachel's lackey but at least he's good company and it does feel like he cares – he has been reading to me, after all.

'We don't need to rush anything,' Rachel says.

'Has anything else come back to you?' Dr Marsden asks. They both stare at me intently and I have a sense that they are nervous. What could be making them so fearful since Rachel has already told me that the worst possible thing that can happen to a person has happened to me?

'Quite a lot of things actually,' I say and Rachel's head jerks up almost violently.

'Like what?' she asks.

'Oh, some mundane things, but also some more impactful things, the type of things that can alter the course of a person's life in just six short months.'

Rachel doesn't look away now and I see that Dr Marsden is leaning forward in her seat, her grey trousers perched right on the edge of the armchair cushion, the pen in her hand tapping hard on the pad, making me wonder if she's always a fidget or if something I've said has made her extremely nervous.

Clearing my throat, I let the moment drag out for dramatic effect before I say, 'Well, I've remembered giving advice that meant that a person didn't get the medical care they needed in an actual hospital and had to rot away alone in their bedroom, perhaps even putting my medical licence at risk.' I raise my eyes and meet Dr Marsden's gaze and find it is like looking into the face of a rabbit caught in headlights. 'Oh wait, that's not me, that's you.'

I laugh softly to show that I'm joking, albeit cruelly, but Dr Marsden stands up suddenly and glares at me as if she is trying to wrestle back control of the situation.

'I think it may be best if we rearrange this meeting for a time when you are feeling more up to it. I know you've had a shock and you must need some time to process it. I don't think we're going to make much progress today.' She says this with an air of finality and I'm tempted to insist that I'm fine, only I know deep down that I'm very definitely not fine.

'OK,' I murmur at the same moment as Rachel says, 'Are you sure you don't want to take your opportunity to discuss your prognosis?'

'There'll be other chances, when you're in a better frame of mind,' Dr Marsden says and leaves the room. The whole meeting can only have taken five minutes but I'm relieved that she's gone.

'Did you really need to be so rude?' Rachel asks, before hurrying after Dr Marsden.

The room feels horribly empty now they've both gone and I do regret what I said, but for one minute, being awful to someone else distracted me from my pain. I wonder if that's the type of person I am going to be from now on, someone who lashes out to avoid facing up to their own problems. My eyes land on the two boxes stacked against the wall and I bite down, grinding my back teeth together and steeling myself, vowing that I won't let myself become that person.

I know what I need to do. I need to open the boxes.

TWENTY-THREE

Pulling back the duvet, I slide out of bed and kneel down on the floor, facing the two boxes, panic thrumming in my chest like the wings of a trapped bird. From downstairs, I catch a whiff of garlic frying that must be Bryce cooking my dinner and my stomach turns. I can't even think about food right now.

Both boxes appear to be identical – small and sealed with silver packing tape – and written on the lid of the top one in Rachel's neat printed letters is 'Marc'. I'm sure I'll find 'Noelle' on the second, but I can't bring myself to look at that one yet. Peeling back the tape, I slowly open the flaps of the first one, wincing as if something is going to spring out and smack me in the face but, of course, nothing happens. When I peer inside I'm slightly disappointed to find a stack of papers and a few other miscellaneous objects that appear on first sight to be no more interesting than a box of bric-a-brac on offer for a pound at a car boot sale.

On top is a plastic wallet and inside it is what looks like a certificate. As I squint at it, I realise that it's our wedding certificate: Jennifer Jane Vincent and Marc Versailles, married in the Kingston registry office on 1 September 2004. I close my eyes and try to think of that day. Did I wear white? Did it rain or did the sun shine and the birds sing a chorus? Shaking my head, nothing comes, but then I realise that underneath the wallet is a photo frame, and when I lift it up I hear myself gasp. It feels as if someone has thumped me in the stomach, forcing all the air out of my body.

It's a plain silver frame and the photo inside is of a much younger me, looking happy and beautiful, with my dark hair down and wearing lots of eyeliner. I'm in a vintage dress with a skirt flared at the knee and funky red shoes that match my lipstick. By my side is a man with his arm around me, gazing slightly up since he's shorter than me in my heels, with the widest grin on his face. The sight of it makes my stomach drop and tears spring to my eyes. Marc, my husband, may still be a fuzzy outline in my memories but seeing his face floods me with an emotion I wasn't anticipating. I expected to feel happiness, but what I'm hit by is a jolt of fear.

I stare at the photo but nothing further comes, and I wonder if I mistook the drop in my stomach for something that it wasn't, so I continue leafing through the box, finding Marc's teaching certificate and his international baccalaureate. They bring me nothing – it's like reading about a stranger. There are some snaps of what I assume is his home in France and his family, but I don't feel a flicker of recognition as I look at the faces of my in-laws. At the bottom of the box is a faded sweatshirt with 'UCL' emblazoned across the front and I take a guess that Marc studied there at some point. I unfold it from the box and bury my nose in the bobbled material, taking a deep sniff and trying to decipher the warm, slightly spicy, earthy tones. Again, I'm confused by the discomfort I feel and some impulse makes me shove the sweater roughly back in the box and jam the lid on.

I can't understand why I'm not feeling a stronger connection to Marc, but I tell myself it must be the fact that I've only just found out about him. Without any memories, it feels impossible to have the intimacy I know must have been there between us. How can you mourn someone you never knew existed?

Turning to the second box, I spot Noelle's name and start to feel jumpy. I'm both terrified that I will and won't remember her – I'm not sure which is worse. My fingers shake as I tug off the tape, flinching at the awful screech that fills the room as it peels off. *You can do it*, I tell myself. Opening the flaps, I lean forward and see that on top is a photo that's been cut into a small square shape. It's of me and Marc and we're holding Noelle between us, and we're all laughing as she reaches up and tries to touch my face. The photo has been printed at a shop on the proper paper, but it's faded almost as if it's from years ago, and something about it snags inside my mind and I feel something whirring in my chest.

Glancing up to the bookshelf, I spot the photo frame that I broke and see the picture of Rachel and me in our swimsuits, splashing on Walberswick beach, and the sliver of chipboard that's been bothering me. I quickly undo the back and try the photo of my family in the frame – of course, it's a perfect fit. As I hold it in my hands, a feeling of calm descends. This is the reason the photo is so faded – it was sitting right here in a frame in the direct sun from the window, exactly where it's meant to be.

Once I've returned the frame to its spot, I go back to the box and see that most of its contents are soft materials that feel like a knife in my chest when I pick them up. I can only bear to look at one tiny Babygro and a beautiful woollen blanket with a llama embroidered on the corner before I shove them back into the box and close the lid, my heart beating hard and tears pricking in my eyes. I may not have made it the whole way through but I'm proud of myself that I've made a start, and while it still hurts, it does feel like a small piece of my icy heart has thawed, telling me that this is what my recovery needs. Truth.

I hear Bryce's heavy footsteps on the stairs and quickly put the boxes back in position because I don't want to discuss them with anyone – I'm not ready for that – but when I turn to get back in bed something stops me. At first I think it's one of the items from Marc's or Noelle's box that I must have knocked under the bed, but as I look closer, I see it's a spiral-bound notebook that I recognise as the one belonging to Dr Marsden. Bryce is almost at the door so, without thinking, I grab the book and throw myself back into bed, shoving the notebook under my pillow then falling still as if nothing has happened.

'I hope you're hungry,' Bryce says as he comes inside, bringing with him a rich and creamy smell of mushroom soup. 'This one is my grandma's recipe so you should count yourself lucky.'

With my fingers clutching the notebook under my pillow, I find myself smiling.

TWENTY-FOUR

Bryce's soup is so delicious that it's no effort to clear my bowl. He sits by the bed while I eat, talking in detail about the different types of mushrooms he used.

'Foraging is one of my favourite things to do. There's a little wood near the newbuild estate where I live that's survived the bulldozers and you can find all sorts of mushrooms. You have to be careful though because some of them are highly poisonous. One bite would kill you.' He wriggles his eyebrows and I can tell he's trying to distract me from the boxes. 'There's a great little book that tells you what features to look out for. I'll have to show it to you one day.'

I smile and nod but find I'm thinking about Dr Marsden's notebook and what may be inside. It feels like my opportunity to learn about what happened to me in the six months I spent in a coma. Dr Marsden took copious notes in the short time she visited me today, so I have high hope that there'll be enough detail for me to piece together my treatment, and maybe understand a bit more about what Rachel has been thinking. It might even improve our relationship if I can get an insight into her motives.

When I'm finished, I expect him to leave but he just clears his throat and says, 'I've been thinking.'

He sounds hesitant so I nod, encouraging him to go on and acknowledging that I'm starting to feel like Bryce is more than my nurse or carer. I'm starting to see him as a friend.

'If there's anything you'd like, I can get it for you.'

I try to work out what he could mean and all I can think of is those prison movies where the guards smuggle contraband in and accept cigarettes as payment.

'Like drugs?' I say, laughing.

Bryce wriggles his eyebrows again. 'Rumbled. Nurse by day, drug dealer by night, that's me. One of the more common career paths for my profession. Everyone needs a side hustle.'

We're both laughing now and I add, 'In that case, then, I'll take some magic mushrooms. I could do with a trip outside my own mind.'

Bryce's laughter fades but he's still smiling. 'We all feel like that some days.'

'I appreciate the offer,' I say, returning to reality. 'What type of thing were you thinking of?'

Bryce shrugs, looking embarrassed. 'I dunno. Maybe a specific chocolate bar or magazine. Whatever little comforts you're missing. We can keep it as our little secret.'

Our eyes meet and I catch a strange intensity before Bryce laughs and scratches his beard. 'Sorry, that sounded a bit unprofessional. I'm not trying to get between you and Rachel, it just feels like you might need a bit of independence given everything you've been through, but just tell me if it's not my place.'

'It's fine,' I say quickly. 'You're right, that's exactly what I need.'

We exchange smiles like children playing a game of secret spies.

'Could you get my phone fixed?' I point to the broken phone on my bedside table.

Bryce grins and puts it in his pocket. 'Of course.' He's quiet for a moment then stands. 'I better do the washing up.'

As he goes to leave, I say, 'Thank you,' and this time it's not just a platitude that slips off my tongue but a heartfelt emotion, and I'm embarrassed by the slight rasp in my voice.

'Don't mention it.' He lumbers down the stairs and I wait until I hear him in the kitchen below before pulling the notebook out from under my pillow. I don't need to open it to be certain it's the same one Dr Marsden was writing in – on the front is a sticker with 'DR MARSDEN MEDICAL NOTES' written in all capitals. I feel a thrill of excitement as I open it to the first page, aware that Dr Marsden surely didn't mean to leave this book behind, but what harm can I do? Your own medical notes aren't confidential from yourself.

As I scan the lines of writing, my heart stutters then sinks. I turn the pages in open-mouthed disbelief. Every word is gobbledygook – made up of squiggles and dots and totally nonsensical. For a moment I consider whether she's written in another language that uses a different alphabet, or that it could even be a code – some people still use shorthand, I've heard – but quickly I'm shaking my head. There's no rhyme or reason to the swirls and scribbles and it crosses my mind that Dr Marsden may have been trolling me. Was she even listening to a word I said?

There are footsteps on the stairs again and this time I don't bother to hide the book. There's certainly nothing in there that I'd need to hide from Bryce or anyone else for that matter. It's totally illegible. The doorknob turns and I open my mouth to complain about Dr Marsden but it's not Bryce who steps inside, it's Rachel, frowning hard with her already heavy jaw set in grim determination. Closing the book slowly, I slip it under my arm without moving too quickly so as to not draw her attention to it. I'm not sure now is the right time to discuss Dr Marsden's state of mind because Rachel already looks utterly furious. She rushes over to the side of my bed, refusing to sit in the armchair, and looms over me, her face flushed and her eyes flashing with anger. I can tell by the way she's holding her arms stiffly by her sides that she's fighting the urge to grab me by the shoulders and shake. I may be much stronger already, but I can't help but feel frightened by her palpable anger.

'Has something happened?' I ask.

'Has something happened?' she explodes, then she raises her eyes to the heavens and lets out a frustrated groan before looking back at me. 'Why don't you tell me.'

An image of Dr Marsden's bright red cheeks and eyes shining with tears pops into my head and I say, 'Is it to do with Dr Marsden?'

'Yes, it's to do with Dr Marsden,' she says icily. 'That woman has been nothing but kind to you and you've gone and threatened her medical licence. How do you think that makes her feel?'

Could what I said be interpreted as a threat? Maybe I wasn't very nice, but she advised my own sister to lie to me. I was lying here thinking I was crazy and that I'd imagined a husband and child, and now I know that they existed all along. It feels like Dr Marsden deserves to stew in her own guilt for a while, as does Rachel, but looking at the fury on her face, I decide it might be best to try to take things down a notch or two.

'I'm sorry,' I say, trying to sound sincere.

'Sorry isn't going to cut it this time.'

I bite my lip, wondering how I've ended up with Rachel mad at me when she is the one who's kept appalling secrets from me, and the doctor she hired for me has clearly got a screw loose. I open my mouth to protest, but Rachel cuts in before I can get a word out. 'You do realise that there are very few people on your side right now, don't you?'

This stings and I find myself blinking hard as I feel the pressure of tears when I think of Marc and Noelle – they'd be on my side if it weren't for the accident. It seems vicious for Rachel to bring that up.

'Let's count them, shall we?' She's still spitting mad and she holds up a finger for every name she says. 'There's me, Bryce and Dr Marsden, so three in total, but after how you treated her today, she has recommended that we find a new neurologist to help you. She gave me some names, but she said it's vital that there's a good relationship between doctor and patient with this type of injury.' Rachel puts one of her fingers down, and when she speaks again her voice sounds like she's talking to a toddler. 'So how many have we got left?'

My hackles rise and I can't say I'm disappointed that Dr Marsden won't be coming back, but I can see that arguing with her in this mood is not going to get us very far so I just say, 'Two.'

'Well done. That's two people looking after you. It doesn't seem very many now, does it?'

I frown, thinking that only a couple of days ago, Rachel said I have many friends. I'm wondering yet again whether I can believe a single word that comes from her mouth. The soup feels like a stone sitting heavily in my stomach and I close my eyes for a moment as the bleakness of her words hits me. Only two people in the world care about me and one of those is being paid to do so. It may have been a bit rash to challenge Dr Marsden, but I didn't warm to her and the note-book proves there's something off about her. Raising my chin, I meet Rachel's eyes and say, 'Maybe it's better to have two people who actually care rather than a third who is no help at all.'

'What on earth do you mean?' she says with a sigh. 'Dr Marsden has been instrumental in your care. She's devised the whole care plan that Bryce and I have been following. You owe her your life.'

'Well, then, why are all her notes written in hieroglyphics?'

I say and a couple of frown lines appear between Rachel's dark eyebrows.

'What do you mean?' she asks.

'Here.' I hold out the book and she snatches it from my fingertips.

'Where did you get this?' she demands. 'Don't you think this is a breach of her trust? I can't believe you would—'

'They're my notes,' I say firmly. 'She left them behind. I don't think I've done anything wrong by reading them. Now you look.'

'No,' she says petulantly and we face off against each other, our jaws set. Looking at her pale face, I realise she's looking more drawn than I've seen her – my care must be taking its toll. I'm not sure how we got on before, but I realise that I don't want to be a burden and I certainly don't want to have to fight against Rachel for every step of my recovery. I need to do things my way from now on.

'OK,' I say softly. 'I can't make you read it but let's just say it doesn't exactly fill you with confidence about Dr Marsden's competence, not that it matters any more if she's quit.'

'I'll try and talk her round,' Rachel says but I shake my head.

'No, don't.'

'Jen, you need help.'

'That may be, but we've tried things your way...'

'Dr Marsden said...'

I don't want to hear any more about Dr Marsden. 'It's time to try things my way.'

Rachel is still standing by my bedside, but her shoulders have dropped. She's now staring at me, her forehead puckered as if she's trying to make sense of where this conversation is going, so I decide to spell it out for her.

'Rachel, I'm so grateful for everything you've done.' She opens her mouth, but I hold up my hand. 'Really. I just think I need a few days to process the news about Marc and Noelle and I need to make my own plans. Physically, I'm on the road to recovery, those are Dr Marsden's words. All your hard work has paid off and got me started on that path and I really am grateful. Thank you. But now I need to work out what to do with the rest of my life. And to do that I need some space.'

Her eyes are wide and I see tears glimmering in the brown. 'What are you saying?'

'I think I need to be alone for a while.'

'I can't leave you,' she says, her voice wavering. 'I'm your sister.'

'You won't be leaving me forever,' I say, 'but why don't you take a few days off. Have a break. Spend some time with your partner. Recharge your batteries while I try and figure things out for myself. I think it will do us both some good.'

None of the tears fall and somewhere in there I'm sure I see a trace of relief as she leans forward and takes my hand.

'Only if you're sure?' she says.

I squeeze her fingers gently as I reply, 'I'm sure.'

'It won't be for long,' Rachel says but already she starts backing out of the room as if she can't wait to get away. 'I'll pop back around in a week or so and I'll keep Bryce on to help you.'

'Maybe I don't need...' I start to say, thinking about what Dr Marsden said about me almost being ready to live without a nurse. But I find I can't say his name. I don't want to be totally alone and I've got used to having Bryce around. More than that, I'd miss him if he was gone.

'Of course.'

'It will fly by.' And with those parting words, Rachel steps through the door. I hear her footsteps almost running down the stairs as if she is desperate to get out of here and I can't help but feel relief as the door bangs behind her.

Goodbye, sister, I think.

TWENTY-FIVE

I wake the next morning with one of Noelle's Babygros clutched to my chest and I take a moment to run through the facts: Marc and Noelle are dead, Rachel is gone, I am alone. Last night I went through Marc's box again but I felt nothing. In fact, I quickly shut the lid. I have no idea what that means but I'm happy Rachel isn't here because it's giving me time to think for myself. I've kept Noelle's box close, feeling comforted by its presence, but I can't bring myself to look through the rest of the contents. It hurts too much.

Fixing my gaze on the light grey linen curtains, I watch the sky in the gap between them as a fluffy white cloud rolls over the bright blue. It looks like a wonderful day. There's a noise on the stairs and I guess it's Bryce coming up with some food. I resolve to ask him to shut the curtains; I'm not in the mood for sunshine.

'Good morning,' Bryce says as he enters the room. I grit my teeth at his chirpiness and don't turn around. 'Actually it's after twelve so I should say good afternoon. I've got lunch for you and a surprise.'

I can't deny that a delicious smell is filling the room and

grudgingly I admit to myself that I am hungry, so I roll over slowly and see Bryce grinning at me with a tray holding what looks like eggs benedict, a cafetière of coffee and my phone with a new screen. Pushing myself up to sitting position, I snatch up my phone and immediately try to turn it on. It takes a moment for the white apple to light up and I feel a whir of excitement as my eyes meet Bryce's.

'The shop said it was quite an easy fix.'

Up pops the password request and I hesitate for a moment before Bryce says, 'One, two, three, four. The man in the shop figured it out. He said it's amazing how many people use the same handful of codes and he wanted to check the functionality. I hope you don't mind but I said that was OK.'

I nod and my face grows warm at the thought that I'm so predictable, but I can't deny that I'm pleased I've been so cavalier. At least I have some connection to my old life and I'm sure I wouldn't have remembered the code. The screen bursts into life and I see an array of icons for banking and shopping and takeaways. Tapping on messages, I see Marc's name at the top and I open the chain. The last message was sent back in early March, and my heart lurches at the thought that I'm looking at the last communication I'll ever have with him, but I grow cold as I read the words.

Don't you dare ignore me.

I'm confused as I scroll back and see there are ten unanswered messages in a row. All short, all demanding I respond to him. The worst one reads:

Bitch.

Quickly, I open the calls function and check my recent

calls. Eighteen missed calls all from Marc on the same day in March. I must have been ignoring him.

'Everything OK?' Bryce asks, still smiling at me, and I don't have the heart to tell him what I'm seeing. All couples argue. That's normal. But something about those phone exchanges doesn't seem normal.

'It's just weird,' I say and he nods understandingly. I slide the phone under my pillow and turn to the food. 'I'm starving,' I say truthfully.

'Breakfast for lunch,' Bryce says. 'Rachel told me she's taking a few days away and she left a list of things you like. Brunch was top of the list.'

A smile plays on my lips as I realise that Rachel must be right because I feel genuinely excited by the plate of food and I'm touched that she's still thinking of me, even now. I still have some questions about Rachel and her role in my life, but I can't deny she's been there for me, again and again. *Nothing makes sense*, I think with a sigh. I accept the tray onto my knee, and Bryce walks around the bed and pushes open both curtains as wide as they will go before taking a seat in the armchair while I tuck in.

'It's a lovely day,' he says conversationally but I'm too busy swallowing the delicious smooth and creamy hollandaise to respond.

'Would you like me to put on one of your records?' he asks but I shake my head quickly. My music reminds me of the person I was before, like the phone, and I don't want to even think of her right now.

'OK. Would you like to sit in the garden today while I do a bit of spring cleaning?'

I grunt, but it does sound like a good idea and it's probably better than lying in bed, wallowing in my misery. I clear my plate in what must be record time while Bryce reads me a couple of pages of Austen, and when I'm done, he stands up and looks at me with purpose. 'Shall we?'

I meet his gaze and nod once and he helps me get out of bed. I make it into the bathroom for a shower by myself. Catching sight of myself in the mirror, I do a double-take as I barely recognise the woman looking back with her short hair and pale face, but I look a bit closer and see that the style does frame my face well. Finger-combing the strands and rubbing on a spot of lipstick, I notice how taking care of myself does make me feel and look a little more human. I get the sense that I was one of those women before who really took pride in her appearance, and it is freeing to have such a low-maintenance look.

Bryce is still in my room but when he hears me coming out of the bathroom, he hurries out and his smile widens when he sees me.

'You're looking more and more like your old self,' he says but his words rankle and I frown.

'How do you know?' I ask, not wanting to be rude, but the first time Bryce met me was when I was in a coma.

His smile doesn't crack as he replies, 'There's a photo in your kitchen that I see every day.' I think of the one he means – the picture of me in my cycling gear. 'You've got such good energy in it.'

It's strange to hear someone thinking of me that way, because I feel like a worm or a grub, something that lolls around waiting and watching the world going on around them, but I smile and decide I much prefer to think of myself as energetic. It's nice having someone look at me the way Bryce does – without judgement.

'Shall we?' he asks, offering me his arm, and I take it even though I'm feeling much stronger and I know I could manage the stairs alone. We make it down to the hallway and he leads me through the kitchen, where he's been preparing dinner already, and there is a rich-smelling stew bubbling on the hob.

'Smells good,' I say.

He seems to appreciate the compliment. 'Red meat is good for iron levels.'

The key to the back door is in the lock and I feel a rush of relief, almost as if I expected Rachel to have taken it home with her to keep me shut up in the house. But there's no reason to keep me locked up any more now I know the full truth. As Bryce unlocks the door and flings it open, I take a deep breath of fresh air and step out into the bright sunlight, blinking as my eyes adjust. It's only a small patio and the low fence either side means that it's overlooked by the neighbours, but it's certainly a sun trap and I feel some of the tension I've been carrying ebb away as I tip my head back and let the sun wash my face.

'This must be pretty much the last day of summer,' Bryce says. 'September has been amazing.'

I murmur in agreement, but I can't believe it's September already. The whole summer is over, and while I know more about my life from before, I'm still a stranger to myself. All I have are glimpses of emotion that tell me the outline of what type of person I was, but I still have no memories to colour in the picture. I wonder if they will ever come back or if this is my new reality. Perhaps it's easier not to properly remember Marc or Noelle. I don't have to truly face losing them if I can't remember having them in the first place.

Bryce settles me on a reclining chair and disappears inside for a glass of water, while I stretch out like a cat on a roof and close my eyes. A bird caws overhead and a car alarm goes off for a few seconds before stopping. I keep my eyes shut, breathing slowly and listening to everything. I hear the sound of footsteps approaching. Assuming it's Bryce with my drink, I keep my eyes closed, but then I hear a woman's voice: 'Psst, Jen, wake up!'

I sit up and see Cathy's red glasses poking over the top of the fence, her eyes darting from me to the kitchen as if she's checking who else is around. She looks like she wants to chat, but as I take in her beady little eyes and her pointed chin that reminds me of Ian's, I feel a rush of anger so strong that it surprises me. This is the woman who burned down my bench and then lied about who I was arguing with that day. She must know about Marc and Noelle, but she failed to mention them when we sat here chatting and she purported to be a friend.

Balling my hands into fists, I clench my jaw, holding in my anger. A cloud passes over the sun, and in the brief moment of shadow I wonder why not just let it out? The person I was before may have bitten her tongue and tried to count to five before acting, but that's not me. I'm a clean slate.

I let out a sound somewhere between a yell and a snarl and manage to push myself to my feet, charging at Cathy in fury.

TWENTY-SIX

Cathy shrieks in surprise and almost loses her footing as she backs up, but I don't care. All the rage and self-pity I feel about what's happened to me comes pouring out and the red mist has totally descended. If the fence wasn't between us, I'm not sure exactly what I would do, but I find myself leaning over the wooden panel, pointing a finger at Cathy, and hissing, 'Why are you pretending to be my friend?'

Cathy's eyebrows knit together. 'Jen, what's got into you? I am your friend.'

'Don't lie to me,' I snap.

She shakes her head as if she can't understand what I mean but I know I have an ace up my sleeve. 'Ian told me what you did.'

Her eyebrows lift in surprise and she murmurs, 'Ian? What's that boy been stirring now?'

'He told me about the bench.' I sweep my arm towards the black scorch marks on the paving stones and Cathy's eyes follow. Her pale face flushes and she flaps her mouth but doesn't say anything, and I feel a certainty that Ian was telling the truth.

'You don't deny it?' I demand.

Cathy shoves her hands deep into the pockets of her cardigan and shakes her head. 'That boy. He's always sticking his nose in.' She says the words with resignation rather than anger and I sense the fight has gone from her.

'Why?' I ask.

Cathy sighs. 'It's complicated.'

Another burst of fury hits me and I blurt out, 'Just tell me.' Why won't anyone give me a straight answer?

'We are friends,' Cathy says. 'Or at least we were. I've been here for you all through your relationship problems, everything that's gone on. I've been a shoulder to cry on. But one day we had a couple of glasses of wine and got into a little disagreement. It was over something silly, but I think we'd both had one too many and we got carried away.'

Cathy pulls a vape from her pocket and takes a long, hard suck. 'Promised Ian I'd try to quit the fags,' she says, shaking her head sadly. 'But it's not the same.'

Rachel did say Marc and I were struggling and I've seen the texts, so those must be the relationship problems Cathy means. I'm glad I had a friend to talk to, but I can't imagine what would have compelled her to set fire to my property.

'What were we arguing about?' I ask, remembering that Ian said it was about him.

'I can't really remember,' Cathy says but I'm not willing to let it go. If it caused her to commit arson, it can't have been something so easily forgotten.

'Ian said it was about him.'

'That boy...' Cathy sighs, taking another draw on her vape. 'Thinks the world revolves around him.'

'So it wasn't?' I ask.

Cathy glances over my shoulder towards my house and I turn to see what she's looking at but there's no one there. She takes a deep breath as if she's trying to work out what to tell me, then looks me straight in the eye.

'Listen, Jen, it's not really my place, but since you already know about the fire, I think it's best you know the circumstances.'

I nod, desperate for her to spit it out and not wanting to interrupt.

'It *was* about Ian. This was last summer, long before your accident. You and Marc seemed to always have it in for him. We'd been sitting out, having a drink, and you were complaining about him again, and if I'm honest, I just lost it.'

I try to search my brain for any feelings I have about Ian. I find him a bit cocky, but a lot of young men come across that way and I can't think of any reason I would have taken against him.

'I thought I got on quite well with your son?' I say. 'Wasn't he one of my students?'

'He was one of your *best* students,' Cathy bursts out. 'That's why I never could understand it. He did well at school and now he's got a place at a good university, but you never gave him a chance. I always felt it was Marc really, but I was so shocked when you started mouthing off, I just snapped.'

I can't imagine why my husband and I didn't like Ian. I felt no animosity towards him when he gave me a lift home from the pub – in fact, I was grateful. Why would I say enough hurtful things about him so as to make his mum lose her temper so spectacularly?

'There must have been something else—'

'You must not remember what you said,' Cathy spits, cutting me off.

I'm about to ask her to tell me when she adds, 'Marc was the worst. He used to come round here and make all these accusations. I had to tell him I'd call the police if he didn't leave me alone in the end, but you know Marc and his temper.'

I realise that although I can't properly remember my husband, her words ring true. Since looking through his belongings, I've sensed something was just a bit... *off* about him – I've felt something akin to fear. Still, I can't help but open my eyes wide since her words feel a bit pot and kettle to me. 'You set fire to my patio furniture!'

'And who drove me to it?' she says.

I'm about to respond when I hear footsteps behind me and Bryce's warm hand closes around my upper arm.

'The gestapo are here,' Cathy mutters but Bryce ignores her.

'Are you OK, Jen?' he says gently.

I realise that my stomach hurts where the top of the fence has been digging into the soft flesh. 'I'm tired,' I say.

'Come on, let's get you sitting down. I've made you tea and there are biscuits.'

I meet Cathy's eye one last time and I swear she rolls them before she says, 'Oh yes, run along and bury your head in the sand again.'

'What do you mean?' I ask, but Bryce pats my arm.

'Come on, there's plenty of time for talking, but we don't want any major setbacks in your recovery.'

I let him lead me over to the seat as Cathy stalks into her house and slams the back door. Bryce lets out a small snort.

'What?' I ask.

He holds my arm as I lower myself into the seat, then he places a blanket over my knees that he must have brought outside. The steaming cup of tea is on the small white plastic table and he hands it to me carefully.

'What is it?' I ask again.

'Nothing, really,' Bryce says. 'It's not my place.'

I wrap my hands around the mug, enjoying the warmth, and meet his gaze. 'Please,' I say, 'I value your opinion.'

Bryce casts a sideways glance at Cathy's house and frowns.

'OK, but I don't usually like to speak badly of people. It's just that woman, does she seem stable to you?'

I sip my tea and my eyes fall on the black marks that must be permanently ingrained in the stone. I try to imagine her clambering over the fence with a can of petrol in her hand and dousing a poor, innocent yellow bench before setting it alight and watching it burn, the flames glittering in her pupils, but it's hard to picture an ordinary person doing such a thing. Surely you have to be a bit crazy to commit arson?

'She does seem like she might have another side to her,' I admit.

'I just think you'd be better off without her in your life,' Bryce spouts out and then stops, blowing out a breath. 'Sorry, have I gone too far?'

'Not at all. We're friends,' I say and a smile flashes across his face.

'I'm pleased you feel that way too,' he says. 'I'm just watching out for you while you're in such a crucial period of recovery.'

Looking over at Cathy's house, I feel like a shadow comes over me and I find myself nodding. Whatever happened with the bench is in the past, and it's my future I have to think of now. And having Bryce here, spending time with him, does feel right. Maybe he could be part of my future? As I think the words, I push them deep inside, not wanting to acknowledge the small lift of hope I feel.

'You're right,' I say. 'I don't need her.'

TWENTY-SEVEN

I wake to another day where the warm weather is clinging on, and the smell of bacon is drifting through my house. My stomach rumbles and I sit up, waiting for Bryce to bring me breakfast. I stretch out, running my hands over my body to feel the changes that have taken place in the short time since I regained consciousness. I could definitely get used to Bryce's cooking.

The boxes containing Marc's and Noelle's things sit accusingly in the corner of the room, reminding me of everything I've lost, but even though it's hard to admit, I feel well again. You can't miss what you don't know, and so little has come back to me about my life before that it doesn't feel real. I wonder if that's a blessing or a curse but as Bryce enters the room with a tray filled with breakfast goodies and a small vase of orange chrysanthemums, I decide to embrace it.

As he sets the tray down carefully on the table, I say, 'Bryce, would you mind doing me a favour?'

'Of course,' he replies.

'Please could you take those boxes and put them in the spare room?'

Bryce hesitates for a moment and I see he's thinking it over. 'Are you sure?' he asks gently.

'Positive,' I say.

'Right you are.'

A minute later, the boxes are gone from the room and I am eating fluffy scrambled eggs with lashings of butter and a heap of bacon, and Bryce is sitting beside me. He's brought a cafetière, which he plunges, and the smell of strong coffee fills the room as he pours me a mug.

'Are you not going to join me?' I ask. There's a pause as he considers it and I wonder if there's a line he doesn't want to cross, but it seems silly when he's helping me so much.

'I can't drink the whole pot,' I say.

Bryce scratches his beard before saying, 'That would be great, actually. I had an early start.'

He pops downstairs for another mug as I lie there savouring the flavours that dance on my tongue. I can't believe I ate half so well before the accident. When he comes back he asks, 'Did you get much from your phone?'

I feel guilt slide over me that it's still stuffed behind my pillow. I know I should be scouring it for hints of my past and using it to connect to my future, but the whole task feels too huge. The future feels overwhelming.

'Not yet,' I murmur.

He replies, 'No rush.'

We lapse into silence as we sip our coffee and my mind drifts to thoughts of when Bryce will stop coming and Rachel will return to her life and it will just be me. Alone with my thoughts. I'll need something to fill my days since I'm no longer a wife or a mother. Perhaps I should visit my extended family in Australia and take up hiking or surfing or whatever it is people do there. It's not like there's anything keeping me here.

'Where were you?' Bryce asks, waving his hand in front of my eyes, and I jump slightly.

'Australia,' I say and he laughs.

'So far. Why don't we return a little closer. I wondered if you fancy a walk today? Just up the road to the little park and back? Test your legs.'

It crosses my mind that he's suggesting it so I don't return to my backyard and get into another argument with Cathy, but a trip to the park sounds nice. I decide not to mention that I've already been to the care home and back since I want to spend more time with him. I'm enjoying his company.

'A walk would be great,' I say.

Bryce goes back downstairs to wash up and I take myself off to the shower, finding I can move reasonably freely. Once I've returned to my room and dressed, Bryce reappears.

'Ready?' he asks.

Taking Bryce's arm, we walk out of the house and along the street. I feel slightly giddy at the prospect of us walking along, arm in arm, and I almost blurt out that it feels almost like a date, but then I bite my tongue, realising how inappropriate that would be. The small park at the end of the street is just a stretch of grass that people use to exercise their dogs and a fenced-off children's playground with a slide, swings and a roundabout. We make it to a bench overlooking the playground and I sink down, finding my eyes are drawn to a little girl in a pink jacket who's pushing the roundabout around and around and laughing gleefully as her dad tells her to be careful.

Her little face is red and happy, and as I watch her giggle I feel a stab of pain. I'm sure that I brought my own little girl here. It hurts to think that I pushed her on those very swings and held her hand when she went down that slide. Sniffing hard, I try not to let tears come, and just as I feel like they might overwhelm me, Bryce takes my hand and squeezes gently, letting me know that he's there. I rest my head on his shoulder and we sit that way for a while until a mechanical tune breaks the silence and I hear 'Greensleeves' playing in the distance but getting closer.

Bryce looks at me with a gleeful grin. 'Ice cream?'

'Why not?' I say with a laugh.

He goes in search of the ice cream van and returns in a few minutes with a couple of 99s, and we sit and munch the flakes before licking the smooth vanilla ice cream. Did I sit here and eat ice cream with Noelle? Was Marc with us? Something tells me that my daughter and I came here but not Marc. No, I can't picture Marc in our little twosome at all. Shivering at the strange thought, Bryce mistakenly thinks I'm cold.

'Time to go home.'

I let him pull me to my feet and we find ourselves standing nose to nose, so close that I can smell the sweet vanilla on his breath, and he looks down at me. I wonder what it would be like to kiss him with that beard and I almost stand up on my tiptoes and press my lips to his. He must sense what I'm thinking because his cheeks flush and he steps back.

'Sorry,' he says gruffly.

'I don't mind,' I say truthfully, and I take his arm as we amble back along the street. I know deep down that Bryce is being paid to be here, but I do wonder if there could be more between us. I'm so relaxed in his company and he seems to enjoy spending time with me. I don't want to get my hopes up, but maybe I do have a future. Perhaps life has more in store for us?

I'm smiling as we return to the house. Bryce goes ahead to open the door and I wait in the sun while he fiddles with the key. A small knocking sound gets my attention, and I realise it's coming from one of the upstairs windows at Cathy's house. Glancing up, I see her shadowy figure and suddenly something comes into view. My heart leaps into my mouth as I see it's a large square of cardboard with a message written in thick black letters:

HE'S LYING TO YOU.

TWENTY-EIGHT

'Everything all right?' Bryce says.

He's back by my side, peering at me oddly as my heart pounds and I try to act like nothing is wrong. Something tells me not to say anything. If Cathy is right, I don't want Bryce to know I'm suspicious of him. My gaze goes to the window again, but the sign and figure are gone and I take a moment to try to collect myself, wondering what the hell Cathy could mean or whether I imagined the whole thing entirely.

'You look like you've seen a ghost,' Bryce says, and I try to smile but my face feels like it's made out of rubber and I know my expression must be closer to a grimace than anything cheerful.

'Ready for a rest?' he asks and I nod, feeling like that's all I'm capable of. Why does everyone I start to trust keep letting me down? Tears prick my eyes, but I fight them back. I don't want Bryce to see me crying, but I feel so stupid that I've allowed myself to develop feelings for him when I don't even know him well enough to know if Cathy's sign is true or false. My instincts are useless. I hang my head.

I let Bryce lead me back into the house and up the stairs. I climb back into bed, although lying down all day is beginning to feel unnecessary, and I try to evaluate things logically. I go over all the things Bryce has said to me, trying to work out which of them could be untrue. Cathy being unstable? I had to drag that out of him and the scorch marks are independent evidence that she didn't refute. What about Rachel asking him to do overtime? Maybe he's here because he wants to be but it's not a crime to want to spend time with me. Cathy couldn't know either of those things anyway. Or could it be something more fundamental than that? I remember my doubts after seeing him remove the needle from my arm and I begin to wonder if that's what she means. But why on earth would Bryce pretend to be a nurse if he's not? I can hardly believe it's that well paid and it's not exactly glamorous work.

I hear him downstairs making tea and it feels ungrateful to be lying here doubting everything he's done for me, and I feel a flicker of hope that Cathy has got it wrong. If she knows something specific why wouldn't she just tell me? Cathy must feel really strongly since she went to the effort of making that sign but she has already proved herself to be someone who likes drama. Perhaps she's the one who's fabricating things? My brain starts to ache as I try to work out what to think. Bryce makes his way upstairs and enters the room with the usual tray.

'Headache?' he asks and I must give him a look of confusion because he says, 'You're frowning.'

I start to shake my head and then an idea comes to my mind, something I can actually *do* to establish the truth rather than just sit here wondering, and I meet his gaze. 'I'm just craving something silly, that's all. You know when you get something in your head?'

'What is it?' he asks. 'Maybe I can pop out for you.'

'I couldn't ask you to do that,' I say, playing on his good nature and hoping he'll take the bait. 'Honestly it's just something stupid.'

'I told you before, I'm happy to get you anything you need.'

My mind is a blank but I know I need to pull something from its murky depths if my plan is going to work so I desperately search for something, feeling a rush of panic as Bryce watches me, until I blurt out, 'Turkish delight!'

Bryce laughs. 'Really?'

An image of a sweet wrapper comes to mind. 'Really. You know those single squares you can buy in the pink wrapper? I think I used to eat them whenever I needed a pick-me-up.'

A wide grin breaks out beneath Bryce's beard and he says, 'Turkish delight was on Rachel's list. It's so great that you remembered.'

I match his smile, feeling relief more than anything that I managed to think of something credible. The little I know of Bryce tells me how generous he is so I feel certain he'll offer to go this afternoon, and I'm not disappointed.

'I'll go now. It will only take ten minutes.'

'Only if you're sure?'

'I'm positive. You sit here and drink your tea and I'll be back before you've even finished the mug.'

I smile at this but I hope he gives me enough time to do what I need to do, and my insides twist with nerves as I try to play it out in my head, imagining the steps I will take.

'Be right back,' he says and I wait until his footsteps stomp downstairs and the front door slams before I scramble out of bed as fast as I can.

I rush back downstairs, aware that the corner shop is only a few minutes' walk away and I need to be quick. I search the hallway, rifling through the coats on the rack and the shoe cupboard, but I don't find what I'm looking for there so I hobble through to the kitchen and search the obvious spots. My heart sinks as each place is empty but I hurry into the living room, giving myself one last chance to search before I return upstairs empty-handed, and that's when I spot it. Tucked between the sofa and the wall, where Bryce must have left it when he arrived this morning, is his bag: a black backpack.

Taking a seat, I haul it onto my knee and unzip the top, feeling like I might be sick with the tension as I strain my ears, listening out for any little sound that might indicate Bryce's return. Once I've pulled back the zip, I see that on the top is a bundle of clothes – a pair of jeans and a T-shirt rolled into a ball that he must arrive in, changing into the navy scrubs here. Lifting them out, I quickly check the pockets, but they're empty. I'm not surprised since most people carry their phone, wallet and keys on their person. Further down in the bag is a notebook and I flip it open with shaking fingers, readying myself for something strange like I found in Dr Marsden's, but the pages are blank and I feel a rush of disappointment. Maybe this is stupid? I'm only going on Cathy's mad behaviour and I'm violating Bryce's privacy, which feels wrong since we've been growing so close. I almost stop but I tell myself I've come this far, I may as well be certain.

Digging my hand to the bottom of the bag, I feel a pouch of material that I close my fist around and pull out. It looks like a bundle of tools in a cloth carry case and I assume it must be medical implements but I tug the string anyway, preparing to see a thermometer and gauze. But what is inside makes my heart almost stop. Bryce is carrying a set of knives, each so sharp I don't dare pick any of them up. My brain scrambles for purchase and I can barely think the words... *What could he possibly need these knives for, here in my home?*

TWENTY-NINE

The front door slams and I almost cry out in fear as I try to wrap the knives back up and shove them back into the bottom of the backpack. Bryce is only a few steps away and the bag and his clothes are on my lap, but I hear his footsteps coming towards me and I realise there's no time to act. I try to work out what the hell I can say when I hear thuds on the stairs – he's gone straight up to my room and I feel shaky with relief.

His confused voice calls out, 'Jen?'

I thrust everything back into the backpack, sliding it into place beside the sofa, and I pick up the TV control from the windowsill and press a random button. The screen crackles to life just as Bryce appears in the doorway and says, 'There you are.'

'I thought I'd see what was on,' I say.

Bryce frowns briefly before handing me a packet of pink-wrapped Turkish delight. 'You're in luck.'

I accept it with a smile but the playful mood between us has vanished and there's a new tension in the air. I wonder if he knows that I was searching his bag but I find I don't really care.

What's more important is that I discover what he plans to do with those knives.

On the screen is some antiques programme that I pretend I'm watching and Bryce slips into the kitchen, muttering, 'I think I'll make a start on your dinner.'

The TV blares but I'm listening to every scrape and beep as Bryce takes something out of the freezer and defrosts it in the microwave. Next he unloads the dishwasher and washes something in the sink before peeling and chopping what must be either potatoes or carrots. Every clink and tinkle makes me jolt but I tell myself this is entirely normal – Bryce makes me dinner every day and he knows his way around my kitchen well. Listening to his footsteps approach, I'm ready when he pops his head around the door and says, 'Would you like to eat in here today?'

'Yes, please,' I say, deciding that lying in bed feels much too vulnerable now I know that Bryce has come armed to the back teeth. My throat feels tight with fear as he reappears, carrying a tray with stew and both potatoes and carrots, which he places on my knee.

'I know it's early,' he says, 'but I thought you might be hungry since breakfast was a while ago now.'

I nod and mutter, 'Thank you,' although hunger is the last thing I feel right now. I fix my eyes on Bryce, ready to move if he goes for the bag. He gives me a quizzical look before saying, 'I'll leave you to it then,' and retreats into the kitchen where I hear the sounds of him clearing up.

The food smells good and I force myself to take a few bites but I can't relax. Why would Bryce bring a bundle of knives to my home? How well do I really know him? I'd like to ring Rachel to ask her where she found him and if she checked his references and I almost rush upstairs for my phone, but something stops me as I realise that Rachel may well be in on whatever he is planning. They've been working together so far and defending each other at every turn. The food I've managed to swallow feels like a stone sinking into the depths of my stomach as I realise that I'm better off keeping the information to myself and acting alone.

It's impossible to know who to trust. All the people closest to me seem to be pointing the finger at each other. Bryce said I should stay away from Cathy. Cathy warned me off Rachel and Bryce. Rachel told everyone that they needed to watch what they say around me. And they've all lied to me again and again. Anger boils inside me as I think of how confused and scared I've been since I woke up. That's not normal and all I want is a normal life. I deserve that much.

Bryce comes lumbering back into the living room and stands in the doorway. I'm once again floored by how huge he is, both tall and broad; by comparison I'm a sickly stick insect that he could swat away with a single hand. He wouldn't need those knives if he wanted to attack me, I realise – he'd need only to bash me with one of those meaty arms or to boot me with a tree-trunk leg. But perhaps he doesn't use the knives because he needs to, perhaps he uses them because he wants to, and the thought sends a shiver down my spine.

'Are you OK?' Bryce asks and I nod quickly.

'Absolutely,' I say brightly, forcing myself to eat another forkful of stew. 'This is delicious.'

He smiles but still sounds uncertain when he says, 'I've cleared up in the kitchen and I think I'll get off if that's OK? I can wash up your tray first thing.'

'Of course,' I say, 'you head off, don't worry about the plate. I can do it.'

He frowns but then just nods and says, 'Right-o. I'll see you in the morning then.'

I give him a cheery wave but he still hovers and I remember his bag just at the moment he says, 'Do you mind passing my backpack?'

I grab it from beside me and pass it across, willing my arm not to shake. He takes it from me and slings it straight onto his broad back on top of his navy scrubs.

'Think I'll change at home today,' he says, clearly desperate to leave.

'Bye, then.'

'Bye.' He disappears from the room and a moment later the door shuts behind him and I leap up.

I know what I have to do – I need to follow him.

THIRTY

As I leave the house, I grab a black wool coat from the rack that's less conspicuous than the leopard-print number, shove my keys in the pocket and snatch up the umbrella that I used as a walking stick just in case we're going far. My body feels like it's getting stronger every day and my steps are becoming more fluent, so I tell myself it won't be impossible to keep up with Bryce, I just need to be determined.

Hurrying out onto the pavement, I see that he's already at the end of the street, ready to turn onto the main road, and my heart sinks. He's walking fast as if he has someplace to be, but I set off as quickly as I can, the tip of the umbrella banging on the ground every step, playing out a marching beat. 'Keep going, keep going, keep going,' I mutter to myself as Bryce turns the corner and disappears from view.

By the time I turn the corner after him, Bryce is already a long way ahead, but I remember the old lady told me this is the way to the town centre so hopefully that's where he's heading. A few spots of rain hit my face and I'm glad to have the umbrella with me, feeling like I can manage to walk without it. Bryce hits the main street just as the heavens open and I put up my umbrella, slowing now I can't use it as a stick, but it doesn't matter anyway because I see Bryce stop and go inside one of the shops.

Slowing as I approach, I try to work out my next move. I want to get close enough so that I can see which shop he's gone into, but not so close that if he comes bursting out he'll see me. I decide to cross the road, so I check both ways and scurry across, ticking off the shops as I get closer. There's a butcher's, an artisan coffee shop, a French restaurant called Chez Richard, two charity shops and a newsagent, and he could have gone in any one of them.

Standing on the opposite side of the road, I lower my umbrella so he couldn't see my face if he happened to look across, and I keep watch on the row, glancing from left to right and back again as if I'm watching a tennis match.

As the raindrops thud on the nylon over my head, everything feels like a mess, and the longer I stand in the rain, the more alone I feel. Tears prick my eyes. I feel like a fool. Why can't my brain just start working again? The already grey sky grows dimmer as I wait and the street fills up with people and cars on their way home from work. I remain in my spot close to a shoe shop, standing in a way that might look like I'm admiring a pair of boots in the window but really watching out for Bryce and wondering what could be taking him so long.

I'm starting to get cold and I begin to worry I've missed him, because he must have been at least twenty minutes. Just as I'm about to give up, I notice a figure walking along the street and I recognise the height and bulk, but I didn't see which shop he came from. I kick myself, but all that matters is that I've found him again, so I set off in the same direction, keeping pace on the opposite side of the street. He's walking slowly, distracted by his phone in his hand; it looks like he's texting someone and it makes him easy to follow. At one point, he stops and I stop, only ten feet away on the opposite side, but he doesn't even look up from the small, bright screen. When he continues, I start again until he reaches a bus stop and ducks under the shelter.

I try to work out what's best to do – should I give up or go closer? Once he gets on a bus, the chase is over since I can't see a way of following him without him spotting me. Deciding I'm not ready to go home, I cross at a zebra crossing, blending in with the other people and their umbrellas, keeping mine low over my head and acting as if I'm just another person on their way home from work.

When I reach the bus stop, I spot Bryce through the glass, leaning up on the bench inside, still transfixed by his phone as his thumb moves quickly on the screen. I wonder what he's typing as I sidle up to the partition, using my umbrella as a shield, but there's no need since he hasn't looked up once. A bus arrives and he glances at it but it's clearly not the one he's waiting for since he doesn't move. People swarm forward and I hang back, and at that moment his phone rings.

'Hi,' I hear him say, and my heart starts to pound in my chest. I'm close enough that I can hear his side of the conversation, but he has no idea I'm here.

'I'll be home in a minute,' he says, 'I'm just getting the bus.'

So he's talking to someone he lives with, I think and find my stomach clenching. I can't help but hope it's a housemate and not a girlfriend, and that little shred of hope tells me that I haven't been able to accept Cathy's warning. Maybe he's taking the knives to a kitchen shop for sharpening, although even as I think this, I have to acknowledge it's a stretch. Do people really sharpen their kitchen knives? I cast about for an alternate theory and admit to myself that I'm trying to disprove her little sign rather than find evidence that it's true. I still want to believe that what Bryce and I have is real.

'I have no idea why!' he bursts out, suddenly sounding angry, and I have no idea in what direction the conversation is going. 'I told you everything. She just suddenly changed.'

It hits me that he might be talking about me and I feel a chill that's nothing to do with the weather.

'Everything was fine, we had a nice morning. We even had an ice cream for God's sake.'

So he's definitely talking about me. I step closer to the glass, not wanting to miss a single word and feeling trepidation as he continues in a raised voice.

'I don't know! It was like a switch flicked.' There's a pause while he listens and then he bursts out, 'We both know she's not right in the head.'

I feel like the air is whooshing out of me like a balloon that's slipped from someone's fingers. That doesn't sound like the Bryce I know. We've been getting on so well but to hear him talking about me so callously makes me feel sick. Another bus pulls up and he starts readying himself to get on, so I step into the queue behind him, so close I could unzip his backpack right there on his back if I wanted to.

He's dropped his voice to a murmur so I miss a sentence or two but as he steps up onto the bus, he spits, 'Amy, please, I'm on the bus now so I'll be home in five – we can discuss it in person.'

My breath catches in my throat and I push my way out of the line and hurry away as fast as I can, my thoughts crashing around in my head like waves on a beach. Now I know I can't trust him.

Who the hell is Amy? Surely it can't be a coincidence…

THIRTY-ONE

The rain lashes down the whole way home, but I barely notice as I march along the slick pavement, feeling every possible emotion as I try to work out who Amy could be and what role she has in my life – could she really be my sister? And if so... who the hell is Rachel? And how have I let her trick me again and again? I'm hurt, angry, disappointed, but I also feel a swell of shame and embarrassment as I wonder if they are all in this together – Rachel, Bryce, Cathy and Amy, whoever she is – and if they are all laughing at me. Stupid, gullible Jen, who can't work a single thing out for herself.

I wish they'd leave me alone, all of them. I'd be better off trying to rebuild my life alone, sorting through my own belongings and broken mind, trying to pull out memories from the rubble. But Rachel and Bryce have robbed me of that opportunity. By trying to control every aspect of my recovery, they have only served to confuse me, making it impossible for me to distinguish the truth from a lie.

I'm almost past the high street when a brightly lit window catches my eye and I stop outside a small pizzeria. Inside is full of young families, crowded together around tables with red-and-white checked tablecloths, sharing humongous pizzas, and the adults are drinking pitchers of beer. The room looks full of light and warmth, and as I'm drawn to the glass, I'm hit by a memory of eating here, sitting across from Marc with Noelle in a high chair, all of us happily eating slices of pizza until... what? Something went wrong and the meal ended sourly.

Tears escape my eyes and run down my cheeks as I press my palms to the pane, wishing I could remember. We may not have always been happy – what family is? – but Marc and Noelle were what I had. My world. I need to figure out the truth for them. I owe them that much.

I notice a couple in the window staring at me oddly, then whispering to each other before looking back at me. The woman mouths, 'Are you OK?'

Blinking back tears, I nod and walk away into the rain, deciding it's time I went home and stopped drawing attention to myself. I have no idea what to do next. I'd like to ask Bryce to stop coming since he's a liar – and judging by those knives, something possibly more sinister – but with Rachel away, he's my only connection to the outside world, and my only link to Amy. And something tells me that I need to speak to her. Whether she's my sister or not, she may know something about my past that can help me unlock my memories.

As I trudge towards home, my shoes and the bottom of my trousers well and truly sodden, I resolve to find a way to follow Bryce again so I can confront Amy. It will be risky but she is the only clue I have. Feeling marginally better to have made a decision, I turn onto my street and hurry the final few steps. It's only as I get closer to my house that I see the two figures on the pavement right outside, their outlines fuzzy due to the torrential rain, but I hear their raised voices so I stop abruptly.

'Get back here,' the man yells, and he grabs the woman's arm and she starts to shriek.

I want to scream for him to get off her since it looks like he could be hurting her but I'm frightened. I'm not yet at full strength, so if he turns on me, I'll be of little use. Perhaps it's better to act as a witness. The man starts dragging her along the street as the woman bucks and kicks and tries to escape. I notice he's speaking in a calm, soothing voice that's at odds with her reaction but it doesn't have the desired effect. They haven't seen me so I make a snap decision and stop behind a lamppost, closing down my umbrella as quickly as I can.

'Get off!' the woman shouts and tries to shake him off again, but he won't let her go.

Neither of them has an umbrella and I know how wet they must be because in the few moments since I put mine down, I've already been soaked. My hair is plastered to my head and freezing-cold droplets run down my collar and back, making me shiver and long to be inside in the dry. The woman's black hair is drenched and hanging in rat-tails down her back. She tries to get away again, but he holds her arm tightly, and as she struggles, she starts slapping and kicking him. He takes the blows without response but continues to slowly pull her along. She lets out an almighty yell and manages to slip from his grip, landing hard on the pavement at his feet. He goes to grab her arm again and I want to tell him that it's no way to treat a woman, but she dives for his legs before I can say anything and tackles him to the ground.

There's a moment where they roll back and forth, their arms locked around one another, before the woman manages to break free and I see that she is little more than a girl. With a lurch, I recognise her and it takes me a moment to place her as the teen who was crying in the pub that night. What is she doing here? She staggers to her feet, and before the man can stop her, she runs out into the road. My heart is in my mouth until I see that there's no traffic, and quickly she's across and onto the other side, picking up her pace until she's sprinting down the street away from us. When I turn back, the man is picking himself up slowly, brushing gravel from his hands and shaking his head.

I stay hidden behind the tree, but he turns my way and I'm sure that he spots me. My hear starts beating even harder as he walks slowly towards me. It's hard to see through the rain and as he gets closer, I wonder whether I should try to run in the opposite direction, but fear and exhaustion keep me rooted to the ground.

Who is this man? What did I just witness? Where was he dragging the girl to and what did he want with her? He gets closer and my mouth falls open as I see his face properly for the first time.

'Ian?'

'Ms V,' he replies, sounding choked up. 'What are you doing out here in the rain?'

'What the hell was that all about?' I ask, deciding he needs to answer my questions before I answer any of his. I want to give him the benefit of the doubt but I'm unable to shake the image of him grabbing that girl and dragging her towards his front door. What was he doing that made her so desperate to escape she would run into the road without looking?

'You wouldn't understand,' he says sullenly.

His eyes meet mine and I'm hit by the coldness in them and the jut of his jaw as he lifts his chin as if daring me to ask him again. Taking in the breadth of his shoulders and his looming height, I realise that Ian is no longer a boy, and whatever I knew of him before, I know nothing of him now. He sounded polite and well-mannered when he gave me the lift home but there is clearly something not quite right about him – what young man tries to drag a woman off the street?

'Try me,' I say.

'You know when someone is doing something that is hurting them more than anyone else?'

I frown and immediately drugs and alcohol come to mind. 'Like addiction?'

'Sort of. I just wanted to help my friend see that what she's doing is wrong. I know how it must have looked but I would never hurt her. I was trying to help her.'

It seems like he wants to say more to me and he steps closer, opening his mouth then snapping it shut with a shake of his head.

'You ought to get out of the rain,' he says.

He turns to go and I feel a swirl of confusion as I try to work out whether he's telling the truth. I don't want to think that he's the type of person that would hurt a woman, but he did have hold of her arm. As he walks away, an idea comes to my mind and I realise I'm going to have to ask him for help. I don't have many options right now, but it turns out that having a potentially psychopathic neighbour might have its advantages.

'Wait,' I call out and he turns slowly. 'I need a favour,' I say, a bubble of hope rising inside me as he tilts his head to one side, and then after what feels like an eternity, he nods.

'Anything for you.'

THIRTY-TWO

The next day, I make sure to smile when Bryce arrives and I eat the porridge with honey and banana he brings me, but inside I'm a wreck and I have to force myself not to flinch every time he comes close. This is a man who has presided over my care while I've been unconscious – he must know every inch of me – and now I think it's a distinct possibility that he's been lying to me the entire time. Perhaps he's even been planning my death.

'Austen today?' he asks and I can't help but scowl, feeling an instant rejection of anything I appreciated from him before. He must notice my expression because a hurt look crosses his face and he gets up from the armchair beside my bed, despite having only just sat down. He looks uncomfortable, as if my bedroom is the last place he wants to be, and I feel the same.

'I wondered if you'd mind if I brought your lunch up a bit early today and left it with you? I've got a couple of things to do at home so I'd appreciate getting off a little early.'

I nod and try not to smile in relief that he's leaving so soon. Not wanting to engage any further, I take my phone out from under my pillow and start scrolling through my messages. Searching for any bit of information, no matter how tiny.

'I'll make sure to let Rachel know so she doesn't pay me for the time,' he says as if that's something I might be worrying about, but I just shrug.

It's strange how little personal information I find in my phone. There are messages from Marc that go way back, and although he appears to have sent ten times the number I've sent to him, they are mostly mundane. Then there are a few from Rachel and several promotions from a hairdresser and a handful of birthday messages back in November, but it's almost suspicious how small my life is. Is it possible that Bryce or someone else has tampered with my phone? He did know the code after all, and once I've had this thought, it's impossible to ignore.

'Right, I'll just go and get a few things ready,' Bryce says.

I think, *Ready for what?* but I just nod and wait as his footsteps stomp down the stairs. I start on my emails but all I find is spam and numerous exchanges with students about lesson times and what pieces to bring that week and I'm shocked by how quickly I become bored with my own life.

I hear Bryce rattling around the kitchen and I strain my ears, half expecting to hear the scraping sound of him sharpening his knives, but all I make out are the usual noises of him unstacking the dishwasher and putting the washing machine on. I wonder if perhaps I'm overreacting since everything Bryce has done for me has been positive, but I know there's no way to silence the voice in my head saying, *Who the hell is Amy?* until I've found out the answer for myself.

Nerves flutter in my stomach as I run through my plan and try to convince myself that it will work. It took a bit of convincing, but after I explained to Ian that the doctor had recommended some physical activity to help with my rehabilitation, he agreed to lend me his old bike since I still have no idea where mine is. My suspicion is that Rachel took it to limit my means of escape, but I can't worry about that now.

Ian dragged his old one out of the shed at the end of his

garden and brought it out to the street. I couldn't risk him seeing me fall off and taking it away again so I didn't attempt to ride it, I just cleaned the bike up as best I could and left it locked to a lamppost further up the street. Today, when Bryce leaves, I'll rush out and jump straight on, but I have no idea if I'll even be able to get back on the saddle. I'm banking on the old adage being true that you never forget.

The smell of onions frying rises through the house and I decide to get dressed in something suitable for a bike ride. Remembering that my cycling clothes are in the wardrobe in the spare room, I move as quietly as I can out into the hallway and slip into the bedroom, closing the door behind me. Breathing deeply, I close my eyes for a moment and I'm hit with a memory of this room painted pale green and a white cot in the centre with a gauzy curtain hanging from the ceiling, shrouding the tiny bed. This was Noelle's room.

My heart races and I find myself hyperventilating, so I open my eyes and bend over, gripping my knees and trying to get myself back under control. Of course, I knew that this must have been the nursery since the house only has two bedrooms, but to see such a clear mental picture has made everything seem all too real, and I'm shaking. It's been easy to block out my grief while I don't remember them. Sitting on the bed, I spend a few moments clutching a pillow to my chest, trying to gather my strength for what I know I need to do.

When I'm a little calmer, I open the cupboard and grab the first item that looks suitable – a pair of cycling leggings – and I swap my pyjama bottoms for them. Next, I pull on an oversized T-shirt that perhaps was Marc's and I pull out a pair of trainers and a black cycling helmet, which I tuck under my arm. Back in my room, I shove the trainers and helmet under the bed and wait impatiently for Bryce to return with my lunch, watching the clouds roll in as the minutes tick by and listening to the occasional clink that's probably him preparing my food.

I go over the plan again but whether it's the warmth of the room or the closeness of the air because of the low clouds, my eyes feel heavy and I start to drift off. Slapping my legs, I force myself awake but my eyelids press down and I realise how warm and cosy it is under the duvet.

A loud bang wakes me and I sit up, my heart pounding, my mouth so dry I can't swallow, and I realise I must have been sleeping with it open. I look around for Bryce, but my eyes land on a tray of hot dogs that he's left on the small table and I blink once, twice, before it dawns on me that the noise must have been the front door. Bryce has left already.

In a panic, I swing my legs out of bed, lurching towards the door before I remember my trainers and I jam my bare feet into them. There's no time for socks or the helmet and I burst out into the hallway, almost flying headfirst down the stairs as I hurry after him, determined to catch him. Outside, I feel a drop of rain land on my cheek as I charge along the pavement, almost tripping over the bike as I bend over and grab the lock and twist the combination to unlock it. I made sure there was only one number to change when I left it so it doesn't take too long to pull apart the lock and chuck it over the handlebars. It's an old black mountain bike that would be discreet other than Ian has covered the frame in stickers of band names and pictures of marijuana leaves.

Swinging my leg up, it takes me three tries to get it over the high crossbar of the frame and I wince in pain as I have to stand up on my tiptoes to sit on the seat. The bike wobbles and I think for one horrifying moment that the whole thing is going to crash over onto its side, taking me with it, but I manage to get one foot onto the pedal and push down.

It's a relief to get moving and after a few turns of the pedals it's like I was never hurt. Cold air rushes through my hair and rain spatters my face but I tip my head back and smile – this is what it feels like to be alive. Turning out from my side street, I cut across the main road and head towards town, searching the pavement for any sign of Bryce. I spot him in the distance and I kick down on the pedals as my whole body seems to throw itself into motion, the movement entirely familiar and filling me with joy as I cycle quickly along the edge of the road. It's only a short journey into town and I quickly bear down upon him, crashing through puddles as thunder cracks in the sky overhead.

Bryce reaches the row of shops and hurries towards the bus stop. A bright flash of lightning distracts me for a moment and I glance up before a loud rumble of thunder follows – and I don't see the bus bombing along the road behind me. And it seems that the driver doesn't see me either, because he veers sharply towards the stop, directly into my path.

THIRTY-THREE

As I'm flying through the air over the bike's handlebars, I remember my lack of helmet, but instead of fear I feel a strange sense of inevitability, like I've been expecting death to catch up with me. I may have cheated it once, but fate doesn't let you escape. Surviving the head-on collision that wiped out my family wasn't the natural order and I think for a moment that this is the end. But I manage to twist my body so I miss the back of the bus and come to a juddering stop on the hard road, the gritty surface tearing the knees of my leggings and the skin on the palms of my hands. The final indignity is my face grazing the ground, and I wince as a jagged stone cuts the skin and I feel a trickle of warm blood drip down my cheek.

'Oh my God!' a woman on the pavement screams and hurries towards me, but I'm already picking myself up and hauling the mountain bike from the gutter.

'I'm fine,' I say quickly.

'You're bleeding,' she says, her mouth hanging open and her face pale. 'Please, let me—'

'Really, I'm fine,' I say more curtly than I intend and wipe my cheek with my sleeve. 'Thank you, though.' So far she is the only person who has noticed my fall and I need to keep it that way. Bryce thinks I'm at home, in bed, and I can't imagine what he'd think if he saw me outside, on a bike, chasing him like a madwoman.

The woman drops back onto the pavement but she's still staring at me and I try to smile as I climb back onto the bike, my palms and knees stinging painfully. The bus pulls away and all I can do is assume that Bryce boarded, so I kick down on the pedal and follow it. Any enjoyment I felt from riding is gone and I just concentrate on pushing through the pain and keeping a safe distance as the bus makes steady progress through the small town centre, pulling in at every stop. I stop too but each time I pull the brake, the pain in my hands brings tears to my eyes.

The rain falls harder as we leave the high street behind, and the bus speeds up as we travel along a long stretch of road that goes down, then up and feels so familiar I know I must have cycled this way many times. Even through my discomfort, some muscle memory deep within tells me when is the moment I need to push down hard on the pedals, cycling vigorously so I can freewheel the final stretch of road before we reach the roundabout.

I'm gasping for breath and know that I can't make it much further when the bus indicates and turns off the main road into a new housing estate made up of identical houses in clusters of three with cultivated green spaces between them. I try to work out if this is a place I can imagine Bryce living, but I don't need to wonder for long because when the bus stops and I pull up beside a tree, I see him hop off and put up an umbrella.

The driving rain helps my cover because he doesn't look around; instead, he ducks under the black fabric and hurries along the pavement, turning at the first cluster of three houses and heading straight to the front door. There isn't time for me to feel excited or nervous because he takes out his keys and lets himself in, and as the door closes behind him, I wonder whether I'm going to discover anything more or if this is all I've come for.

Wanting to get closer, I lay the bike on the wet grass and follow Bryce's footsteps towards the front door. It's painted a shiny black and there's a silver number 63 nailed to the wood. I think about knocking but what good would that do? Instead, I decide to walk the perimeter, edging towards the front window first – a bay window with white plastic frames. I crouch down so only my eyes and the top of my head are visible over the sill and I peer inside to the living room within. There's a white sofa with jazzy cushions and a lovely big painting on the wall behind. The room has a feminine feel and I wonder if that's Amy's handiwork, whoever she may be. I'm about to continue edging around the house when the living room door flies open and Bryce comes barrelling into the room. My mouth falls open, but I don't drop from view – I want to see the face of the figure who enters behind.

It's a woman with a mass of curly hair, and from their body language I can tell they're arguing. Bryce's arms are raised and she reaches to grab him so he spins back around to face her.

'She needs to trust you!' I hear the woman shout and my spine stiffens – I'm sure she means me and my head spins as I wonder what motive these two could have for meddling in my life.

Bryce responds in a low voice that's too deep for me to make out any words, but I peer at the woman's face, trying to find something familiar in the slight curve of her nose and heavy-lidded eyes. Nothing comes, but then she lifts her gaze and her eyes lock with mine. We both stare at each other for a moment as I think, *I know you*, and then she starts to scream.

THIRTY-FOUR

All thoughts of trying to speak to Amy disappear from my head and I feel a sudden desperation to be as far from here as possible. Hobbling as fast as I can, my knees and palms still stinging from the fall, I make it back to the bike and climb on just as I hear the front door open behind me and she calls out, 'Jen! Stop! Please!'

I swing my leg over the high crossbar and get back on the bike, my foot slipping from the pedal on the first try but connecting on the second, and I swerve out into the road. The ride home is horrible as the rain falls and I have to drive my legs to get back up the hill, and all the while my mind is racing, trying to pinpoint exactly where I know her from and what role she and Bryce play in my life. It seems like an odd coincidence that the nurse Rachel hired lives with someone I know and I feel a ripple of disbelief. I don't believe in coincidences.

By the time I reach my street, I'm utterly exhausted, but the fear that Bryce or Amy may be following me keeps me going until I can see my front door up ahead. I'm looking for a place to park up when it hits me that this bike might be my only means of escape, so I need to find somewhere safe to keep it. I don't want anyone tampering with the brakes or slashing the tyres to restrict my freedom, and while I'm aware I may be paranoid, how can I trust anyone when everyone seems to be lying to me?

Towards the end of the street, I spot a bush with a railing behind that's the perfect spot to conceal the bike and keep it safe. Arranging the branches so it's well hidden, I limp along the pavement as quickly as I can and unlock my front door with shaking fingers. When I get inside, I try to calm down but all I can think is, *Bryce has a key*, so I cast around for a way to secure the door and my gaze lands on the coat stand. Dragging it over, I lay it down on the floor in front of the door but then I think of Bryce's built shoulders and burly arms and I decide I need something heavier. It takes me several trips to and from the kitchen, but I drag through each of the four dining chairs from the small table and stack them against the door, but still I fear he could shove them aside.

Using the last of my strength, I heave an armchair from the living room and push it up against the pile, and finally I add my boxes of records that I drag from the shelf. Once I feel like my home is secure, I haul myself upstairs. I need to change out of my soggy clothes and clean up my knees and palms where gravel is still embedded in the skin, but there's something I need to do first.

In my bedroom, I go straight to the bookshelf, drag it forward and carefully ease out the photo album. I don't want to dirty my bed, so I perch on the edge of the pink armchair and begin turning the pages until I reach the one I'm looking for. It's Rachel's sixth birthday party and she's blowing out the candles. I'm knelt on a chair next to her, enraptured by the flickering flames, and watching are several children but my gaze is drawn to the little girl with the shock of dark curls. Almost four decades have passed, but as I stare at the snub nose and freckles, I know that this little girl has grown up into the woman I just saw – this is Amy.

Tears of frustration spring to my eyes as I try to remember a single thing about her but, unsurprisingly, I draw a blank. I can't believe there was ever a day when I took my memory for granted; when waking up and knowing who I was and what my place was in life was not a luxury beyond my grasp. I feel the pull of despair trying to drag me down as I consider what reason I have to keep going. My family is gone, destroyed by my own hand, and my sister, my neighbours and those I might have called friends won't tell me the truth. And my mother's brain is broken too.

Allowing a sob to overtake me, I let my tears fall before sniffing hard and wiping my face. I know I've never been one to give up easily – in fact, I'm sure I've been called stubborn more than once in my life – so I resolve to take the photo back to Mum, to see if there's anything left in the depths of her memory. She may have been unpleasant when I visited her, but she's suffering too and I think she may be the only person who hasn't actively lied to me.

My eyes are dry and I feel a steely determination. I won't let this beat me. I go into the bathroom for a shower but the sight of my face in the mirror stills me. One half is covered with dried blood from the gash in my forehead, and my cheek is speckled with grit and grime. My hair is plastered down and I realise I look like some sort of monster that's risen from a ditch. No wonder Amy screamed.

I'm about to force myself into the shower to wash away the sweat and grime when a noise roots me to the spot with fear – the sound of the key in the lock as someone tries to open the front door.

THIRTY-FIVE

I meet my own gaze in the mirror and my eyes are those of a hunted animal. It's hard not to burst into tears at the sight of my messed-up face – how have I ended up here? There's a rattling sound downstairs that must be someone attempting to open the door, then I hear Bryce call out, 'Jen, please, let us in.'

My heart pounds and I feel a rush of anger that he's made me feel so unsafe in my own home. What right does he have to be here, yelling at me? Who does he think he is?

'Jen, honey. It's Amy. We just want to talk.'

The warmth in her voice sets my teeth on edge. Why has this girl from my childhood grown into a woman who now thinks I owe her something? If she really wants to help me, why hasn't she been here in my hour of need? Instead she's stayed away, sending Bryce – whoever he is – to gain my trust. For what purpose? I can't even imagine.

The banging continues and it sounds like Bryce is throwing his shoulder into it. I wonder how long my makeshift defences will hold and I feel a squirm of worry that they'll be inside in a few minutes and I'll be trapped. Should I arm myself? Or call the police? Or should I go round to Cathy's and ask for help? I'm paralysed with fear but then I hear another voice.

'What the heck is going on out here?' It's a woman. 'How dare you beat down the door of a woman?' I realise it's Cathy and the hairs lift on my neck as I hear the fire in her tone. 'I've already called the police, so I'd say you've got around five minutes before you're answering to them instead of me.'

There's a muttering that I imagine is one of Bryce or Amy trying to plead with her, but Cathy explodes, 'No, I will not lower my broom. This is my street, and my neighbour, and if you threaten her, you threaten me.' There's a banging sound from outside and I wonder what she's doing with the broom before she yells again, 'And don't come back! Good riddance to you!'

I slump against the wall and slide to the floor, feeling relieved that they've gone and grateful to Cathy for helping me. Breathing deeply, it takes a few minutes to get myself under control. I keep listening out for a siren that never comes and I realise that Cathy must have been bluffing. I resolve to call the police myself, but then doubt starts trickling in. Rachel mentioned that the police want to speak to me about the accident and I wonder if I'm ready for that conversation. I don't have all the facts yet, and a little voice inside whispers that they may blame me for what happened.

Letting my head rest on my knees, I feel hopelessness threaten to overwhelm me. I have no one to turn to. The only person I can rely on right now is myself. Deciding that all I can do is push on with my plan to visit Mum, I force myself to rest. I'm going to need my strength.

It's a fitful night, and as soon as dawn breaks, I get up and dress in a simple blouse and smart trousers – Mum made it clear that she does not like jeans, and I'll do anything to put her in a good mood. Combing my hair and adding a quick dab of lipstick, I spend half an hour trying to conceal the grazes on my face until I decide I'm as presentable as I can be, and I slide the photo out of the album and fold it carefully so I can fit it into my back pocket.

Downstairs, I survey the state of the hallway and I'm shocked by the size of the blockade I created. In the light of day it seems ridiculous that I felt the need to stack half of my furniture in front of the door, but then I remind myself that Bryce and Amy persisted long beyond what is reasonable, and with a shudder, I wonder what they might have done to me if they'd got inside.

I clear the furniture and then I peer out of the front window for a few minutes, scouring the parts of the street I can see for any sign that Bryce or Amy might be waiting outside for me, ready to pounce. My heart beats wildly in my chest and I try to calm myself, but it's hard when they behaved in such a strange way last night. If Cathy hadn't confronted them, they would have forced their way inside, and then... I shudder to think.

I know I owe Cathy for what she did but it's also hard to see her role in this mess. She's certainly kept things from me too but at least she's also tried to help me. That's more than I can say for some. Taking one last look around my cramped hall, I realise that I've started to feel like a prisoner in my own home and, as I draw in a deep breath, I'm suddenly hit by the certainty that I won't be coming back. This house is not a happy place and I will not be trapped here any longer. I fling open the door, striding out onto the street, trying to convince myself that it's broad daylight so I must be safe.

THIRTY-SIX

The Hollies is a hive of activity when I pull up onto the gravel driveway, and I get off the bike and find a spot to leave it in the bushes out front. There's nothing to lock it to but I decide that the chances of a criminally minded pensioner coming across it are low, and it's hardly like Ian took good care of it before. It was rotting in their shed before he lent it to me.

Smoothing my clothes as best I can, I put my shoulders back and my head up and walk to the front door, trying to act as if this is just a normal visit. I buzz in and smile at the passing nurses as I pretend to sign in – writing a fake name in the book, which may be over-the-top but I don't want to take any risks – before tailgating another visitor into the main entrance hall and taking the grand staircase up to the dementia wing. I take a couple of wrong turns, but I keep the smile pasted on my face and act as if I know exactly where I'm going until I find the door to Tulip wing.

There's a keypad to enter the code and I try a couple of times to see if my muscles will remember the number, but the door doesn't budge and I wonder how many times you can get it wrong before a silent alarm is triggered. I'm about to take another loop of the building when the carer with the pink hair appears; she does a double-take when she sees the state of my face but she just winces and says, 'Back again?'

I smile and we share a slightly awkward hug as I'm unsure how well I know her, but she clearly knows me.

'I'm pleased I ran into you again,' she says and I nod but she seems to want to say something more. I notice her glance around as if checking no one is within earshot.

'This may not be my place and I really don't want to offend you,' she begins and my mind starts to race. Is she going to tell me that my breath smells or that I'm wearing my top back to front? 'I just remember a few of our chats and I wanted to give you something, in case you ever need it. Something that helped me once, a few years back.'

She pulls a small card from her pocket and slides it into my hand. I turn it over and read the words: 'Sofia's Women's Refuge – A Restful Place for Women and Children'. Surprise must be written all over my face because the woman flushes and I'm suddenly sure she's read the bruises and scrapes all wrong.

'Just put it in the bin if it's not for you,' she says. 'I must get on, I've got the tea round to do and I'm sure you want to get up there to meet Rachel.'

'Rachel?'

The woman frowns, looking worried she's said something wrong again. 'Rachel always comes at this time on a Saturday, usually with one or two family members so it's quite the party. But I don't need to tell you that – the two of you came together on Saturdays for years.'

She bustles away and I stare at the card but instead of looking for a bin, I slide it into my pocket. Is it possible that my relationship with Marc was much worse than even Rachel let on? Our messages don't tell a happy story and I have had some strange feelings about him that seem to back this up. Maybe instead of just drifting apart, our relationship was something worse? Something dangerous.

My heart thuds with anticipation as I stride along the corridor towards Mum's room. After wishing Rachel would disappear, I'm suddenly thrilled at the thought of having the opportunity to interrogate them both at once. And the nurse said she sometimes brings people. Who could it be? Rachel's partner perhaps, but the woman said sometimes more than one. All I can do is hope and pray that it's someone who will be honest with me.

Reaching the room, I pause by the ajar door and peek inside. Mum is lying in bed, her head on the pillow with the blankets pulled up, looking to be asleep. I'm about to go in when it crosses my mind that it might be better to observe from the outside first. Maybe I can listen to what Rachel says and glean something that way since asking her questions directly hasn't revealed much so far.

Glancing back down the corridor, I see I'm alone so I quickly try the door opposite Mum's and discover that the room is empty and cold, the bed made up but no personal belongings anywhere. Deciding it's a safe place to hide, I stand by the door, ensuring that it's open a crack so I can peer through.

Ten, twenty minutes pass. Lying in bed for days is good preparation for a stake-out since I don't get bored quickly. It's easy to let the time pass me by as I stand there, telling myself that this is the best way to get answers. I feel like I'm almost in a daze when Rachel strides into the corridor, walking quickly and bursting into Mum's room with a loud, 'Good morning, Mother.'

From my position across the hallway, I can't hear anything else that is said, nor can I see anything other than a tiny sliver of wallpaper on the far wall. I'm about to slip out and move closer when someone else appears and enters Mum's bedroom.

I only glimpse their face for a moment, but I'd recognise them anywhere.

I slump against the wall, gasping from the shock. I feel bile rising up my throat and I lean over, clutching my knees.

It's my husband, Marc.

THIRTY-SEVEN

It's all too much. I have to press my lips together to stop myself from yelling out in anguish. My brain can't fathom a single reason why Rachel would tell me that my husband is dead when he's clearly alive and well. What could I possibly have done to make them want to torture me so much? The past week has been one falsehood after the other, leading me on a path to total and utter confusion.

I feel like sinking to the floor in disbelief, but enough is enough, I need to confront them both here and now. Grabbing the door handle, I'm about to pull it open when I spot something that makes my whole body go slack. Someone I can't believe I am seeing and I can't compute. It's like my brain is stuck.

All I can do is gape as a young woman walks along the hallway staring at her phone. My jaw drops open, slack. My heart rate begins to race.

It's the girl from the street and the pub – the one with the jet-black hair and heavy eye make-up. She must be only fifteen or sixteen and she's clearly fragile, but it's not that which makes me gasp for breath.

I know this girl.

I feel a pull of protectiveness. My palms are sweating. I can't believe it. I can't bring myself to even think it.

She pauses for a moment to tap out a message before joining them inside the bedroom. I long to get closer, to study every pore and split end, to see this girl under a microscope. I feel like my whole body is trying to tell me something. This girl is important; and then it hits me – she's everything.

I pause before I even dare to think her name, but when it comes into my head I feel as if my head has split open and a million stars have burst out.

Noelle. This girl is Noelle. My small, red-haired baby has grown up, and most importantly, she's alive. The memories that have come back to me must be from years ago. For some reason, I've only remembered that tiny, helpless baby up to now. But seeing her up close, I know exactly who she is. It feels like I could never forget that face, despite what's happened since I woke up. Somewhere, deep down, Noelle has been imprinted on my heart.

Creeping out into the corridor, I edge closer to Mum's room because I need to catch another glimpse of her, and I spot them crowding around her bed. They look like a cosy family unit, and I feel a tug of jealousy as Rachel touches Noelle's arm to get her attention before saying something that makes Noelle smile.

Her smile makes joy bloom inside me, and as I watch my daughter and my sister, I'm torn between love and hate – the strongest love in the world, a mother's love, and the blackest hate reserved for a person who tells you that your child is dead. It's an unimaginable betrayal and I don't know how I could possibly ever forgive her. I want to storm in and demand answers. But I can't stop staring at Noelle.

My baby has grown up and discovered make-up and hair dye, concealing those familiar features with smears of black and white. The incense stick I found in the spare bedroom must belong to her and I picture her filling the house with pungent smoke. I wonder if I objected to her choices before my accident, if I wished more of that baby remained, but all I feel is an intense joy that she's here and she is herself. What else would a mother want their child to be?

And what of Marc? I can't direct all my fury towards Rachel because he clearly deserves some fire. He's a grown man after all and he's allowed his wife to go through recovery alone, cared for by a stranger, all the while playing happy families with his sister-in-law. As I watch them smiling and laughing, I feel like barging into the room and locking them inside. Demanding they tell me everything. But as I try to imagine what possible reason they could come up with, I can't think of a single thing that could justify what they've done.

Other words start entering my head. False imprisonment. Cruel and unusual punishment. Torment. How else could you describe what they've done to me? I know that there is no coming back from what's happened. Some part of my life is about to fracture again – the accident may have created a before and after, but this is the real moment of split. Mistakes can be forgiven, but lies? They can't be forgotten.

My rage propels me out into the corridor and I know I should calm down before I enter, but I can't stop myself. I bang open the door and they all look at me as I hold on to the door-frame to stop myself from falling down with the shock of it all. I see matching shock and horror etched on each of their faces.

'Jesus Christ!' yelps Rachel.

Marc's face turns entirely white, but it's Noelle's reaction that hurts the most.

'No!' she screams. 'You can't be here!'

'Please—'

But before I can beg her to just talk to me, Noelle barges past me and I smell her perfume – a smell that if it was bottled would be called 'Noelle' and I would buy up all the stock in the world – and then she is gone. Rushing off down the corridor and letting the door to the ward slam behind her.

It takes me a moment to gather myself before I look up at my sister and husband. Mum is in the bed, her head slack and her gaze lost in the middle distance and I hope she is far enough gone that she doesn't realise what is going on. She doesn't deserve the hurt of knowing what one of her daughters has done to the other.

'How could you?' I say, my voice trembling.

Rachel is crying softly but Marc doesn't seem ruffled. His cold eyes meet mine and he says, 'Here is not the place.'

'Do you realise what you've done is a crime? You can't treat me like this.'

Marc takes a couple of steps towards me. He's only slightly taller than me and of slight build, but there's a strength in his wiry frame, and something about the way he moves reminds me of a big cat. Sleek and deadly. I shrink back as he grabs me by both arms and kisses me once on each cheek.

'*Ma chérie*,' he says. His pale grey eyes are bright. 'I've missed you.' He doesn't seem genuine and his words leave me cold.

'I demand that you tell me what is going on.' I feel almost hysterical, but I force myself to speak evenly.

'It is all so complicated.' He says this in a scolding way as if I am the one who has made it so. I feel like a silly schoolgirl who has got the maths homework wrong again, but then I look back at Rachel and see the devastation on her face and realise that I'm in the right. Marc should not be dismissing me as if this is some trifling matter. This is deadly serious.

'I must go to Noelle,' he says. 'We'll talk later.'

I try to grab his jumper but he stops, gives my hand a long look, and I feel a frisson of something that makes me drop my arm slowly. We listen to his footsteps until the door bangs and then I turn to my sister.

'What have you done?' I stammer.

She is crying softly and lets out a quiet whimper that seems to shake Mum from her daydream.

'Are you girls arguing again? You're like cats and dogs. I thought you agreed to stay out of each other's lives so we wouldn't have this constant yowling.'

'Did we?' I ask, keeping my eyes on Rachel. 'I thought we were close.'

Tears run down Rachel's cheeks and she draws in a juddering breath. 'We were close, as children. But when you got married you pulled apart from me and everyone else who was close to you. Marc preferred it that way.'

I frown now, wondering how she could have allowed us to be pulled apart if we were close. But Rachel has done many things I feel like I will never understand.

'I know this is stupid, given all the lies I've told, but I honestly thought your illness might bring us back together. It's what I hoped anyway.' A loud hiccup escapes her throat and she shakes her head. 'I know it doesn't seem like it, but I've always done my best. I tried to think of what you would do.'

My mouth falls open. 'Don't put this on me. I would never behave like you. You're evil.'

Rachel weeps at this and I would feel bad if things were different.

'Girls, please,' Mum says, sounding agitated.

Rachel manages to stop crying long enough to say, 'I promise, I'm going to make you understand. But now's not the time.' She nods at Mum. 'There are some things she shouldn't hear.'

I nod grimly, not wanting to upset my mum any more than she already is, but I can't be left in the dark any longer. 'You and Marc need to explain everything to me, today, or I will go to the police.'

Rachel's eyes widen but she doesn't argue. 'OK.'

'You have until this evening,' I say.

She nods, draws in one big shaky breath and says, 'I'm sorry, Jen, I really am.' And then she kisses Mum's cheek before rushing out.

I stagger over to Mum's bed, my legs feeling shaky from the shock, and slump into the chair by her bedside. As the tears fall down my cheeks, she closes her eyes and I'm relieved she's not asking any more questions. I rest for a moment, but soon I feel like I can't sit still, like I need to do something, so I get up to leave but then I remember the photo and I pull it from my pocket.

'Mum?' I say softly and her eyes flutter open. 'Do you recognise the little girl with the curly hair?' I ask, moving the photo into her eyeline and pointing at the child.

Mum takes the photo from me and moves it close to her face but quickly she lets her arm drop and looks at me as if I'm mad.

'Of course I recognise her,' she says brusquely. 'I may be old but I'm not stupid. That's Amy.'

I close my eyes in frustration. 'And Amy is... ?'

'Our next-door neighbour, of course. She was the same age as Rachel, and her brother was the same as you. You were always running around, the four of you, causing mayhem wherever you went. The number of times I had to speak to their mother about the scrapes you got in. Not that she did anything about it. Frivolous woman. Now, Amy's brother... what was his name again?'

My eyes snap open and a possibility crosses my mind that I turn over. *Could it be?*

'Odd name, I always thought. American-sounding, though they were local for generations. Probably thought it made them sound exotic, but that was his mother through and through. Always wanting to be something she wasn't.'

My instinct must be right. There's only one person it could be.

'Bryce,' I say softly.

'That was it – Bryce.'

And all I can think is that I've been betrayed by all the people closest to me, the very people I should have been able to rely on. But why?

THIRTY-EIGHT

By the time I make it back downstairs and out of the front door of The Hollies, there's no sign of any of my family and I imagine they all scarpered as quickly as possible, desperate to get away from the evidence of what they've done – me.

I get back on my bike slowly, the weight of what has just happened making every movement an effort, and I set off along the driveway, the gravel crunching beneath the tyres, trying to come to terms with what I have discovered. Marc and Noelle are alive. I know I should be bursting with joy at the news, but it's hard to feel ecstatic when I know that the people closest to me are the ones who let me think that they'd died.

As I try to come up with a rationale for their behaviour, my brain veers from an inheritance tax scam to sheer sadism, but nothing quite feels right. I run through the people that were in on it – my sister, our oldest friends, my husband and even my daughter; how can there be a good reason for what they've done to me? My feet go round and round as I pedal but I'm barely concentrating on where I'm going. I know I don't want to go home. I can't face returning to that house, which has become my prison. It's impossible to imagine there were any happy times that took place within those four walls and I decide that I'll put it on the market. And while I imagine the house belongs to Marc and me, after what he's put me through, I think he'll find it hard to refuse me if I tell him I want to sell.

I think of what I'll miss if I leave and the only thing that pops into my head is Cathy. She may be a little zany but through this period of recovery, she's been there for me, and our friendship means a lot to me. We've clearly had our ups and downs but something tells me that she's one of the only people who's been honest with me even if there have been shades of grey.

Looking around, I see that I've come into town. I blink at the busy pavements and people bustling around doing their shopping, and I feel a surge of envy. Why can't I be one of them, with my biggest worry being what I'm going to buy for dinner? I slow down to watch a couple who are holding hands and peering into the window of the estate agent. The woman points to a listing and the man nods and says something in her ear and she laughs. I imagine them working out where their sofa will go and which room might become the nursery and it crosses my mind that they're the type of people who deserve to live in my house – a proper family.

I'm about to pick up my speed again, deciding I've stared enough, but the row of shops where Bryce disappeared before catches my eye and I decide to lock up my bike and have a closer look. It was a couple of days ago, but I'm still intrigued to know which shop he spent over half an hour in, and I'm happy to have something to distract me from my despair.

The first shop in the row is a charity shop, and it's hard to imagine what Bryce could have been doing in there for so long unless he was replacing his entire wardrobe. Next up is a newsagent, which again feels unlikely, but the restaurant next to it, Chez Richard, catches my eye and I go up to the window to take a closer look. Could Bryce have treated himself to a slap-up meal? The lights are off inside and the door is closed and I can tell it's not open yet or I might have gone inside and ordered some lunch. Spotting the menu in a gilt-edged frame in the window, I stop and read the dishes of the day.

It's even fancier than I thought and I'm shocked by the prices – almost fifteen pounds per starter and close to thirty for the mains – and there are quite a few ingredients I've never heard of. I wonder if this is the type of restaurant Marc and I would eat at – he is French, after all – but something tells me we prefer simpler food and I can't imagine we'd spend so much on a meal. The dessert list is the only thing that draws me and there's a chocolate delice with a Turkish-delight-flavoured ice cream that makes my mouth water – I guess I really have always loved Turkish delight.

My eyes fall on something at the bottom of the menu that makes me gasp. There's a single line that most people probably don't even notice but as soon as I read it, I understand exactly what Bryce was doing here: 'Executive Chef – Bryce Gordon.'

My body goes from hot to cold as I realise that the man who's been coming to my house daily and changing my nappies and sponging me down isn't a nurse at all. He's a chef who works at the fanciest French restaurant in town. The *executive* chef, no less. I let out a strange laugh as I think that his profession at least explains the delicious meals I've been treated to and the bundle of knives in his bag. But why on earth would a man with such a busy job spend his days caring for me?

I'm pleased that Bryce isn't a deranged madman who carries a murder kit everywhere he goes, but I'm struggling to know how else to feel. The secrecy and lies overshadow everything else, and while he may have been my lifeline in my darkest moments, I can't help but feel like he's responsible for keeping me in the dark. Suddenly I'm not hungry any more, all thoughts of dessert gone from my mind.

I'm about to leave when I spot movement inside and I see

Bryce himself coming out of the kitchen door in chef's whites. Without thinking too much, I knock on the window and he stops stock still, staring at me like he's seen a ghost, before hurrying over and unlocking the front door.

'Jen, please, come in. You must be going out of your mind.'

I frown at his choice of words. 'You have no idea,' I say, folding my arms.

'I promise you that all Amy and I wanted was to help you. You're family to us.'

'So you decided to torture me?' I say and he winces.

'I know it must seem like that but we had our reasons. Look, come inside and let me make you a coffee and explain, please. At least let me tell you our side.'

I think this over and finally say, 'On one condition.' He looks hopeful. 'Ring Amy and get her to come here too. I can only face having this conversation once.'

'She'd expect nothing less,' he says.

I let Bryce show me to the table closest to the door and wait while he calls Amy, tapping my fingers on the white tablecloth while my heart thrums. I only hear his side of the conversation, but it doesn't take much persuading for her to agree to come and then Bryce makes us coffees. The machine hisses and spits while I wait until Bryce brings over a tray with coffees and what look like fancy little biscuits, and by the time he's placed them in front of me, the door opens and Amy rushes in. Her wild curls are held back from her face by a headband and her face is lined and pale – she looks like she hasn't slept since I saw her last.

'Jen, darling.' She holds out her arms as if expecting a hug, but I refuse to stand, and after a moment, she lets them drop limply at her side. 'I'm so sorry. This has been horrible for us too. I can't even imagine what it's been like for you.'

She starts to cry softly and her brother puts his arm around her but I feel my insides harden. Whatever she's been through, I've been through worse.

'Why didn't you just tell me the truth?' I ask, starting with the simplest question. But the simplest questions are often the hardest.

'We wanted to,' Amy says. 'You won't believe how much we wanted to. But Marc and Rachel had a plan and they insisted that they knew best. We questioned, we argued, we almost disobeyed them, but in the end we decided to go along with it, even though some of their decisions felt pretty strange.'

'Pretty strange?' I burst out. I think that might be the under-statement of the century. 'But why? Why go along with some-thing so horrendous that you can't even look me in the eye any more?'

They exchange a glance. I feel like they're going to hold something else back and I want to scream. But Bryce says, 'One reason, and one reason only – Noelle.'

I lift my eyes, surprised, and look at him. 'Noelle?'

Amy takes the seat next to me. 'She came to us on the night of the accident. Honestly, Jen, if you'd have seen her... She was totally beside herself, screaming, crying and threatening all sorts of things.'

I frown but before I can ask, Bryce says to Amy, 'She needs to know everything.' Then he turns back to me. 'I'm sorry, Jen, but Noelle said she was going to kill herself if we didn't go along with the plan they'd concocted. Look, this is going to be hard for you to hear, but she admitted to us that she lost her temper and intentionally caused you to crash your car.'

I try to picture my daughter forcing the steering wheel but it's hard to imagine when I still can only really remember her as a baby.

'She told us you were badly injured and she was so scared that you'd go to the police and she could be charged with attempted murder. Of course, we told her you'd never want her to get into trouble, but we couldn't calm her down. She said that in the brief moment after the accident before you lost consciousness, you threatened to call the police—'

'She was terrified that you were going to die,' Amy interrupts. 'She thought it was all her fault. We did our best to reassure her but you can see how difficult those months must have been for her. She's needed a lot of help. I really thought we might lose her.' There are tears in Amy's eyes and I picture that broken girl, sobbing at the pub, and all I want is to wrap my arms around her and hold her together.

Amy continues, 'Marc came up with a plan to look after you at home until you woke up from the coma. We all agreed that once you were on the road to recovery, it would be easier to gently explain what had happened, and we were all sure you would forgive Noelle immediately.'

I nod vigorously, absolutely certain I would forgive my daughter anything, but then I stop, frowning as confusions spreads through me. 'You didn't gently explain anything – you allowed me to believe that Noelle was dead. What changed?'

'When you came round with such complete memory loss, it took us all by surprise,' Amy says. 'Neither of us was there, but Rachel said that when she saw you awake, she panicked. And she decided to tell you as little as possible because she wasn't sure what to do. And once she started the lie, it became harder and harder to unravel.'

I'm still frowning in disbelief – I can't accept that it was easier to lie than tell the truth.

'Surely you realised I would find out the truth sooner or later? Or were you planning on keeping me locked up like a prisoner forever?'

'We begged Rachel and Marc to tell you the truth,' Amy says. 'Honestly, we tried so many times, but they insisted that we wait until Noelle was stronger.'

Bryce cuts in, 'Amy, to her credit, refused to be involved.'

'I agreed to support Noelle,' Amy says. 'But I couldn't come to your home and see you lying in that bed. It didn't feel right.'

'What about you?' I turn on Bryce accusingly. 'You pretended to be a nurse!'

'Jen,' he pleads, 'I know you don't remember much, but you and I have always been close. I weighed it up and decided the old you would have wanted me around, and I honestly believed that me being there was helping you recover faster. I wouldn't have stayed unless I thought I was doing you good, and Noelle begged me to help. She wanted someone close to you looking after you.'

I think back to all the things he did for me. The sponging and cleaning and cooking and wiping, and although there was certainly kindness, I can't help but feel rising indignity. He should never have put me in that position and I still don't understand why my husband and sister would have allowed it.

'Where was Marc all this time? Why wasn't he the one looking after me?'

Bryce looks like he's about to say something, but Amy puts her hand on his arm. 'I think that's for you to discuss with him. But I'm sure he had his reasons for staying away. He had a lot on his plate looking after Noelle. They stayed at your parents' house, but Noelle went into a residential unit for a few weeks and Marc stayed nearby.'

I'm shocked to hear that Noelle's mental health was so bad that she needed in-patient care, but I feel like I'm starting to understand a little of what Bryce and Amy must have been feeling. It doesn't justify what they did, nothing ever could, but it's something. I think we all realise at the same moment that there's nothing else to say. It's as if something has broken between us that can never be repaired and we've all heard the crash and seen the splintered fragments of our relationship.

'We're so sorry,' Amy says as tears slide down her face.

Bryce's eyes are too bright and he stands up before

slumping back down again as if he's not sure what to do with himself. 'I never wanted to hurt you,' he says, his voice thick with emotion, but there's nothing I can say to that. They've hurt me beyond belief.

'I think it's time for me to talk to my husband and sister,' I say, pushing back the chair. Neither of them stops me as I stand to leave, my coffee untouched, and as I go to the door, I hear Amy say softly, 'Just don't be too harsh on her.'

Stepping out into blustery air, I wonder whether she means Rachel or Noelle.

THIRTY-NINE

I get back on my bike and start pedalling with purpose, deciding it's time for me to go home, but instinctively I know that I'm not headed to the home I made with Marc and Noelle, but the one where it all began and where Marc and Noelle have been living – my childhood home. My feet know exactly where to go, like a homing pigeon that will always come back.

I cycle along the long road that leads out of town, going up and down over the small hills, and I pass the turning to the newbuild estate where Bryce and Amy live but I know that isn't where I grew up. The memories that have come back to me are of an old house with a large back garden. And I already know that there's an oak tree in the front, one big enough to do serious damage to my skull.

The road winds into a narrow bend and the houses either side begin to get further apart. Soon I'm in what feels close to countryside although I know it isn't far from the built-up town. The wind whistles through my hair and I kick down on the pedals, enjoying the feeling of freedom and the moment when my brain is occupied by the movement and I don't need to think about what they've all done, but it doesn't last long. As I huff up a big hill, I begin to feel dread building inside me and I shiver even though I'm warm from the ride. I zoom down the other side and go around a sharp turning and then I see it.

Most of the house is hidden behind an overgrown hedge, but as soon as I glimpse the tiled roof and ivy growing up the face, I know that this is where I grew up. There's a car in the driveway and I'm not surprised that someone is here – in fact, I feel certain that this is where my family have gathered, but before I investigate, there's something else I need to see. Slowing right down, I cycle along the hedgerow and it doesn't take long to spot the gap in the bushes near the boundary of the property where my car must have exited the road and crashed across the grass verge. The hedge is sparser here and I ditch the bike on the grass and hurry through into the front garden, where I see the oak stretching far into the sky.

Walking slowly towards it, I ready myself, expecting something to happen like a flashback or a memory floating to the surface like a bubble in a pond, but nothing of the accident comes to mind. There are no tyre tracks in the mud, and the bark of the tree is gnarled but there are no cuts or gashes that might indicate the scene of a serious accident. But it was over half a year ago now and nothing in nature is permanent. Already the tree has healed and its scars have closed, which is more than I can say for my brain.

I run my fingers over the thick trunk and look up at the leaves that are starting to turn a rich amber in colour. It won't be long before they fall to the ground and the tree is bare. I don't remember the accident, but I can see myself as a child, hiding behind here in games of hide-and-seek and kicking leaves as Rachel squealed and told me to knock it off. I wonder if we played here with Bryce and Amy too and I peer over the hedge at the roof of the house next door, certain that was where they lived and sure we spent as much time in their garden as we did our own.

A noise comes from the house and I glance over to see the front door opening. My heart leaps into my mouth as Noelle comes out, her black hair loose to her shoulders and rippling in the wind. I wish I could see the beautiful red I know is hidden beneath but as I stare at my daughter, I realise that as long as I can see her face, I don't care. The idea of her gone from this world drained everything of colour, so to have her here, alive and well, suddenly feels like anything is possible.

'Noelle?' I call out and she looks over to me. I smile and wave and pick a path out from beneath the tree but her face instantly crumples with what looks like fear.

'What are you doing here?' she asks, her hostility plain.

'I... I... Well, to be honest, I'm not really sure,' I say.

Noelle's frown deepens. 'I have literally never heard you say that,' she says.

'Say what?'

'That you don't know. You always think you have the answer to everything.'

Her words strike their mark and I say, 'I'm sorry, that sounds annoying.'

And for a moment, Noelle forgets her anger and laughs. 'It *is* annoying and you've never said that before either.'

'Maybe I'm different now,' I say gently.

'I doubt that,' Noelle says and I wonder what exactly happened to take my daughter from that smiley baby I remember to this guarded young woman.

'Well, for one thing,' I say brightly, 'I don't know who anyone is.'

'Yes, Uncle Bryce said.'

Uncle, I think, my eyebrows shooting up, but all I do is smile and nod.

'It's true. Rachel had to introduce herself.'

Noelle laughs. 'That is mental.'

'But I did remember I like to go to car boot sales.'

Noelle groans and rolls her eyes. 'Mum, you are obsessed. Trust you to remember your most boring hobby. It's always freezing and you insist on looking at everything twice, just in case you missed something the first time.'

We both laugh now and I can't believe how normal things feel. There are so many things I could ask her, but all I want is to stay in this moment, chatting and making jokes with my daughter. Surely she must know that I would never report her to the police for anything – that feels all wrong.

'You know I will always love you,' I say softly. 'There's nothing you could do that would change that.'

She freezes and her eyes flood with tears.

'I wanted to come and visit,' she says. 'I thought of you all the time. I sent flowers, did you get them?'

I nod, suddenly feeling a rush of understanding over the note I found. My darling girl was sorry because she believed she was responsible for the accident. I want to tell her that she may have done something she regrets, but I'll never hold her at fault. I'm her mother, I should have protected her. I open my mouth to speak again but we hear a car approaching and both turn to see it swing into the driveway.

It takes me a moment to place it but before the driver's door opens, I realise it's Ian's car. He gets out slowly, wearing a pair of sunglasses despite the weak sun so I can't see his eyes. He raises his arm and calls out, 'Ms V!'

'Hello, Ian,' I say as he looks from me to Noelle and back again.

'I take it you've figured out who this is?' he says, and though his words are callous, I don't think he means them unkindly.

'I have,' I reply. 'It may have taken longer than it should, but I don't think anyone could ever truly forget Noelle.'

'I did try to get her to come and visit you,' he says and my mind goes to the image of him trying to drag her to what I assumed was his front door, and I realise it could easily have been mine. I thought he was being too rough with her but, looking back, I wonder if that was the case or just a product of my paranoid mind. I was in a state of heightened anxiety but I'm not willing to dismiss my fears without further questions.

'Do you feel safe?' I ask Noelle gently.

'With Ian?' she asks, her eyes growing wide in surprise.

'I saw you two arguing,' I say.

She glances at him and they both burst out laughing. 'He's a pussycat,' she says. 'An annoying pussycat, but Ian would never hurt me. He's been trying to get me to talk to you for days.'

'I just wanted it all to be over,' he says quietly and I nod because that's all I want too. 'I was only trying to bring her to you because I was so sure that if you had a conversation you could sort out this whole mess.'

I glance at her and realise I have to say what I'm feeling out loud. 'You know that whatever happened, I'd never have gone to the police.'

There's a long silence and I seem to have said the wrong thing because a frown flashes across Noelle's face and she says, 'I can't do this. Come on, Ian, let's get out of here.'

She stalks across the driveway and yanks open the passenger door, getting inside without another word. There's so much more I want to say, so many memories to try to rediscover, but I realise we have plenty of time and I need to repair whatever damage there is between us. Ian doesn't get into the car right away and I feel him watching me.

'You OK, Ms V?' he asks.

There are tears in my eyes, but I blink them away and nod, and he follows her and gets into the car, leaning over and kissing her softly on the cheek. Of course, they are a couple – I'm surprised it didn't come to me before. They look good together, but I wonder how old he is. Cathy mentioned he was at university and Noelle must only be fifteen or sixteen so it is a big gap, especially at that age.

All these thoughts run through my head while he starts the engine and reverses too quickly on the driveway and I want to shout at him to be careful but I bite my tongue because I've said enough for now. They are about to leave and I wave them off but suddenly the car stops and Noelle leaps out. She comes running towards me and I brace myself, unsure what is about to happen until the moment she throws out her arms and wraps them around me. Hugging her tight, I never want to let go and I feel like this is the moment I've been waiting for – the thing that makes me whole again – but then Noelle drops her arms and steps back.

Mascara is streaked down her cheeks and I lift my hand to wipe her tears.

'Sweetheart, what's wrong?' I say.

Noelle chokes on a sob and says, 'I love you, Mum.'

'I love you, too, of course.'

I smile but she's clearly not done and she shakes her head.

'I'm sorry,' she says before turning on her heel and running for the car.

FORTY

I wait until Ian's car is gone from sight before walking to the front door of the house. I'm not sure who I'm going to find inside but the car remains on the driveway and I plan to find out who it belongs to. It hurts to see Noelle so torn up and I vow that now is the time for my sister and husband to explain the whole story to me. I can't have my child thinking anything after the accident was her fault when there are adults around who should know better. My sorrow is replaced by anger as I stand in front of the house, wondering whether to knock or go marching right in.

I lift my hand but then stop as I see the lock and it triggers a memory. Putting my hand in my pocket, I pull out my key ring and see the ornate gold key that seemed not to fit anything at my home. Even without trying it in the lock, I know it will fit. Of course, it's the key to this house and I know that it turns with a heavy thud, always giving us away when we tried to sneak back home late at night. I'm smiling as I push open the door and step into the hallway with its pink-striped wallpaper and creaky wooden floor. The air smells slightly musty and I close my eyes, breathing deeply as I picture Dad playing records in the bright yellow front room and Mum cooking Sunday lunch in the terracotta kitchen, yelling through at him to turn the music down every few minutes.

I'm drawn to the living room, where I sense my dad spent most of his time, and as I push open the door, I see two people sitting close together on the sofa who spring apart the moment I step inside. Rachel is one of them but it's the person next to her who makes me gasp – her blonde hair may be down today in a swishy style and she may be wearing sweatpants instead of a suit, but I'd recognise her anywhere.

'Dr Marsden?' I say, my voice filled with disbelief.

The woman flinches as if I've slapped her. She looks from me to Rachel and back, her pale cheeks swiftly turning pink, before saying in a shaky voice, 'Don't call me that.'

Rachel puts her arm around the woman and clears her throat. 'Jen, there is no Dr Marsden. We will explain every-thing, but first I want to introduce you to someone who is very important to me. Someone I put in a terrible position, who really didn't want to deceive you in any way, and someone I owe a huge apology to. This is my partner, Laura.'

I see Laura's quivering lip and the way she's twisting her hands together as her red-rimmed eyes meet mine, and she says, 'Jen, I'm so sorry. I didn't know what was the right thing to do and Rachel begged me to pretend to be your doctor. She said I was helping you.'

'It's OK,' I say, accepting her apology because it feels like one of the smaller wrongs in the whole mess. 'We've met before, haven't we?'

She smiles weakly and nods. 'Rachel and I have been together ten years.'

We all laugh at the absurdity of the introduction, but my smile fades and I turn to Rachel.

'Now,' I say, 'start at the beginning.'

Rachel hesitates. 'Shouldn't we wait for Marc? He's just gone for a walk to get some air. He won't be long.'

I think this over but shake my head. 'Just tell me everything you know. You owe me that much.'

Rachel takes a deep breath and Laura nods at her encouragingly.

'OK, but the beginning is a long time ago. We've had a rough few years as a family,' Rachel says, and Laura squeezes her arm. 'First Dad died, then Mum's dementia became unmanageable. She was grouchy before, even though she always had our best interests at heart, but the dementia made her difficult.'

I frown, finding it hard to see what that has to do with the accident.

'You were struggling and it affected your home life. Things were bad between you and Marc...'

'You confided in me that they'd been bad for a long time,' Laura adds quietly. 'I don't think Marc has always been very good for you.'

'You were devastated after Bryce left,' Rachel takes over the story. 'You two were inseparable as teenagers, but then he went off to train as a chef, first to London, then Copenhagen, and I'm not sure you ever got over it. But you met Marc and had Noelle and you were making the best of it...'

'And then Bryce came back,' Laura says.

'To be honest, we were happy because for the first time in a long time, you had your spark back. Things with Marc had deteriorated to the point where you and everyone around you thought you'd be better off apart and when Bryce came back, I think it reminded you that you have so much life left to live. You fell for him all over again and he so wanted a second chance. You shouldn't blame yourself but things developed into a relationship.'

Rachel is choosing her words carefully, but it dawns on me that I must have had an affair with Bryce and I feel my scalp prick with shame. I can tell she doesn't like Marc but I feel like I should have worked harder at my marriage, but I'm confused about why she's raking it up now. Do we really need to go over everything I've done wrong when they're meant to be explaining *their* actions to me.

'Why are you telling me this?' I ask, angry at the direction they've taken. 'I want to know about the accident.'

'We're trying to give you the back story because those difficult years particularly affected your relationship with Noelle,' Rachel says gently.

I give her a sharp look. 'Noelle? How?'

'It was typical mother and daughter stuff at first. She felt like you were being too hard on her and you felt like she was pushing the boundaries too far. But soon you couldn't bear to be in the same room as each other, and every family event turned into a screaming match.'

I try to play this out but all I can think is that Noelle is only a child – my child. How could I have argued with her?

'Surely I rose above it?' I say. 'I'm her mother.'

There's a beat and Rachel and Laura glance at each other as if they're unsure how to respond.

'I saw some pretty epic rows,' Laura says. 'You both gave as good as you got and Marc seemed to fan the flames rather than act as peacekeeper. It was like he enjoyed you being on different sides.'

I'm speechless but I'm still not sure what this has to do with my forced quarantine.

'It got worse when Noelle discovered your affair with Bryce,' Rachel says.

'Noelle knew?' I'm horrified. I wish she were here right now so I could go and tell her how sorry I am, that no child should have to witness their parents behaving in that way.

'You were planning on leaving Marc, which I don't think was too much of a surprise to anyone, apart from Noelle. And when Noelle found out, everything fell apart. She refused to be under the same roof as you and went to stay with Cathy and Ian. Marc moved out. It was only because it was the anniversary of Dad's death that you were all in the car together that night. You were coming here, to pay your respects where we scattered his ashes.'

Without needing to ask, the oak springs to mind. I know instinctively we mixed Dad's ashes in with the soil by its foot – a place that means a lot to me. Rachel takes a deep breath and Laura reaches for her hand, patting it gently, and Rachel goes on.

'It was Noelle who caused the accident,' she says quietly and I nod, because this is what Bryce and Amy already told me. 'Marc was in the back and the two of you were arguing, and he saw her grab the wheel and force the car off the road. You hit your head and the force of the seat belt seemed to have broken a couple of ribs, and Marc told us that what you said before losing consciousness terrified Noelle.'

'That I'd call the police?' I ask and Rachel's eyes grow wide with surprise. I feel a rush of power that I've found something out before she's told me.

'You remember?' she asks.

'No, Bryce and Amy told me,' I admit. 'They said that Noelle was suicidal and that's why you all lied, but I still don't understand it. I'm not sure I ever will.'

Rachel's eyes fill with tears. 'All I can tell you is that was the scariest phone call I've ever received. Marc said you were hurt and all I could think was that he'd done something to you... but then he said it was Noelle.'

'You know how much she means to us all,' Laura interjects.

'By the time we got here, it seemed like Marc had decided everything – he made it sound like we had no choice because of what you'd said, so we agreed to take you home. We never could have imagined you'd be unconscious for so long, and once the plan had been set in motion, we didn't know how to reverse it.' Rachel wipes tears from her cheeks. 'I wanted to come clean so many times but I just didn't know how. We were in far too deep by that point.'

I close my eyes and try to get a sense of whether any of that rings true but I realise I barely know who I am; I feel like a slate that's been wiped clean. Would I really have called the police on my own daughter? It doesn't feel right but, then again, I'm shocked that I allowed things to get so bad with Noelle that she refused to live with me. How could I have driven my own daughter away? How could I have let her discover my affair? Shame washes over me as I realise that I've been picturing myself as the innocent party but no one's hands are clean in this mess.

'I just want you to know that we would never have agreed to it if Noelle hadn't been so fragile,' Rachel says, her voice thick with emotion. 'She was self-harming and we were scared that she'd go through with her threats. I honestly thought she wouldn't survive an arrest, let alone a trial, and I can't even begin to think about prison.'

'Was prison a real possibility?' I'm surprised that they believed Noelle might have gone to prison.

'Marc said she could be charged with attempted murder, given the extent of your injuries and the fact that you'd had a screaming row before you got in the car. He said that witnesses heard her say, "I wish you were dead."'

I feel numb at the thought of such a horrible day. I try to put myself in their position.

'It was awful seeing you like that, but deep down I told myself that you would have wanted us to protect Noelle at any cost. Even if that cost was yourself.'

I think over her words, weighing them in my mind as I turn to look out of the window at the branches of the oak, swaying in the wind.

'You were right. I would die for Noelle. But why not be honest with me when I woke up from the coma? Six months had passed.'

Rachel and Laura share another look before Rachel speaks again. 'It's hard to admit, but a small part of me enjoyed taking care of you. Ever since you married Marc, things had been strained between us and I could never understand why you allowed him to keep us apart. So when Noelle insisted that the only people who could see you were me and Bryce, it felt like an opportunity to have some time with my sister again. And when you came round with no memories, something inside me just said it was best for you to keep thinking that I was all you had.'

I'm shaking my head and opening my mouth to ask how on earth she could ever have thought that was the right thing to do, but it's Laura who speaks first. 'Rachel loves you. I love you. And you always loved us. But it's Marc who came between us.'

Rachel puts her hand on Laura's arm, but Laura shakes it off. 'No, she needs to hear it. Marc has always been such a domineering force in your life and it doesn't surprise me that at the very moment you were about to break free of him, something awful happened. I've never liked him – neither of us has.'

At that moment there's a scuffling sound from the doorway and we all look up to see Marc. But instead of looking hurt or sad, there's a wide grin on his face.

'Oh, good – it's all coming out now,' he says.

FORTY-ONE

Marc's cheeks are flushed from being outside and his thinning hair is windswept. He strides into the room and I notice the muddy boots on his feet and feel a rush of anger that he's tramping mud into my parents' house. He's certainly making himself at home. He doesn't seem bothered that Rachel and Laura don't like him; instead, it appears like he's getting a kick out of the situation.

'Shall we leave you two to talk alone?' Rachel says and I see a flicker of hope in her eyes that she might get to walk away from the carnage.

'No, stay,' Marc says. 'You're as much a part of this as I am. You both are.'

Rachel looks down at the floor and colour rises in Laura's pale cheeks. They both seem uncomfortable, but I can't worry about that now.

'We've all done some things we regret,' Marc says to me, 'but you must accept your part. All this started because of your behaviour.' I realise he's looking directly at me with fire in his eyes. 'Jen, *ma chérie*, you brought this on yourself.'

I open my mouth to deny it, but I'm speechless at the suggestion. How could I possibly deserve this?

'Let's just think of what you've done. First,' he holds up one finger, 'you jump into bed with the first man that looks your way.'

Laura's mouth falls open and Rachel says, 'That's not fair, Marc. You would be the first to admit that your marriage has been volatile—'

'Was I the one caught by our daughter sleeping with a chef?' He spits the word in distaste. 'I think not.'

My cheeks start to burn and I remain still, bowing my head because it's clear that Marc has more blows he wants to rain down on me.

'Second, your unreasonableness drove our daughter to despair.'

I sink further into my armchair, tears springing to my eyes. Even Rachel and Laura said that things between me and Noelle weren't good. How could I have made her hate me so much that she'd want me dead? The car crash was the fire that lit the match and that was my fault.

'And third,' Marc goes on, 'you never put our family first. That's the true cause of all of this. You've spent your whole life living in the past, wishing you were back here with your parents, playing in the garden with your neighbours and sister.'

He flicks his wrist towards the house next door and his face is set in a dismissive smirk. I can tell it's a topic that Marc and I have argued about many times. I keep my mouth shut, wanting to give his anger a chance to burn out.

'Do you remember your ridiculous bench?' he spits.

I nod slowly, thinking of the yellow bench and the scorch marks on the paving stones.

'You found it in a scrapyard and convinced yourself you were some sort of restorer of the arts as you put it back together.'

'OK...' It doesn't seem that offensive to me that I rebuilt an old bench but the venom in Marc's eyes tells me he thinks of it as almost a mortal wound.

'You gave that hunk of wood more of your time and attention than either me or Noelle. That ugly bench really captured your heart.'

'Did you set fire to it?' I ask, incredulous that it could inspire so much vitriol and wondering if Cathy and Ian were lying.

Marc laughs. 'I wish I did but no, that was our neighbour. I must say I was happy it was gone though.'

'Why did she do it?' I ask.

'Noelle told you she was dating Ian and you decided to tell his mother that he wasn't good enough for our daughter. Never mind what Noelle wanted. Never mind what I thought. You said all these horrible, terrible things about Ian, and was it any surprise that Cathy decided to get her own back? I think we were lucky it was just the bench that went up in flames.'

I try to square away what he's saying with how I feel about Noelle and Ian, but it doesn't quite fit. Marc clearly feels righteous anger and I can tell that once I might have felt the same and we would have been on opposite sides, shooting poison at one another until one of us landed a fatal blow for the argument and the other one stalked away, but now all I feel is a creeping shame at his words and I wonder just how bad things could have got between us.

'Did I really say anything that bad?' I ask.

Marc rolls his eyes as if he can't truly believe the question. 'That bad? Of course, you'd been drinking, you usually were, but that's no excuse. You called the poor boy every name under the sun and you even brought up Cathy's ex-husband. Some of those things she'd told you in confidence, so you can imagine her horror when you screamed them over the fence.'

'Marc,' Rachel says his name like a warning, but I can tell he's enjoying unleashing on me.

'Why didn't I like Ian?' I ask.

'It's not about Ian,' Marc says. 'It was about you not being able to control Noelle any more.'

'Did I really behave that way?' I look at Rachel for the answer.

'I think that's a harsh characterisation but you were erratic. You'd been through a lot,' Rachel says. 'Dad's death really knocked you for six.'

'Do you know what the funny thing is?' Marc says, cutting in.

Rachel frowns but I say, 'What?'

'You hated your mum, but you were turning into her.'

'Marc!' Rachel says. 'That's not helpful.'

'She has a right to know,' Marc says. 'Nothing anyone around you said or did was good enough for you. The school I taught at didn't pay enough. Noelle didn't want to study music. She dated the wrong boy. You goaded Noelle into causing the accident. She may have turned the steering wheel, but you were the reason. And after when you threatened her with the police...'

His eyes are wide and there's colour in his cheeks. He mutters a stream of French and then says in English, 'You may as well hear everything. You hit your head, but you walked away from the accident and we all came inside. But once I heard your threats and saw the impact on Noelle, I had no choice but to find a way to keep you quiet.'

Everyone stares at him. The room is silent, other than my own breaths coming short and sharp. My heart is pounding. Out in the hallway, the grandfather clock ticks on. What does he mean?

'I knew your father's medication was here, so I found something strong – benzodiazepines that I crushed into your drink at first then added to your saline drips later on. That's why I got them delivered here before passing them on to Bryce.'

Rachel starts sobbing, shaking her head in disbelief. 'I didn't know, you have to believe me.'

Laura shushes her as I just stare at my husband, who really is no more than a stranger who wants to cause me harm.

'How could you?' Rachel whispers and Marc turns on her.

'Have you not been listening? Everything I did was for my wife and daughter. You think our relationship would have survived the accident had I not intervened? My darling, I wrapped you in cotton wool and kept you safe while I nursed Noelle back to health. And when she was strong enough, I cut back the dosage, and look at you... you've made a full recovery! I saw you and Noelle out there. She gave you a hug, yet a year ago she wouldn't even be in the same room as you. You ought to thank me.'

Listening to him, I can see he truly believes that he's the hero of this story. And me, the person who spent six months lying unconscious, drugged in her bedroom, I am the villain. How could it be that my relationship with my husband and child became so twisted?

'How have we ended up like this?' I ask Marc sadly.

There's a flash of emotion in his eyes and he comes over to me, kneeling at my feet. 'I only ever wanted to be a family, but you've made it so hard.' His voice sounds choked. 'You let that man into our bed.'

I wince and allow him to take my hand, shocked at how hot and clammy his skin is and the glimmer of what looks like madness shining in his eyes. He appears to have orchestrated everything and he clearly believes that he's acted in the best interests of our family, but what he's done is a crime. How can someone treat another human like this, let alone their wife? I long to rip my hand from his grip and scream that I never want to see him again and yet... What about Noelle? Where does she fit into this picture? I have to be sure that pushing away Marc won't take her from me.

'Yes, you've caused an awful lot of damage,' Marc goes on, 'but you'll be relieved to hear that I've decided to forgive you for the sake of our family. I've talked about it with Noelle...'

'Noelle?' I breathe.

'Yes, our daughter has always been at the heart of *my* decisions.'

I bow my head at the insinuation.

'I discussed it with her and we agreed that the three of us can have a fresh start, living together again, another chance. Isn't that what you want?'

I look up and although tears fill my eyes and my stomach is churning with horror at the very idea of forgetting everything that's happened to me, I want to have a better relationship with Noelle than the one he just described. And even Rachel admitted that I've done things that weren't rational.

'OK,' I say softly and Rachel gasps.

'You don't need to do this,' Laura says softly but Marc grins triumphantly and holds out his hand.

'Come,' he says.

'Where?'

'I'd like us to go outside and keep talking,' he says. 'That's the only way for us to rebuild our family. You, me and Noelle, as it is meant to be.'

Rachel and Laura grip each other's hands and exchange a glance. I see their hatred for him radiating from their eyes and their desperation for this to be the end of it. But no one is blameless here, certainly not them, and it is my life, my family. I have to take control.

Allowing Marc to pull me to my feet, I move into his arms and close my eyes. Those months of darkness have left their mark. There's only one person I can fully trust now – myself – but I'm willing to go with my husband, to try to sift through the wreckage of our marriage, for one reason only: Noelle.

'Come,' Marc says, striding from the room, and I take one last look at my sister and Laura, huddled on the sofa.

'Jen, please,' Rachel begs, 'You can be free...'

'I'll never be free of what you all did.'

I follow Marc out to the garden, into the blustery wind, where I find him standing at the foot of the oak tree, smiling at me in a way that tells me he feels like he's won. But there are no winners here. All I feel is a hollow dread, knowing that I must go on, that I have to keep putting one foot in front of the other to rebuild my life and my family. The irony not lost on me that we are starting again in the very place where everything was smashed apart.

FORTY-TWO

SIX MONTHS LATER

Marc

The smell of roasting chicken drifts through the room as my wife opens the Aga to baste the meat. As I watch her spoon the clear liquid over the top of the chicken, I smile at her in wonder and I can't help but think, *What the hell have you done with her?*

It's impossible to think of this woman as the same Jen who was making my life a misery only a year ago. My beautiful, impetuous Jennifer. The woman who thought she might have a better life with a chef. *Well, we can all cook a chicken*, I think, and as I watch her smiling to herself, I see how happy she is to have put that part of her life behind her. We can both acknowledge that Bryce was a huge mistake and we're better together – stronger, happier. Couples always are after their relationship has been forged in flames.

We moved into her parents' old home with Rachel's blessing. She could see that Noelle, Jen and I needed a fresh start, someplace we could rebuild our trust and our relationships, and there was no way we could do it under that old roof. It feels like Rachel is just happy to be as far away from us as she can be and that suits me just fine. Jen despised our old house after her months of rehabilitation, and I have my own reason to hate it. She doesn't remember but that was the place Noelle walked in on her and Bryce and it sent everything into motion until ultimately we crashed into that tree.

Looking out of the front window, I can see the tough old tree out there now, the branches bare and quivering in the wind – one of the few English things that has my unwavering respect. It does not bend or sway on a whim. There's something reassuring in knowing that it's been there since long before any of us were here and will remain long after we're gone. Somehow that makes what happened feel less significant. We may have had a little accident, a misdemeanour, but we're back on track and everything is totally fine. Jen doesn't even remember her affair with Bryce, which I must admit gives me some satisfaction. *He must have been rather forgettable*, I think whenever his name comes up, which thankfully is not very often since he's thrown himself into work. He's trying to get a Michelin star, apparently – well, good for him. Let it keep his bed warm at night.

'How's the gravy?' Jen asks and I stir the liquid in the pan as it reduces.

'Thin,' I say, 'but it will thicken once we add the meat juices.'

'That's the magic,' she says with a grin, returning to her famous stuffing, and I return her smile.

We're eating at the big wooden table in the kitchen and Jen moves on to setting it for seven. Noelle and Ian are upstairs, and Rachel, Laura and Cathy will arrive any moment. It's been almost miraculous how smoothly things have gone since we admitted everything to Jen. There's that odd English expression about waiting for the other shoe to drop and I must admit to occasionally feeling a ripple of anxiety as I think, *Are we really going to be allowed to be this happy?* But it's been months now and things are working out better than any of us could have hoped.

It's hard to imagine that I even considered increasing the dosage until she... I can't bear to think it, but I think it's understandable that sometimes I longed for a simpler life after everything Jen put me through. It was a huge leap of faith to let her wake up and return to us after she'd been so hateful, but I gave her the chance and it's blown me away how far we've come. I'd read that benzos can cause memory issues and she did have a hard bang on the head, but it's been almost poetic how much of her past has been wiped clean. No more reminiscing about the good old times with Bryce and Amy, no more endless stories about her father teaching her the violin.

It may sound callous but I'm just thinking about the future – our future together. For me and Jen, it is like we are teenagers again, falling in love for the first time. She plays me her favourite pieces on the violin and listens to me rant about the English and their love of bureaucracy, or the laziness of my students, and we laugh together. After all the tears and shouting, I never thought I'd laugh with my wife again.

Abandoning the gravy, I intercept her as she's putting out the wine glasses. I kiss her, wrapping my arms around her and feeling grateful that we're back together.

'Please,' comes Noelle's voice from the doorway, 'get a room.' But I hear the happiness in her voice, and as we pull apart, I see she's smiling.

'Just ignore my parents,' she says to Ian. 'They are disgusting.'

'Why thank you, darling,' says Jen lightly, and Noelle goes to her and accepts a hug.

Their relationship has undergone the biggest transformation and it brings me joy to see them together. They are so much alike with their sharp minds and stubbornness but also the intensity with which they love.

'What's cooking, Ms V?' drawls Ian from the doorway.

'Roast chicken and all the trimmings,' she says.

'Delicious,' he replies. 'My mum loves a roast, too.'

Rachel and Laura are picking up Cathy on the way and she'll complete our little dinner party. Thankfully, Bryce and Amy are no longer welcome here and that brings me joy. I shouldn't have to share a table with the man who slept with my wife – it's one humiliation too far. But I'm pleased that Cathy is joining us; it's nice to get to know her better, especially since Ian and Noelle are planning to take off next summer to visit the rest of Jen's family in Australia. I'll admit I thought the boy was rather arrogant at first, but we've put that a long way behind us and I've grown rather fond of him.

'Shall I put some music on?' he asks.

'Yes, please, but nothing too offensive to the ears,' Jen says, teasing him.

Noelle and Ian go over to the record player and I try to squeeze Noelle's hand as she passes but she sidesteps my outstretched hand. Her rejection stings, but I cover up my reaction by returning to the gravy and stirring it vigorously. If there's one area of life that isn't quite so satisfactory, it's my relationship with Noelle. I suppose it would be too much to ask for everything to be perfect, after all. When a family has been through such a huge trauma, there is bound to be a scar.

Our scar is small and well hidden, but it's there nonetheless. Noelle and I don't speak of it, but we both know it's there. The little lie we had to bury for the sake of the family. The truth that can never come out. I never meant to drag my little girl into it all, but I knew it was the only way we could stay together. What mother could hold a grudge against her daughter?

But if Jen knew the truth – that it was me in the passenger seat, me who pulled the wheel, me who didn't care if we lived or died in that moment... Well, would she be so forgiving? I think not. And none of us likes to think of everything that happened after. It's better if we just put it behind us.

The doorbell goes and Jen beams. 'They're here!'

She rushes off into the hallway as Ian puts the record player on and Fleetwood Mac fills the room. I turn to Noelle and say, 'I love you, *ma choue*,' but my little cabbage doesn't even smile.

Jen returns with Rachel, Laura and Cathy, bringing a breath of fresh air and a couple of bottles of wine, and happiness and laughter soon fill the room. And as I stir the gravy and watch over my family, I smile and think that everything has been worth it. One day, I'm sure, Noelle will agree with me.

FORTY-THREE

Jen

It's an effort to sit here and chew my roast chicken like there's nothing at all wrong. Each swallow is like forcing down a golf ball. But I take regular sips of my wine to assist and keep the passive smile on my face. It's an expression I've got used to wearing ever since my memories started to come back. A smile that says I'm happy, when inside I'm on fire.

It was Noelle who triggered the first memory. We were painting our nails together in the sunny kitchen at the back of the house, both laughing as she drew a smiley face over my bright yellow thumbnail, and I suddenly remembered watching her play the piano when she was much younger. Her small fingers tripped over the keys and I remembered cringing at the poor timing, incorrect notes, all of which I took as a personal insult because she clearly hadn't practised at all since we'd last sat down. I remembered snatching up her hand in mine and squeezing her bony fingers hard, in a way that I knew would sting, and saying, 'If you've got time to paint your bloody nails, you should have time to practise your pieces.'

I'm not proud of that memory, and the most pain I've felt since I woke up from my accident has come from learning that I wasn't a perfect person, or a perfect mother, but then, who is? I've sought professional help since things started coming back to me – a lovely young man named Rajiv, who I sit down with once a week and I just talk and talk. It helps. Occasionally Rajiv interjects and I see links between events that I hadn't noticed before, like spiders' silk connecting everything in one big web of memories.

That awful piano practice with Noelle wasn't long after I lost my own father, and music was one of our greatest loves, something that bonded us. It doesn't take a great stretch to see that perhaps I was trying to seek connection with Noelle and interpreted that her lack of commitment wasn't just a lack of love for piano, but also a lack of love for me. My own neediness is something that's shone through in the memories that have come back, and that's something I'm working on putting behind me. Rajiv says I'm making good progress and I believe him – I am finally feeling like myself again, only a better version. Someone who is able to learn from their mistakes. What happened may have been one of the worst things that could happen to anyone, being betrayed by everyone you love, but it has given me one thing: a fresh start. Only I haven't yet started again.

As I look around the table, I see that almost everyone who I love is here, there's only Bryce and Amy missing, but also nearly everyone who I hate. There is a fine line between the two after all, and it's always the people we love the most who hurt us the most. Only for most people, hurting your loved ones doesn't include causing them to drive into a tree, then drugging them for six months and keeping them locked in a room, unconscious. Whatever I was like before, whatever I said or did, surely I didn't deserve that?

My eye catches Rachel's as she tops up Laura's glass and

she gives me a brief smile but looks quickly away. My own sister knows what she did is unforgivable – she may not have known Marc was drugging me, but she should have made it her job to find out. Why did she trust him when I know that she and Laura never liked him? She won't pretend that we can just slip back to our old ways, and I respect her more for that.

She and Laura – or Dr Marsden as I like to call her just to watch her pale skin blush and to hear her stammer another apology – have kept their distance, only really coming around for special occasions like today, the anniversary of my dad's death, and also a year since my accident. Rachel tried every excuse going to avoid coming, but after everything she did, she had to bow to my pressure in the end. I wanted her here because I'm not ready to let her off the hook just yet. Everything has a price and even poor, lovely Laura has to pay it.

She's sitting on Rachel's left, with Cathy on her other side, and the three of them are chatting about the Canaries. Cathy goes every year and Rachel and Laura are planning a trip, only they can't decide between Tenerife and Gran Canaria.

'It's the black sand that puts me off Tenerife,' says Cathy. 'It's just not right, not right at all.'

I laugh along as if I'm engaged in the conversation, but really I'm thinking, *So you're worried about black sand but not about a neighbour who was locked in her house for half a year?* I know Cathy is not really to blame, since she didn't know I'd been drugged, but sometimes I think she could have done more. Why hold up a cryptic warning sign rather than marching around and banging on the front door? She's usually as bold as brass, but something held her back.

My gaze swings round to Ian and Noelle and I wonder if it was Cathy's motherly love that stopped her from acting. She knew how her son felt about my daughter and perhaps she truly believed that Noelle might go to prison if she called the police. None of us wanted that outcome, of course, but she couldn't know I felt the same way, because she couldn't ask me. No one could.

And so I have to look at my husband, my darling Marc, squeezed between me and Ian. He tried to slip into the seat next to Noelle, but it escaped no one's notice that she instantly leaped up on the pretence of getting a glass of water, and Ian shifted across one. The unspoken dance that has been going on since we moved here – Noelle avoids Marc at all costs. And as soon as I noticed, it got me thinking. Why does Noelle hate Marc so much?

Marc is the one person who is at the heart of everything. He was in the car with me and Noelle the night it happened. He was the person who convinced Rachel that I would report Noelle to the police if they didn't keep me out of the way. And he came up with the crazy plan to keep me in the dark for as long as possible, with a little input from Rachel. My darling puppet master. I smile at him and he reaches across and squeezes my knee. It takes every ounce of strength I have not to flinch and to return his smile as if his touch makes me happy. But I can't remember a time when it ever did.

I understand how Noelle feels about her father, because I feel the same way. Whenever I see his beady little eyes with the scrubby goatee he insists on having because he believes it gives him an air of Gallic sophistication, I feel an overwhelming revulsion. From what I can piece together, the passion in our marriage died out not long after Noelle was born but we limped along until Bryce returned. How can someone like Marc compete with a man like Bryce? That's a rhetorical question since there is no answer.

Bryce is music, Bryce is heart, Bryce is love. It's hard sitting at this table, knowing he is only a few miles away, working at Chez Richard; he's been putting in every hour there because he can't be with me – that's what he told me anyway. It sounds like a stupid teenage romance, but that's probably because it was exactly that for so long. As soon as I went up to my childhood bedroom in this house, I remembered the hours and hours I would lie on my bed, dreaming of Bryce. And later, lying there with Bryce himself.

But then he broke my heart, disappearing into the labyrinth of kitchens in London's West End and a famous restaurant in Copenhagen. And then I went on the fateful trip to Paris and met Marc, and by the time Bryce returned home, we were two very different people in two very different places. I didn't immediately fall back into Bryce's bed. Thankfully, as my memories have returned, I have realised just how hard I worked at my marriage, how much I wanted things to work out with Marc, for Noelle but also for me. That was the life I'd chosen but Marc was never satisfied.

The picture everyone here has painted of me during those years was not very rosy. I was difficult, I was tempestuous, I argued with my teenage daughter. Yes, all those things are true, but I loved them fiercely, could also be funny, and spent time and effort making that house a home. We may not have had tonnes of money, but I put everything I could into making that place feel fit for a king. But it wasn't good enough for Marc, and neither was I.

Ultimately, it was a memory of my bench that made everything fall into place. My silly, inconsequential bench that seems to have been a turning point for so many things. I remember the pride and care I took in that bench, rebuilding it by hand as a way to carve out a little space and time that was just for me, away from the arguments with Noelle over silly teenage things and the heavy cloud of resentment that was building between me and Marc. I put so much love into it that by the time it was sitting proudly in the backyard, it turned that unassuming space into a battleground.

I'd sit out there with Marc and he'd tell me everything he felt was wrong with me and our life and especially our daughter. We weren't disciplining her enough. I wasn't setting a good example as a mother or a wife or a woman. We were letting that boy next door *rape* her. That's what he said when they began seeing each other, when she was fifteen and he was eighteen. I told him I didn't think they'd even kissed yet, but he went on and on until I took Cathy aside and had a word. It wasn't a good idea to speak to her after we'd shared a bottle of wine, and an even worse idea to use some of the language I chose.

That was the night my bench burned to the ground and I remember waking up to find Marc standing by the window, his face lit up by an eerie orange glow, but the thing that shocked me the most was he was laughing.

'Pass the gravy, please,' Marc says and I offer him the jug and watch as he drenches his plate, his second helping, tapping his straining paunch before tucking in again.

Marc felt right at home the moment we moved in here. It was as if this was what he'd been waiting for – a kingdom of his own to preside over. He has big plans to knock down the old conservatory and rebuild a modern monstrosity in its place, and I've nodded along, all the while certain that he will never get the chance. We've been through every room, pinning up curtain samples and testing squares of paint colours on the walls, ready for the big redecoration that's due to begin tomorrow, and I've gone along with all of his choices. Only the whites and the beiges and the greys will never go up because tomorrow isn't going to come, not for everyone here today.

They say revenge is a dish best served cold, but I have decided to serve it stewed, blended and strained. It's taken me months to forage for the right type of mushroom – the kind I found in a little book in the library called *Fungi of Britain: Everything You Need to Know*, which I read in situ, of course. No one who's about to be involved in a scandal like this one needs that on their library card, so I have been very careful. Who would suspect anyone in this happy little family of anything criminal when it comes out? I'm certain the world is going to put it down to a second tragic accident in a single year. And if anyone figures out it's happened on the anniversary – well, what an awful, poignant coincidence.

My special stuffing has been served to everyone here, and as I watch them all eat up, I can't help but feel a grim satisfaction. No one deserves to be spared some pain, not even my darling Noelle. But I reserved a special portion for Marc. He is the target after all; the others are just needed to divert suspicion. And unfortunately, I've had to include myself in that.

I watch until Marc clears his plate and see him let out a little belch. He gives me another of his possessive little smiles that make my skin crawl and I decide that this is my moment. Lifting my knife, I tap my glass gently and the *ting, ting, ting* swiftly stops the gentle hum of conversation. Everyone looks at me expectantly – well, everyone except Rachel, who still won't meet my eye. Smart woman.

'It's been an eventful year,' I say – they all laugh and Noelle rolls her eyes good-naturedly. 'But it's wonderful to be able to sit here, with my family around me, and put it all behind us.'

'Hear, hear,' mutters Rachel.

'I know we've had some ups and downs, but I want you all to know that I love each and every one of you. And I'm so glad we have the rest of our lives to spend together.'

Noelle and I share a smile and I mean every word as I look at my daughter. She's the person I've done this for. I didn't set out to become an adulterer, and I certainly never thought I'd be a murderer, but life sometimes takes us in strange directions and we have to make the best of them.

'Cheers,' I say, just as I hear a strange groan come from Ian. He pushes back his seat and darts from the room.

A moment later, we hear him vomit noisily in what I hope is the sink. His action seems to set off a chain of events, like the conductor at the orchestra counting everyone in, and soon we are a mess of hurling and moaning and people running in every direction, trying to find someplace appropriate to empty the contents of their stomachs. I remain in place, though my own guts are cramping and I know that soon I will need to retire somewhere private, and strangely enough, Marc remains stoically upright by my side.

I feel a glimmer of worry that perhaps I have managed to cock everything up, and it will all be for nothing, until he vomits spectacularly, clear across the tablecloth, and I'm flooded with relief.

You see, the gravy boat was lightly contaminated, a gentle grating of poisonous mushrooms to ensure we all had a rough night, nothing more, because I needed everyone to suffer for it to be plausible that this was an accident, but it was Marc's plate that took the most careful preparation. His contained a large serving of the special stuffing I make – his was slightly different today, though it seems he still enjoyed it. I know I need to be very careful to wash any leftovers on his plate down the sink, and that will be my next task, only now I plan to remain here and make sure that the job is done.

When one's own child is frightened of their father, that is enough motivation for drastic action. And then there was the attempted murder – not once, but twice. It was after a session with Rajiv when I was cycling home, all pleased with myself that things were finally falling back into place, when I turned the corner and spotted the oak, that I finally remembered everything that happened on that awful night.

It was the night of the accident, in the driving rain, in the midst of the mother of all arguments, when an arm leaned over and grabbed the wheel, but it wasn't Noelle in the passenger seat – it was Marc. He was so furious that I had moved on, that I was planning a future with Bryce, that he drove the three of us into a tree, not caring if we lived or died.

But somehow, miraculously, we all walked out of that car

and nothing had changed. I was devastated, but I was resolute, and that's when he attacked me. The head injuries I suffered were not caused by the impact with the sturdy tree, but by the sole of Marc's boot when he stamped on my head. And Noelle saw it all. So when Marc made her promise to never tell or he'd kill us both, she agreed, because she believed him. And I believe him too, which is why I've had to do what I've done tonight.

Marc forced them all to go along with his plan. He sent Noelle to Bryce and Amy with the instruction that Bryce must look after me, because Marc needed someone he could control. Marc himself rang Rachel, but all the while he used our daughter and played upon her real devastation. Imagine almost murdering your child's mother then making them tell everyone it was their fault? I'm shocked at the arrogance it took to believe that he could control them all, and the only mistake Marc made was letting me wake up. I won't be making the same one.

After this is all over, I'm not sure what will happen between Bryce and me – there's a long and complicated history between us, but perhaps we'll find a way to forge a new path, together. The only thing I know is that I've freed Noelle from a lifetime of fear and worry and we can truly all put that dark night behind us.

Bon appétit, mon cher, I think as I watch Marc slowly slide further and further down in his seat.

A LETTER FROM HOLLY

Dear reader,

I want to say a huge thank you for choosing to read *Everyone Is Lying*. If you did enjoy it, and want to keep up to date with all my latest releases, just sign up at the following link. Your email address will never be shared and you can unsubscribe at any time.

www.bookouture.com/holly-down

I hope you loved *Everyone Is Lying* and if you did I would be very grateful if you could write a review. I'd love to hear what you think, and it makes such a difference helping new readers to discover one of my books for the first time.

Thanks,

Holly

PUBLISHING TEAM

Turning a manuscript into a book requires the efforts of many people. The publishing team at Bookouture would like to acknowledge everyone who contributed to this publication.

Commercial
Lauren Morrissette
Hannah Richmond
Imogen Allport

Contracts
Peta Nightingale

Cover design
Emma Graves

Data and analysis
Mark Alder
Mohamed Bussuri

Editorial
Lucy Frederick
Melissa Tran

Copyeditor
DeAndra Lupu